THE LITTLE THINGS IN LOVE

M.C. ROTH

The Little Things in Love
ISBN # 978-1-80250-754-6
©Copyright M.C. Roth 2024
Cover Art by Kelly Martin ©Copyright September 2024
Interior text design by Claire Siemaszkiewicz
Pride Publishing

THE LITTLE THINGS IN LOVE

Dedication

For Q

Chapter One

Elgin

Something was wrong with Wallace. There was a paleness to his cheeks as he flitted his eyes across the busy restaurant, tracking random people as they passed by the small cove that obscured their table. He was usually so focused, so spirited, but ever since Elgin had come home for dinner, only for them to immediately turn around to head out to the restaurant, things had been *off*.

"Is it a sex thing?"

Wallace spluttered, grabbing for his glass of wine and smothering his laugh against the rim. It was clearly too late. His eyes were already sparkling, color flushing into his cheeks again. His soft cheeks and the smattering of freckles were some of the first things that had made Elgin realize he was in love.

That hadn't changed...not for years.

"Are we getting dessert and leaving early?" asked Wallace, waggling his eyebrows. The server chose that moment to walk by, a grin touching her lips as she swiftly changed direction.

"No way." Elgin shook his head, running his finger along his lower lip. *I must've been imagining things.* Nothing had changed. They still had the same jokes and laughter. Maybe it was time for him to give Wallace a break. The man was a CEO and worked for a living.

Wallace leaned in, pushing his half-eaten soup to the side so he could set his elbows on the table. "Then do tell. What is 'the sex thing' — and when are we having it?"

Anyone who looked at Wallace probably had no idea about the mouth on him — or that dirty mind that was locked behind blond hair and blue eyes that were so expressive he could see the world in them. He was the type of guy who stopped to help someone pick up their groceries if they dropped them or would fund a kid's university tuition because the teacher had called him up.

Elgin was the only one who really *knew* him.

"Did you see the bathroom at this place? There's a couch in there, along with crested hand towels. Not many places have that type of thing anymore." It helped that they would drop a thousand dollars between the two of them over dinner. The hostess would probably stand guard at the bathroom door if he tipped well enough. *Which I always do.*

"A bathroom?" Wallace quirked his lips. "Kinky."

The door to the restaurant must've shifted open, as a bit of cool air swept into their bubble. They always had the same spot in the private area just inside the place. It was far away from the kitchen, so it was quiet, and it was the best place to people watch. Most didn't notice the small inlet tucked to the side that had a view of most of the main dining room.

Two men shuffled by their little hiding spot, the second one catching Elgin's eye. "He's going to propose. I bet you five— No...twenty dollars." He narrowed his eyes. "The excessive cologne, tie and the way he's overdressed makes me wonder if it's a surprise. And the way he keeps reaching for his pocket tells me that's where he must have the ring."

Wallace let out a soft sigh, running his hands over the tablecloth. "I love weddings." His smile brightened. "Oh, look. We'll have a front-row seat."

The couple was seated just outside their bubble of privacy, the scrape of their chairs audible against the floor. They would be able to hear every single word from their spot.

The hostess reached over, lighting the small candle at the table before sweeping away and leaving a trace of her perfume. With the low lights and soft ambiance, the candle was almost the brightest thing in the room. Elgin strained to catch every detail.

The one who was reaching into his pocket every few seconds was tall, with visible sweat gathered at the edge of his dark hair that was styled to fall just above his ears. His gaze wandered the restaurant as he shifted, pulling his chair up tight to the table before he rested back again. He fiddled with his napkin, running the material through his fingers over and over.

"He's so nervous, poor guy," said Elgin, staring shamelessly. Glancing at Wallace, he was momentarily caught. "What? This is exciting."

Wallace's cheeks were flushed, his lower lip red as he released it from between his teeth. The sweater he wore was perhaps a size too big, but it dragged Elgin's thoughts to how light Wallace would be when he tossed him onto the bed later.

"It's okay," said Wallace, his eyes dark. "You're just really invested in another man right now."

As if. Wallace was his everything, and he meant that in every sense of the word. His husband was sweet, like a cinnamon heart that had the hidden bit of spiciness he was never expecting. But that wasn't the half of it.

"You just don't want to bet against me," said Elgin.

The second of the pair had no nervousness to speak of and didn't seem to notice his partner's state — or much of anything, really. He was buried in his phone, the glow of the white screen flashing against his glasses with the video's reflection glaring on the pane.

"This is a nice place. Do you like it, Ralph?" the nervous one asked, running his hand through his hair. He must've had gel in it or something because he scrunched up his face, wiping his palm on his pants a moment later.

"Meh." Ralph shrugged, running his finger over his phone screen. "I told you I didn't care, Annan. Sophie was here last week, and she didn't like her vegetables much. She said they weren't even cooked."

Elgin turned his head away from the scene, taking a sip of his water. *Poor guy.*

"I might take that bet, after all," said Wallace, smiling at the server as she brought their main course. Elgin's steak appeared seared to perfection and topped with a crusting of cheese and two thin spears of purple asparagus. Wallace's portion was tiny in comparison.

"Fifty bucks says Annan will back out. Another fifty if Ralph leaves before the main course arrives," said Wallace as soon as they were alone again.

Elgin glanced at the couple out of the corner of his eye. "It doesn't seem like as much fun without a wedding at the end." He wiped his cheek dry of a pretend tear. "I could have been the best man."

Wallace bit his lips as if he were struggling to keep the smile off his face. "You're right. Everyone should propose the way you did—no chance of rejection that way."

That's not fair. Elgin shook his head, grabbing his fork and knife and cutting into his steak. The blue cheese coated his tongue as it melted in his mouth, a groan catching in his throat. Ralph didn't know great food if he was worried about a few al dente vegetables.

"I gave you a heads-up when I proposed," said Elgin, eyeing up Wallace's food. "Is that all you're going to eat?"

"Gotta save room for dessert." Wallace licked his lips, dragging his gaze over Elgin's form.

How fast can I finish this steak? Elgin wondered.

"But sending me a message on social media is not a 'heads-up'," said Wallace, laughing as he shook his head. "I'll never forget when Lenny called to congratulate me when he saw a picture of the ring on your feed and told me that you had updated your profile to 'engaged'."

"Hey." Elgin pointed his fork at Wallace. "You're telling it all wrong. I got down on one knee just a few days later when you got back from your business trip. The post *was* my heads-up."

Wallace sent him a light glare. "You are as romantic as a jar of peanut butter—sweet, satisfying and unexpectedly dangerous."

"Please put that on my tombstone." Elgin framed his hands. "Here lies Elgin, sweet and unexpectedly dangerous."

Wallace's smile dropped as he swirled his spoon in his bowl of soup. He'd barely touched it, a few vegetables floating around the top of the thick cream base. There was bread on the side that was sprinkled with herbs and a dusting of cheese that smelled divine.

"Are you sure you're feeling okay?" Elgin lowered his voice. "We can get the rest to go, and I can light the candles and get the massage oil out. You look tired."

Wallace rubbed his forehead before shaking his head. "No. I'm fine—really. It's just been a long week. Rachel at the office thought it would be a great idea to bring in a crock pot of chili for the potluck this week, and everyone got food poisoning. Two general managers and the COO were all out of commission. The vegetarians were safe, at least."

"Thank God," said Elgin, shoving another forkful of steak into his mouth.

"Besides, I can't miss this." Wallace looked to the side, his not-so-subtle gaze focused on the couple. Ralph still hadn't looked up from his phone, and Annan was pulling at his tie, his hair ruffled and shiny where sweat dotted his temples.

"I feel bad for the guy," whispered Elgin, leaning his head on his hand. He'd never admit it, but he'd been too terrified to propose to Wallace in person, taking the easy way out and telling the world first to give Wallace a chance to make a break for it while he could.

It had been worth it to see his husband laugh when Elgin had picked him up in the airport, holding a 'future Mr. Bekker?' sign in his hand. And every time they revisited the story, Wallace's eyes lit up. *Worth it.*

The nervous one named Annan shifted in his chair, and Elgin perked up, turning sideways so he had an even better view. With one hand in his pocket, Annan stood, rounding the table and dropping to one knee. He winced as he landed, grabbing for his tie as if it had choked him.

"Aww." Wallace reached across the table, tangling his fingers with Elgin's.

Ralph raised one eyebrow without looking up from his screen, his posture stiffening in his chair. "What are you doing? Unless you fell, get back in the chair. You're making a fool of yourself, Annan."

Ouch. Elgin winced, trying to look away, but he couldn't. Annan seemed like a nice guy, in a rugged sort of way, with blue eyes and a five o'clock shadow that was genuinely attractive. His throat bobbed as he swallowed, pulling a small case out of his pocket.

"Ralph," Annan started, clearing his throat when his voice caught. His voice was deep and smooth but had a nervous waver to it.

You can do it, buddy. Elgin gripped Wallace's hand tighter. All joking aside, he was fully invested, just about ready to grab Ralph's phone from his small hands and toss it across the restaurant.

The server paused her approach, turning around and heading back to the kitchen. She, at least, had qualms about eavesdropping on what should have been a beautiful moment. *Not me.*

"Ralph—"

"Seriously, Annan, get off the floor." Ralph slammed his phone on the table, the sound of the hit putting Elgin on edge. "I'm leaving." He reached for his coat that he'd hung on the back of his chair, despite several hooks being available.

"Can I ask you a question? Then we can go home, Ralph. I promise." Annan seemed to falter, clutching the box tight in his hands. His knuckles were white, the little velvet package looking close to buckling.

"No." Ralph pushed his chair back. "I can't believe this." He shook his head, his eyes going wide.

"Oh no," said Wallace, squeezing his hand tighter. "Elgin, I can't watch. Tell me when it's over."

Elgin couldn't look away, every muscle in his body going progressively tighter. He knew how fucking hard it was to be in Annan's position. *At least give the guy a chance.*

"Will you marry me?" Annan blurted out, his fingers slipping on the box as he tried to pry it open. After a moment of fumbling, he managed to reveal a thin black band nestled on a pillow of white. The jewel in the center was small and barely noticeable in the low light, but it was beautiful, nonetheless.

Ralph snorted, covering his mouth with his hand as he laughed. The high-pitched sound drew every eye in the restaurant, another server peeking around the corner as the room went quiet. Forks and knives hovered above plates, as people held their collective breath.

"No," said Ralph, slipping his coat over his shoulders. "Why the hell would I want to marry *you*?" He spat the last word, an icy venom dripping from his lips. The way he crinkled his nose gave him a semblance to a pig who had just rolled in its own waste.

Elgin narrowed his eyes.

"Why not?" Annan muttered, dipping his gaze to the box to stare at the ring. His hands were trembling and his gaze unsteady as he stared at it. It was tiny in his large hands, and Elgin could almost smell the sweat that seemed to pour from him.

"Don't get me started." Ralph shoved his phone into his pocket. "You're boring as hell, you don't have any friends and you're not even that attractive—not to mention, all you care about is your stupid animals, who smell terrible, by the way. I can't stand getting into bed with you, even after you've had a shower, because you reek, just like they do." A cruel smile spread across Ralph's lips. "To be honest, I'm just here for the food."

Wallace gasped, ducking his head while Elgin clenched his jaw.

The box fell from Annan's hand, and he dropped his arm to his side, slowly standing. His head was ducked, his eyes glassy as he looked at the floor, his forehead scrunched. "I have friends."

"No, you don't, because there isn't a single person in this world who can stand you."

Elgin rose to his feet, releasing Wallace's hand before he even knew what he was doing. Crossing the short distance, he strolled to the couple's table, relishing in the way Ralph's gaze snapped to him, his eyes going wide.

"Annan, is that you?" asked Elgin, grinning as he stopped a pace away from the table. "Oh wow, it is! I haven't seen you in years." He didn't spare Ralph a glance as he held his arms out, pulling Annan into a bear hug.

A woodsy, earthy scent tickled his nose, along with something else he didn't recognize as he embraced

Annan. Their heights were near level, but Elgin was broader, his frame dwarfing Annan a bit as he drew close to his ear, whispering quietly, "Just play along."

Elgin drew back, catching Annan's eye and releasing his grip. Annan blinked, his forehead still drawn in confusion. "Hell, it's so good to see you. It's been, what? Six years? You look great."

He did look even better up close. His hair had some natural curl to it that was trying to break free from the product, little wisps going astray. That, and he was built under his suit that didn't fit all that well.

"Elgin, remember? Elgin Bekker." He spied Ralph's eyes widen in recognition. It felt good to throw his name around a little for a good cause. Wallace was probably hiding his head in shame, though. "We met at the retreat. Those were some of the best weeks of my life."

He patted Annan's back, turning to Ralph for the first time. Letting his smile drop, he stood a touch straighter. Wallace always claimed that Elgin had the patented 'resting bastard face', and the best part was, it was as natural as breathing.

"It looks like your friend is leaving. Care to join us for dinner?" asked Elgin, dismissing Ralph with a glance and putting his back to him. Annan was holding onto himself, his eyes still shiny but dry. "It will be my treat."

"Sure." Annan drew out the word as if he wasn't exactly sure what he was saying. He glanced to the floor, spying the box that had snapped shut and rolled under the table.

Elgin ducked down, grasping the small velvet box and pressing it into Annan's hand. "Wouldn't want to lose this."

"I can stay. I don't have anywhere to be."

Elgin turned at the sound of Ralph's voice, giving him the same unimpressed look. Ralph's gaze was flitting from Elgin's watch to the cuff links on his jacket, then down to the very expensive shoes he'd worn to the restaurant. He would have much preferred sandals, but he'd dressed up for Wallace.

"I'm afraid I don't know who you are," said Elgin, grabbing Annan's chair and hefting it off the ground. "Here, Annan, follow me. I've told my husband so much about you. He didn't believe me when I said I saw you in the same restaurant where we were grabbing dinner."

With his back to Ralph, Elgin held out his arm, looping it through Annan's. The poor guy still looked as if he were in shock, staring at the box in his hand. Helping him across the space was an easy task, and he tucked the chair at the end of his own table, clearing away the breadbasket and the tiny plates so Annan would have room.

"Wallace, this is Annan." Elgin grinned at his husband before peering back over his shoulder. Ralph was staring at them, his jaw hanging slack and something like determination in his gaze.

Elgin narrowed his eyes at the man, jerking his head toward the exit. *Get the fuck out.* Ralph stumbled back, nearly tripping over his chair in his rush to get away. It was the same way a new intern would scurry away if they didn't realize that ninety percent of Elgin's body was made of dry humor and sarcasm, and that he had only fired two people in his entire career.

Wallace groaned, holding his hand out to Annan as he shook his head. "Elgin, you are in so much trouble."

Chapter Two

Annan

There were a few things running through his mind, so jumbled that he wasn't sure what the hell was going on. He was also pretty sure that Elgin Bekker was either insane or very confused. Ralph had seemed to know who he was, which didn't bode well, but the guy seemed nice, if not a little intimidating.

Looks can be deceiving. Looks had drawn him to Ralph, and Justin before him and Henry before that. He'd had the ring through the last six relationships, and not a single one of the men he'd offered it to had even appeared the least bit interested.

"Fuck." He sat hard in the chair Elgin had dragged over to the table for him before dropping his head into his hands. He was soaked with sweat, his cheap suit that he'd rented probably ruined. He'd never worn one in his life, and he'd hoped this was the last time. "I can't fucking believe it."

"I know," said Elgin's husband, reaching across the table to pat his arm. "Sorry about Elgin. He probably didn't mean to kidnap you, so I'll hold him back if you want to run now."

"Wallace…" Elgin let out a pouting whine, his lower lip sticking out just a touch. "I couldn't just keep watching that without *doing* anything."

"Sorry, honey," said Wallace, patting Annan one last time. "You, okay?"

Annan looked to his hands. He wasn't shaking anymore, which was a plus, but his palms looked rough, thick calluses coating his palms. Maybe Ralph was right. No matter how many times he washed up, he never fit into the stereotype of a city boy. He had country blood through and through.

"Sure." Annan cleared his throat, leaning back in his chair. "Sorry you had to see that." He glanced over his shoulder. He hadn't realized that this little room was there until now, the light low with a black curtain blocking a touch of the entrance. His previous table was smack-dab in the middle of view and close enough that he could see the candle sputtering in its holder. "I should go."

His jacket was hanging over his chair, so Elgin must've grabbed it. The ring could have stayed on the table as far as he was concerned. The jeweler wouldn't want it back, and no man seemed to want it, either. It was essentially worthless.

"Wait," said Elgin, sitting up straighter. Annan tried not to wilt. The guy was intimidating as hell, with shoulders that stretched for days. They were close to the same height, but Elgin was all severity where Annan was softness. His husband was the opposite—

cute, tiny and with fluffy blond hair that flipped out at the tips.

"Did you need a ride?" asked Elgin. "I have a feeling your—uh—friend took off with the car…unless you came separately."

Annan shook his head. "Of course." He couldn't stop the laugh that bubbled up from his throat. Ralph would chop his own legs off before he spent a dime himself, especially when it came to transportation. "Guess I'll be walking for a bit."

It wouldn't suck so much if he hadn't lived thirty minutes outside of town, where the city lights were only visible as a distant haze in the middle of the night. He could see the stars there—pure, clean and unblemished on clear nights.

"I'd report it stolen," said Elgin, shrugging when Wallace sent a glare his way. "What? The guy seemed like an asshole. It would serve him right."

"Elgin." Wallace spoke through clenched teeth. "Don't you think that's a little inappropriate? I'm sure he had his qualities." He pushed the bowl of whatever he was eating to the side, smoothing his hands over the white tablecloth. His fingers were delicate and pale, like the rest of him.

Qualities? At first, Annan had fallen for Ralph's looks alone and the way he had moved to the music from across the bar. The sex had been decent, if not a little unenthusiastic, but that was about it. Their relationship was pretty bleak, now that he thought on it. Looking back, most of them had seemed that way.

"I don't think Ralph had any," said Annan, licking his bottom lip where he'd been biting it repeatedly for the last few hours. Scratching at the gel that clogged his hair, he tried to think. There had to be something.

"Was he a good cook, maybe?" asked Wallace, leaning his head on his hand and tilting his head. His eyes were sparkling in the candlelight, his lips turned in a soft smile.

"No way," said Annan, wincing as he recalled the single time Ralph had made dinner. He'd wondered at the time if his tastebuds would ever recover. "And not one for other housework, either." Dish and laundry soap gave Ralph rashes, but only if he touched them directly. How that stopped him from picking up his clothes and towels was a mystery.

The first time Annan had been to his apartment, he'd wondered if Ralph had been robbed, with things lying all over the floor and dirty dishes piled in the sink. He'd been willing to overlook it at the time.

"Maybe he was really sweet? Did he buy you little gifts or leave you notes telling you to have a good day?"

Annan shook his head. That was so opposite to Ralph that it gave him shivers. Ralph had never been the gift giver but loved getting little treats himself, not that he ever thanked Annan for them.

"I know," said Elgin, a smirk on his lips. "He gave amazing head."

Annan choked, covering his mouth to smother the sound as another laugh bubbled forth, this one laced with a touch of disbelief. *Is this guy for real?* "Definitely not."

Elgin shrugged. "Guess it was doomed."

"Elgin." Wallace reached across the table, standing so he could swat his husband's shoulder. Elgin let it slide off with a grin.

"I'm just saying—a man's *technique*—so to speak, is half the picture. One half handsome, one half a devil in bed and the rest will work itself out." Elgin turned to

Annan, his face completely serious. "Wallace gives *amazing* head."

"Elgin!" Wallace flushed, pushing his chair back and crossing his arms as Elgin chuckled, the rich sound filling the space. "You better pay now, because we're leaving."

"Come on. I'm just trying to make the guy laugh. He just got his heart broken, so give me a break," Elgin said, reaching for his wallet and abandoning the rest of his steak.

The strangest thing was that Annan *was* feeling better. He was laughing right along with Elgin, a grin spreading over his face as Wallace flushed brighter. They were two strangers, but he was laughing harder than he had in months.

"I'll get the car," said Wallace, wincing a little as he looked at Annan. "Annan, we can drive you home if you like, or we can call you a cab—whichever you prefer." He turned, lightly stepping toward the exit. The server zeroed in on him as he left before glancing to where Elgin was seated with his card lying on the table.

"I don't know what I'm going to tell my parents." Annan let out a groan, combing a hand through his hair. His finger came away sticky and gross from the amount of product in it. He rarely styled his hair, and he'd admittedly gone a bit overboard. "I told them I was going to marry Ralph. What am I going to say? First, they think I should quit my job because of the fire, now my boyfriend dumps me."

"I might try wording it a bit differently," said Elgin, his eyes sparkling.

Annan chuckled, the sound coming from deep in his gut as the ache in his chest throbbed. *How did I think this guy was intimidating?* There was something familiar about him—something soft that Annan hadn't expected when he'd been pulled into that first shocking hug. "You're a shit disturber."

Elgin winked. "Sure am. I don't mean to belittle your feelings, but you're very handsome when you laugh. I can't seem to help myself."

Annan swallowed, turning his head as his heart rate picked up. *He* was not the handsome one. Wallace was gorgeous, and Elgin was something else. His suit was obviously custom, but it still hid his figure in a similar way that Wallace's oversized sweater had. Annan could imagine Elgin was ripped under the layers of clothes and Wallace was small, soft and perfect. But they were also married.

"You should come back to our place for coffee," said Elgin, flagging the server down as she hovered by the table. He turned to her, the grin gone from his face. "Can you wrap mine up, along with another of the same from the kitchen and a fresh order of soup? My husband didn't have a chance to enjoy his."

"No problem, sir." She took his plate, bustling off to the kitchen.

"Coffee?" Annan rolled the invitation around in his head. "I'm more of a tea person, especially at this time of day." Even with tea, he probably wouldn't be able to sleep all night. There was something about the warmth that invigorated him.

That wasn't the biggest problem. Every time he'd invited someone over to his place for coffee, there tended to be zero drinking and a lot of fucking. The two went hand in hand—like Netflix and chill, or a massage. *I'll keep my hands to myself if they do.*

"Sure." He grabbed the jewelry box from the table, shoving it deep into his pocket. "Wait. You guys aren't swingers or something, are you?" A rebound was great, but he probably shouldn't sleep with someone an hour after he broke up with his ex-future hubby—even if it helped with the emptiness, if only for a little while.

"Like a playground?" Elgin furrowed his forehead. "We have a pond out back and a nice raised garden, but no swing set."

You have got to be kidding me.

A smile spread across Elgin's face. "I'm just fucking with you. No swinging. We're a little kinky, but who isn't?"

Me. Annan swallowed hard, wiping the sweat from his palms onto his pants. "Sure, coffee sounds great. I don't have anywhere else to be at the moment except—"

He cut himself off as the memory of smoke flitted through his senses. Everyone had gotten out safely when the fire had started, but it had still been a complete shock to his system. He'd been so powerless as the flames had consumed a chunk of his life and livelihood, the screams of animals and humans forever implanted in his mind.

There were times in his life that he'd spent every waking moment there, but now it was almost exhausting just to drag himself to work, shuddering as he looked to the few remaining ashen scraps where one of the barns had stood.

The owner had done her best to get the build and recovery moving along, but he could still smell the remnants of burning whenever he went to that part of the property. *It could have been so much worse.*

"Excellent."

The server arrived with two boxes and something similar in bowl form, and Elgin paid with a tap of his card. "Follow me, Annan. Wallace will have the car out front by now. He'll probably be surprised you didn't ditch us after all."

Annan shrugged, kicking his shoe along the carpet as they made their way to the exit. "Like I said, I've got nowhere better to be."

It was so true that it was like a knife to his gut, twisting and turning until it stripped him of the last drops of life. Since the fire, he'd only had home and Ralph. Now he just had home, he supposed…*and tea.*

"I don't believe that for a second." Elgin held the door for him, stepping in behind him as the sun hit their faces.

It was still bright, the summer sunlight streaming through the spaces in the slatted roof that marked the entrance of the restaurant. Most of the trees were full green, but there was still a touch of spring flowers in one of the shaded beds. The front of the place was impressive, with massive wooden doors and two decorative fire pits that flickered with blue and orange flames. It looked expensive — and like a great place to get engaged.

His stomach grumbled, the rich smell of food leaving him unsatisfied. His knees still ached from being on the floor for those few moments, every eye but Ralph's on him. He wished he could say he'd never been so embarrassed in his life, but that would have been a lie.

"After you," said Elgin, sweeping his arm toward a car as it pulled up to a spot before them.

Annan's jaw dropped, his throat going tight. Wallace and Elgin were both well dressed, and the restaurant was expensive as all hell, but he hadn't expected a car like *that.*

"That is one pretty car." He closed the space, hovering his hand above the reflective blue paint that shifted colors, even as he stared at it. "I didn't think you could even get them in this color." The window rolled down, and Wallace waved at them from the driver's side. The sunglasses on his head were keeping his hair pinned back as he gripped the wheel, seeming so small in the large seat.

"It's a custom," said Elgin, pulling the passenger door open and motioning for Annan to step inside.

"Oh." Annan held his hands out before taking a small step back. "I'll be fine in the back seat." It looked spacious, so he wouldn't be cramped, and if he somehow ruined the leather, it was less likely they would notice. His ass was not worthy of sitting in the front seat.

"I insist." Elgin dropped his voice in the same way that had made Ralph scurry off. His stomach flipped, his gut sparking. The only way to cover his reaction was to duck inside, fumbling with the seatbelt with his head lowered.

"You doing okay?" asked Wallace, his voice soft and gentle. His cheeks were flushed, probably from the heat pouring through the vents, but Annan didn't dare turn it down. Instead, he nodded, keeping his mouth shut and propping his arm up on the window.

"Jeez, Wallace, it's like a sauna in here," said Elgin as he ducked into the back seat. "I don't want Annan to get hot and bothered."

Annan chuckled, tipping his head back into the headrest. The car smelled of new leather, which was something that called to his very heart. The cool seat pressed into his back, sweeping the last of his discomfort away as Wallace reached for the heat and turned it all the way down.

"Sorry, baby. I've got a chill." Wallace rubbed his arms even as he said it. His wrists were exposed, little goosebumps breaking out over his skin. Annan stared at the delicate blue lines on pale wrists that were thin enough that he could easily wrap his fingers around them.

He clenched his fist at his side, dropping it along the door and out of view. He should *not* be thinking about pinning Wallace's wrists to a bed, or kissing Elgin's jaw line when he'd barely been single for half an hour.

"Are you sure you're okay?" Elgin leaned between the seats, touching Wallace's face with the back of his hand. "I can drive if you want."

Wallace grasped his hand as it slid over his cheek, turning and placing a kiss on Elgin's palm. "No way. This is my baby."

They have more than one car like this? Annan let out a pained groan, rolling up the window as Wallace pulled out of the parking lot.

"Which way to your place?" asked Wallace, whipping his head around to eye up traffic. A horn blared in the distance as the city rush-hour heightened.

"*Our* place," said Elgin from the back seat. "We're going to have a tea party."

Annan craned his neck around, his eyebrows nearly hitting his hairline.

"Is that some kind of code?" asked Wallace, hesitantly pulling out into traffic before gunning it halfway through the turn. Annan pressed into his seat, holding his breath as they scarcely missed a car. His heart pounded, his gut going tight as he reached for an imaginary brake pedal before him.

"One thing I've learned about Elgin is that it's always a code for something," said Wallace, his hand flat on the wheel as he whipped them around the next corner, narrowly missing a red light and a Honda who had attempted to cut them off. "His mind is dirtier than a gutter."

If this is the way I'm going to go, I'm fine with it. Annan relaxed further into the seat, flexing his toes when they started to ache in his restricting shoes. "I think he's talking about tea bagging."

Elgin spluttered, smacking his knee as he laughed. Annan chuckled along with him, even as Wallace scrunched up his face in obvious confusion.

"I knew we were going to be friends," said Elgin, squeezing Annan's shoulder and letting his hand linger, hot and heavy. "As soon as you walked into the restaurant, I knew you would be hilarious. Fuck, I should have dragged you to our table sooner."

Fuck, that felt nice. Being wanted was like finally touching that unreachable peak that he'd been staring at for his life. He'd been popular in school, but that had dwindled in adulthood as people had moved on with careers and families while he stayed in the same place, putting himself at risk on the daily.

"What's tea bagging?" asked Wallace, slamming the brake as a squirrel ran across the road. Annan grabbed for the handle above his head, holding on for dear life.

"Other than a great idea?" asked Elgin. "Hopefully on the table. That's up to Annan."

His mouth was so fucking dry. They were way out of flirting territory and only a step away from foreplay. He couldn't remember his last real hookup that hadn't ended with more, and he rarely even snagged a rebound when he inevitably broke his heart. But it could be worse than two attractive and rich men who had excellent taste in food and each other.

"It's on the table," said Annan, risking a glance at Wallace out of the corner of his eye. He knew some couples who were open, but sometimes that changed after they were married. From the rings on their fingers, and the little ways they looked at each other, they were definitely in love. *Something I have no place in.*

"I'll get the teapot out of storage, then," said Wallace, all innocence as he made another turn. Elgin only snickered.

"This is going to be so much fun."

Annan couldn't help but agree.

Chapter Three

Elgin

This could go one of two ways, very, very quickly.

On one hand, Wallace could figure out exactly what they were talking about, turn the car around and demand to take Annan home. He'd be pissed and riled, and maybe a bit horny—hopefully horny enough to ride Elgin like a cowboy—or take him from behind to teach him a lesson.

Elgin moved his legs wider, shifting on the leather seat as he looked between his husband and his new best friend. Annan had relaxed, only tensing when Wallace tried to defy the law of physics while driving, which was often enough that he'd totaled four cars in three years. Luckily, the only casualty had been their bank account.

Option two, Wallace would figure it out and agree to the first threesome of their lives. They'd talked about it before, as he was sure most couples did, always in the midst of passion when blood pressure and mouths were running hot. But it was something he'd never expected to do.

Wallace was more than enough for him, but something had to be said about having a bit of fun. There was no question as to if Wallace would figure it out. He was a smart man who was spicy to the core.

Annan looked around as they pulled into their driveway and the metal gates closed behind them. He leaned forward in his seat, ducking low so he could presumably get a full view of the house. "This is your place? Wow."

"This is home," said Wallace, hitting the remote for one of three garage doors before pulling inside. "We used to have a penthouse downtown, but it was too close to work, and I'd spend the entire week away. Living here means we have somewhere to relax, where work is just far enough away that you can't make an excuse to stay."

"What he's trying to say," said Elgin, unbuckling his belt and stepping out of the car. He got to Annan's door in time to hold it open for him. "Is that he's a workaholic who got sick of his boy toy showing up at work to drag him home to a place that looked identical in every way, except for the fancy printer. And I wanted a garden."

Elgin moved to open Wallace's door next, wrapping an arm around his waist and leaning in close as Annan looked around the garage. "You okay with where this might go?"

Wallace set his jaw, nodding. His eyes were determined, a small flush on his cheeks that was absolutely adorable. His lashes were long, the pale strands brushing his cheeks as he blinked. He looked tired, but his stubbornness seemed to win.

"I call the shots, though," said Wallace, giving him a quick hug before stepping toward the door. Annan was looking at them as he tugged his tie looser. The first order of business would be to divest him of the entire ensemble — or maybe they'd just ruin it and buy him a new suit that actually fit him.

"Let me get the kettle," said Wallace, walking past Annan and opening the door. "I'll have to see what we have for actual tea bags, and if they're any good. It's been a while."

"Don't inconvenience yourself," said Annan, following Wallace a step behind. His eyes kept getting wider as he looked from the rich floors to the high ceilings. Elgin's personal favorite accents were the bookshelves at the top of the stairs, but they probably wouldn't have time to tour them today — not if he had his way.

"You're our guest," said Elgin, shifting the food he'd retrieved from the car, so he could shut off the light for the garage. The food smelled heavenly, and he was still hungry from rushing out of the restaurant. "And we can finish dinner while Wallace looks for the kettle."

Leading Annan to the kitchen, he set the food on the island, motioning to one of the tall chairs. They'd turned the dining room into a reading room, but it was no loss when they had ample space in the kitchen for breakfast and dinner. They rarely had people over for dinner — preferring to go to restaurants so they could maintain their privacy. This home was theirs and theirs alone. *Except for tonight.*

He could make the exception.

As he grabbed a few plates, Annan took a seat, leaning close to the marble countertop and running his hand over it like he couldn't quite believe what he was seeing. The white surface was cut with shimmering lines, something that was both beautiful and impractical. Elgin had managed to chip a small spot from the surface before he'd realized that they needed to seal it often.

"I'm fine," said Annan as Elgin set a plate before him, along with one of the boxes from the restaurant. His stomach chose that moment to let out a loud growl that had Elgin smiling.

"You should eat," said Elgin, taking up a fork of his own and grabbing the box with the remains of his own dinner. Wallace had barely touched his soup, but Elgin put the extra bowl in the fridge. There were some days he couldn't convince Wallace to eat. Most of those were when he was so wrapped up in his work that he forgot where he was, but those days were getting fewer and farther between, thanks to their new home.

"It's good." Annan let out a groan, his eyes sliding shut as he took a bite. "This has to be one of the best steaks I've ever tasted."

Elgin glanced to the far end of the kitchen, where Wallace had yet to appear. He may have been upstairs washing up after dinner and brushing his teeth. It was probably better that he was out of the room for this part.

"Have you fucked a man before?" asked Elgin before sucking a piece of steak from between his teeth.

Annan paused with his fork halfway to his mouth. He blinked, looking from Elgin to the entryway of the kitchen. There were no traces of embarrassment, like Elgin had expected. "Yeah."

Elgin nodded. "I figured you were a top, but I didn't want to assume. What about getting fucked?"

Now a flush worked its way across Annan's cheeks, and he ducked his head. "Do you interrogate everyone you bring home like this?"

"Only the ones who we might have sex with." *So only you.* He didn't want to say that out loud and somehow scare Annan off. Damned if he didn't want the guy.

"Yeah, but you might say I'm a bit rusty." Annan rubbed the back of his head. "Condoms are a must, either way."

"Sounds good," said Elgin, chomping off another bite. The steak was delicious, even though it had cooled. "I'll make sure to oil you up. That should help you with the rust."

Annan shifted, moving his steak around with his fork. It was almost half gone, but he made no move to finish it. Juice oozed from it as he poked it before sliding it back into the container. "Just be gentle, yeah?"

"Elgin is always gentle."

Elgin looked up to see Wallace at the entrance to the kitchen with a kettle in one hand and a teapot in the other. His shoulders were tense as he turned to set both on the counter before pulling a few bags from his pocket.

"Okay," Annan said softly, staring at his food.

Now that just won't do. "You say the word and I'll call a cab and get you home. Hell, we can play a round or two of poker instead, if you'd rather. We are up for a little fun, but only if you're up for it, too."

"No, it's fine." Annan dropped his fork, looking between the two of them. "I've just never done anything like this, so I'm not sure what I'm supposed to do. You already got me out of a crappy rejection, brought me dinner and gave me a ride. I don't have much to give you in return."

"You don't need to give anything," said Wallace, closing the distance and putting his hand over Annan's.

"Like Elgin said, it's a bit of fun. We aren't going to suck you dry or anything."

"Well," said Elgin, crossing his arms as he leaned back on his stool. "If Wallace gets his mouth on you, he may suck your soul out through your cock. I can't count how many existential crises I've had because of his mouth."

Annan chuckled, a grin on his lips. "I'm good to go — really. Just don't expect much."

Elgin nodded, regarding the two of them. *Is it go time?* He wasn't sure if he was supposed to wait for a signal or something. When Wallace gave him a small nod, he folded his container along with Annan's, putting them both into the fridge for later.

"Elgin is a great teacher," said Wallace, leaning against the counter. The lid to the kettle was sitting next to him and apparently forgotten, the tea bags probably destined to go back exactly where they'd come from.

"You okay if Wallace calls the shots?" asked Elgin, moving around the table until he was leaning next to where Annan was seated. Reaching for Annan, he grasped his hand, turning it over to see his palm. Calluses lined his palm, along with a small blister right at the center that had broken and scabbed over.

"Yes."

Annan swallowed audibly, and Elgin watched his throat bob. The cheap cologne had mostly faded, leaving that woodsy scent, along with thick leather that hadn't just come from the car. He looked nervous, fresh sweat tainting the air.

"Did you want me to drive you home?" asked Elgin, sliding in even closer. Wallace was shy in public, but in the bedroom, he was a wildcat. Annan was so different from him — insecure, unsure and nervous. Elgin wasn't quite sure how to react. It had been so long since he'd thought of pleasing another man who wasn't Wallace.

"N-no." Annan's voice trembled. When he looked up, his gaze darkened, and he licked his lips. Even if he was nervous, he was ready.

Elgin paused, his neck cramping as he held his position and kept their gazes locked. The hairs on the back of his neck prickled as he caught the sound of shifting cloth and Wallace's footsteps as he walked closer.

"I think you two should kiss," said Wallace.

Elgin turned his head to see his husband leaning on the island with his elbows on the surface. He had that same determined focus, but his eyes had taken on a soft shine. *How long have you been planning this?*

"You okay, baby?" asked Elgin. He'd imagined Wallace and Annan together, or Wallace between the two of them. He hadn't expected to share the first kiss with Annan.

When Wallace gave him a nod, Elgin shifted beside Annan's chair, turning it so their legs were tangled together. Annan flitted his gaze quickly between Wallace and him, his pupils wide and dark.

Sliding his fingertips over Annan's jaw, Elgin tilted his head up until their gazes met. He held it, the seconds passing by as he searched for any hint of hesitation. Annan was shaking, his hand unsteady as he touched Elgin's. But he didn't look scared.

"Nervous?" asked Elgin, dragging his thumb over Annan's lower lip. He was soft, warm and wet from when he'd licked his lips.

"Yes."

As he opened his mouth, Elgin dipped his thumb inside, drawing along the inside of his lower lip. Annan parted them farther, darting his tongue out to reach him.

"I'll be gentle."

Chapter Four

Wallace

He *needed* to know.

Elgin was a puzzle with too many jagged pieces that didn't match any jigsaw on the shelf. It was so rare to find someone who matched him and fit into those slots like they belonged.

Wallace had thought he was the only one.

He clenched his hand into a fist, his gut burning hot at the sight before him. The two of them were so beautiful together.

But he *had* to know if it was real.

Chapter Five

Annan

His heart was pounding, his gut burning as he held Elgin's gaze. Elgin wasn't doing anything, just touching his lip and staring, his eyes saying a hundred things that Annan couldn't understand. Between Elgin's sharp gaze and the way he crowded in closer, he looked ready to devour — to fuck, to destroy.

But he just stared.

"I'll be gentle."

Annan swallowed. Elgin didn't look like he was capable of being gentle. He was all dominance and strength, his muscles rippling beneath his clothes until the expensive seams strained. Wallace was the delicate one, with a look of utter determination the only thing that made Annan realize he was the one who was in control.

How many times have they done this? Maybe it wasn't flattering to realize that he was going to be a notch in the belt for two kinky guys. Marriage had to be boring, and Annan was probably meant to be that spark to liven things up.

But something told him that wasn't quite the case. It was too real to be practiced — too hesitant.

What is he waiting for? He was at his limit. Elgin was so close, heat rising to his skin as the distance between them shrank to nothing. But still, Elgin didn't kiss him, cupping his chin, but dropping his finger from his lips. They buzzed with the echo of his touch, tingling as Annan chased the feeling with his tongue.

Elgin watched him, following the movement with his gaze before wetting his own lips. He was clean shaven, his face looking so much smoother than his own, but different from the men he usually kissed. He was bigger — stronger — than anyone Annan had ever been with.

But Elgin didn't fucking move.

Annan raised his hand, threading his fingers through Elgin's hair. It was soft and warm, a hint of lavender shampoo and something else reaching him as he played with the strands. Tilting his head, he straightened in his chair, getting them as close as he could without pulling Elgin his way. He didn't want to rush, even as the anticipation thrummed through him.

"Do you trust me?" asked Elgin, whispering directly against Annan's lips. His breath was hot, tickling over his skin. Annan's mouth was bone dry as he nodded, unable to comprehend the question.

How could he trust a stranger who he'd known for an hour at the most? He couldn't even trust himself to pick out a man.

One thing was for sure — Elgin was dangerous. Annan licked his lips, struggling against the urge to lean in and *take*. He didn't care if he was being played. He *wanted*. Hell, he *needed*.

One moment, he was sitting on the stool, and the next, Elgin had him by the hips, bringing him around and setting him atop the kitchen island. A fork clattered to the floor as everything was pushed to the side, Annan's breath leaving him in a huff.

It took a lot of man to toss someone like him around. And yet, Elgin was still waiting, his eyes open but so close that Annan was seeing double. Elgin moved his hands from his hips to his waist, and Annan arched in response.

When their lips met for the first time, Annan almost didn't see it coming. The touch was soft and sweet, quickly deepening as Elgin slipped his tongue inside his mouth. He let out a groan, tilting his head to give Elgin better access as he looped his arms around his neck.

Holy hell, he can kiss. If he would have been standing, his knees would have gone weak, sending him sprawling on the polished flooring. He let out a long moan as Elgin took him apart, tightening his grip and bringing them closer.

There was no violence to it — no teeth or rough hands or anything like he'd expected. His gut thrummed, his cock already hard, even though it was just a kiss.

It was hard to call something like this *just* a kiss. Elgin had said Wallace would suck Annan's soul out through his cock, but it was already halfway there, brimming at the edge of his lips and ready to pour forth...*from a kiss.*

Annan let out a groan, gripping his hands tighter. He didn't need to breathe, not when he was being possessed in a way he'd never thought possible. Elgin seemed to know exactly where he was sensitive and how hard to stroke his tongue that twisted with Annan's to make him shudder. A clock ticked on a far wall, the silence of Wallace astounding.

Elgin turned his head to the side, breaking the kiss and heaving in huge breaths that matched Annan's. His lips were red and wet, a string of saliva caught on the lower one. Annan reined in the urge to lick it off, shivering when he realized it was *his* spit that marked the rosy stretch of Elgin. Maybe that would be cum soon, with Elgin's lips red, bruised and stretched around his cock beautifully.

"Wallace." Elgin's voice was broken, his eyes soft as he looked over Annan's shoulder. Annan followed his gaze, trembling when he caught sight of Wallace. His face was flushed, his hair messy as he stared at them with dark eyes and his lip red where he was biting it. It matched the spot on Elgin's lip where Annan longed to touch and stroke with his tongue, soothing any hurt he may have caused.

"You two are hot together," said Wallace, shifting his legs wider before rubbing his palm over the front of his pants. The luxurious fabric did nothing to hide him, stretched and uncomfortable-looking.

"Did you want to join?" asked Annan, unable to drag his gaze away from the tent in Wallace's pants. At least he wasn't the only one who was hard.

"Not yet." Wallace dragged his hand away before strolling across the kitchen toward the exit. "Meet me in the bedroom."

Elgin grasped Annan's hand, pulling him out of the kitchen and toward the stairs with Wallace only a few paces ahead. He was breathing fast, his gaze focused on his husband. *So much for Elgin being the dominant one.*

Annan had a feeling that Wallace could wave his baby finger and Elgin would follow whatever order he gave.

The grand wooden staircase passed by in a blur, a few doors and a reading nook a shadow in his periphery.

"On the bed," said Wallace, pulling his shirt from his shoulders and dropping it to the floor before sitting at the edge of a massive bed. The blankets were dark blue and plush, dipping as Wallace shifted. It made him seem pale, despite the flush on his cheeks, and so frail against the darkness.

It brought forth the strangest surge of protectiveness.

The entire room was immense, with a thick wooden frame on the bed and another nook to the side with a circular chair that overlooked a window. There were a few doors, one open and displaying a peek of a walk-in closet, while another exhibited the first few feet of a bathroom.

Elgin released him, sitting on the bed and reaching for the buttons on his own suit jacket. He couldn't seem to drag his eyes away from his husband, but Annan could only watch Elgin and the way he moved as he frantically tried to undress. Wallace stopped him with a light touch to his wrist.

"I want Annan to undress you."

Shit. That shouldn't sound so hot. Annan's cock throbbed, and he shook off the last of his doubt, strolling to the bed with every bit of confidence he could muster. He'd been with men before, and one couldn't be that different from two.

But there was something to be said about Wallace watching him, his eyes dark and predatory with his lithe hands clasped and his legs crossed as if he were ready for the next business meeting.

Grasping the edges of Elgin's suit jacket, he tugged, glancing to Wallace for approval. The fabric resisted him, and he flushed when he realized the buttons were still done up. He rushed to free them, his hands shaking as he pulled a little too hard, the fabric straining.

"Annan." Wallace reached for him, placing one chilled hand on his wrist. His hands were soft and light, leaving only the barest impression of him ever being there. "Put on a show for me. Go slow. Make him wait. It's so much better that way. Don't let anyone in the world make you rush. Cherish it."

Cherish it? This was a threesome, not a slice of cheesecake. *But...*

Elgin bit his lip, looking to Annan's hands, where he still grasped the material of the suit. He spread his legs a little wider, bracing his hand behind him as he squirmed the tiniest bit. Annan knew that move because he'd done it before himself — when he was hard but knew there was no escape anytime soon.

Sliding his hand along Elgin's chin, Annan tilted his face, a mirrored echo of what had happened in the kitchen. He brought their lips together in a puff of breath, slipping his eyes shut as the warmth and longing nearly overwhelmed him. A hand brushed against his own, and he didn't have to look to know it was Wallace, guiding him to the buttons on Elgin's jacket.

The suit jacket fell wide, and Annan dipped both hands inside, slipping over the smooth silkiness of Elgin's shirt as his skin prickled where Wallace's touch had disappeared. He could have shoved Elgin back and climbed aboard like a few guys had done to him, but instead, he deepened the kiss, slipping his tongue alongside Elgin's and letting out a soft moan at the pure sensation of it.

"Did you want to see him?" asked Wallace, his voice near. "He's beautiful."

Annan let out a groan as he eased away, his lips tingling as he nodded. His hands were shaking again, but he managed to slip a finger between the buttons of Elgin's dress shirt, popping two with zero effort.

The first peek he got of tanned skin and sculpted muscle had his mouth watering. He couldn't wait for more, his hands moving of their own accord and parting the fabric one button at a time, exposing more of a perfection that made his throat close up.

Beautiful. He glanced to Wallace, admiring the view of his bare chest. He was lean and lithe everywhere Elgin was broad, with a touch of softness to his features that made him that much more desirable. It was one thing to long for a hunk of a man, but Wallace was the type you would come home to and wrap up in a hug that would carry every ill away.

When every button was released, Annan slipped the suit jacket and shirt from Elgin's shoulders, tugging it free and tossing it behind him. With so much before him, he could only stare, his hands itching to touch but his mind frozen.

"Have you gotten your fill?" asked Elgin, a smirk on his face as he flexed, his muscles standing to attention. Annan shook his head, bringing his hands up before dropping them back to his sides.

"When Wallace said slow, I don't think he meant glacial," said Elgin, glancing at his husband with a grin.

Annan flushed, dipping his head. He was so far out of his league, and he couldn't even laugh about it.

These men were both beautiful and he was just — well, as Ralph had said — boring, friendless and *him*. "I'm not sure if I can do this."

Elgin's smirk disappeared in a moment.

"You're both so much, and I'm just…" He trailed off, blinking away the memory of the barrage of breakups from over the years. They had been alarmingly consistent. He'd never heard the 'it's not me, it's you' line. It had always, *always* been him. "I'm no good."

Elgin nodded, his gaze softening as he touched Annan's hip. His hand was hot and heavy, burning straight through the cheap suit fabric. He never should have rented the damn thing, nor the ring that was still burning through one of the pockets.

"Maybe not for anyone else," said Elgin, petting his thumb over the spot. "But I think you might be good for us." His smile flitted back, his eyes sparkling. "I mean, this is the most turned on I've been in ages, and I have a new best friend. What's better than that?"

Wallace smiled softly. "I think what Elgin is trying to say is that *we* want you to stay. It doesn't matter what anyone else thinks right now. It's just us, in a room — "

"Trying to get naked." Elgin cut him off with a grin before wilting under Wallace's light glare. "Oh, come on. Here, just let me — " He reached into his pants, adjusting himself and letting out a sigh. "That's so much better. I was getting a permanent bend."

These two are absolutely ridiculous. Annan shook his head, letting out a laugh as he sat on the edge of the bed next to Elgin. Even if they were ridiculous, he didn't want to leave. He just wasn't sure he belonged.

"Only if you want me here. I'll understand if you call a cab and send me home," said Annan, playing with the edge of his dress shirt that had somehow come untucked. The fabric was nearly see-through and rough against his fingertips.

Elgin grasped Annan's hand, dragging it over his lap and pressing it to the bulge at the front of his pants. "This here is for you—at least, seventy percent of it. Wallace still gets thirty, even if he hasn't touched me yet. That kiss was *hot*."

When he felt the heat and the hardness thudding against his palm, Annan let his eyes slide shut, reaching for Elgin's face by memory and dragging him close. Elgin met him in a kiss, groaning as Annan's hand twitched against his cock.

The kiss was just as sweet as the first one until Elgin touched the back of his head, holding him close as he leaned them onto the bed. Annan hit the blanket with a soft moan, twitching as Elgin climbed over him. When he reached out his hand, Wallace was there, squeezing him once before letting go.

"Get in the middle of the bed and, Elgin, take the rest of your clothes off."

Elgin leaned back as they both scooted across the bed until they were in the middle with Elgin straddling his hips. He flexed his abdomen as he reached for his pants, giving Annan a show of popping the button and dragging the zipper down. When Elgin tried to push them off, they clung on, his legs spread too wide to get off.

"I didn't think this through," said Elgin, probably to himself as he rocked back onto his feet, standing above Annan as he dropped his pants. "Or maybe I did."

Annan dragged a hand over his own abdomen, pausing at his groin and giving in to a gentle touch. He had the perfect view of Elgin, now naked as he tossed his socks away, his cock springing upright and already red and wet at the head. He was fucking starving for it.

When he glanced over to Wallace, he caught sight of naked skin. He didn't know when Wallace had undressed — maybe when Elgin was putting on a show, but he instantly regretted missing it. Wallace was perfect and unblemished, except for a small scar lower on his abdomen, a dusting of fine blond hair covering his body. That smile, though — shiny with a touch of warmth — was the real draw.

"I didn't know it would be like this," said Annan, not knowing what to do. He relaxed on the bed and stretched his arms out on either side of him, touching the tips of Elgin's toes.

"What did you expect?" asked Elgin, going to his knees and resuming his position of straddling Annan's hips. His flesh burned through his clothes, his cock most of all, as he settled down.

Something hard, fast, painful…cold. Anything but this. "Not this."

"It feels good." Annan's clothes were like a barricade, giving him an edge when he needed it most. Even as Elgin moved back in for a kiss, Annan still had the upper hand. He gave in, welcoming Elgin to him and running his hands through his hair. He would have loved for Elgin to do the same, but the gel was nasty — something they both seemed to realize.

"Use your teeth," said Wallace. Annan blinked, his heart pounding as Elgin ducked below his lips, kissing the slight scruff of his neck. He let out a hiss, curling his toes even as he tilted to give him better access. *Maybe a bite won't be so bad.*

It was strange how some guys thought he was some sort of chew toy. Bites in bed rarely felt all that good, but he could bear them well enough for his partner's sake.

"Relax," said Elgin, sucking at his ear lobe before scraping his teeth over it ever so gently. It didn't hurt, only called to something deeper in Annan that dragged a moan from his chest.

When Elgin dipped to his chest, he expected a bite on his collar where the top two buttons were already gone. He braced himself as Elgin grabbed the next button in his teeth, tugging it off and spitting it on the bed as it came loose.

"Use your teeth."

His eyes rolled back as he realized what Wallace had meant, gripping the sheets so he didn't reach down and pull Elgin's hair. At this rate, it was going to be over before it even started. With Elgin's breath tickling his skin, and his clothes slowly falling away, nothing else mattered.

Elgin whined, nosing at Annan's belt when he reached it. The leather was thick. It was probably the only thing he was wearing that truly suited him. The thing had cost almost as much as renting his entire suit, which was now mostly ruined.

"Should I help him?" He turned his head to Wallace. He may have been the one being stripped, but Elgin had been right. Wallace was calling the shots.

"If you want," said Wallace, shrugging as he stroked himself. "It's finally nice and quiet in here, so I wouldn't mind if you want to watch him struggle for a bit."

Elgin chuckled, kissing the looped leather. "You love my mouth."

"I do," said Wallace, his gaze steady. He looked to Annan, his expression going soft. "Help him."

Annan jerked at the leather, nearly whacking Elgin in the face in his rush. Elgin only chuckled louder, ducking to the side as the belt came undone.

"My teeth thank you," said Elgin, going for the button on the slacks with renewed vigor. It only took a moment for the pants to be opened wide. Annan sat up, pulling his shirt and pants the rest of the way off and shivering as his hot skin hit the cool air. Their gazes were hungry — devouring, as he exposed himself.

Wallace let out a soft groan. "If I would have known all that was hidden under your clothes, I would have suggested you get naked sooner."

Annan flushed, falling back as Elgin nudged him and placed a kiss on his neck. He used his hands to pull his boxers down as he sucked a bruise into Annan's pec, the suction insistent...but not painful in the way he knew it could be. When Elgin moved to Annan's nipple, he almost lost it.

He'd always been sensitive, but Elgin seemed to know exactly what to do to him, and just how to touch to make it feel the best. He swirled his tongue, reaching for Annan's cock and touching it for the first time.

"I'm gonna—" Annan cut himself off as he tried to hold on. *How fucking embarrassing.* He might as well have come in his pants.

"I am *that* good," said Elgin, leaning back with a smirk before he moved toward the edge of the bed, grabbing a handful of things from the bedside table. Annan throbbed, his legs twitching with the power of his missed orgasm.

"One condom for me, and one cock ring for you," said Elgin, tossing each item on the bed as he counted them out. "Make that two condoms, and a pile of lube for shares." He grinned, crawling toward Annan and grabbing the cock ring as he went.

"The first time Wallace and I got together, he busted before I could get him in my mouth," said Elgin, casting a look to his husband.

"Lies." Wallace narrowed his eyes. "The first time I gave Elgin a blow job, he came all over my face before I'd even touched him."

These guys.

"But you looked so good," said Elgin, tapping the cock ring against his chin. "It was a compliment."

Annan closed his eyes, letting his head thud against the mattress. He'd never been so turned on while laughing at the same time. His cock was flapping around with each chuckle, which was an interesting sensation, to say the least.

"What about your first?" asked Wallace, lying flat next to him as Elgin paused with his hand hovering with the ring just above Annan's cock. Annan opened his mouth to speak but was cut off as Elgin touched him, pushing the ring to the base of his cock and stretching the flexible silicone around his balls.

"My first threesome…" Annan trailed off, his breath hitching as Elgin stroked him from base to tip. "I lasted longer than anyone else."

Lies.

Wallace grinned. "I'd figured this was your first time with two men."

"It definitely is," said Elgin, moving to straddle him. "I'll take it as a challenge. What do I get if you come first?" He rolled his hips, bringing their cocks together and dragging along the sensitive skin.

Annan trembled, grabbing Elgin's thighs and sinking his nails into the soft flesh. "That depends on where you're sitting. If you were on your knees, your prize would be a boatload of cum on your face."

"Winner, winner." Elgin leaned in, pressing their naked chests together and stealing Annan's breath in another kiss. This time there was no sweetness — only hunger as Elgin divested him of every rational thought. Moving down his body, he kissed a path over Annan's chest and abdomen while pointedly avoiding his cock.

"Did you want Elgin to eat you out?" asked Wallace, leaning on one elbow and stroking himself with his other hand. He didn't seem in any rush and looked to be simply enjoying the view. "He's very good at it."

Annan nodded, his face flushing bright as Elgin sucked another bruise onto his chest. He was going to be covered in marks, some of the small red spots already blooming purple. Without a word, Elgin grabbed Annan by the hips, flipping him over.

Jesus, he's strong.

Pressing his face into the bed, Annan burned as he was exposed, Elgin kissing one ass cheek, then the other. He flinched as something touched his rim and Elgin made a soothing noise, stroking him.

He could count on one hand how many times he'd been in this position. He could use that same hand to tally the guys who had rimmed him in a way that he had actually enjoyed.

His breath caught as Elgin licked a stripe along his perineum, pausing at his entrance and wiggling his tongue all the way inside. Annan felt his body part with a long moan, and he gripped the sheets, his knuckles aching from the strain.

Without the cock ring, he would have come already, spurting into the sheets and staining them with his mark. As it were, his cock twitched and leaked, his entire body jolting every time Elgin wiggled a bit deeper.

"Jesus." Annan bit his lip, squishing his face into the sheets. Elgin deepened his touch, spreading Annan's cheeks wide and thrusting his tongue inside. "Fuck, I can't."

He was so close, the edge a prize that was just beyond his reach. He couldn't keep still, kicking his legs out and moving his hands as he tried to get more — to get away — to come.

"I think he's ready," said Wallace. Annan looked to him, his eyes watering from the onslaught. He wasn't sure what he was ready for — or who — but he didn't care. Fingers, a cock... Hell, even a dildo would be fine. As long as it was in him *now*.

Elgin touched Annan's cock, rolling something over it from tip to base. Annan couldn't look away from Wallace, caught in his gaze that was all softness.

"Roll over," said Elgin, grabbing Annan by the hips and urging him until his back hit the bed, his sweat soaking into the sheets. Elgin's lips were red, his cheeks flushed and drool smothering his lips before he wiped it away.

Face to face? Everything had been so personal and intimate that it really shouldn't have been a surprise. When Elgin straddled his hips again, Annan furrowed his forehead in confusion. It wasn't until Elgin grabbed Annan's cock, pressing it against himself and bearing down, that he truly understood.

He was *fucking* Elgin.

Elgin threw his head back as he lowered himself, his chest flushed and his ass so tight that Annan knew he hadn't gotten much prep, if any. He was hot, his body pulsing and already milking him.

He wasn't going to last long.

"Fuck, that's good," said Elgin, reaching up and pinching at his own nipples. Leaning to the side, he grabbed for Wallace, who had risen to his knees to get a better look at where Elgin had impaled himself. Wallace dodged his outstretched hand.

"I want to watch you get fucked," said Wallace, scooting back so he was out of reach.

If there was one thing in the world that Annan was good at when it came to sex, it was the fucking part. He'd been rolling his hips for so long that it was almost second nature. *Maybe there's one thing I can teach Elgin.*

Taking Elgin by surprise, he reversed their positions, grabbing Elgin's knees and pushing them to his chest. He was surprisingly flexible for a man of his size, his arms bulging as he grabbed at his own legs and held them wider.

It was so practiced the way he did it, telling Annan all he needed to know. Wallace had been in this same position, fucking Elgin into the mattress with urgency and dominance.

Slowly, Annan sank all the way inside, nudging his hips to move his cock deeper as he claimed Elgin's lips in a kiss. He knew he found the spot when Elgin cried out, his mouth dropping open so Annan could devour him.

Nothing in the world could have made him go faster as he kissed Elgin within an inch of his life, slowly fucking him and nailing his spot each time. His cock throbbed from the tightness of the cock ring and from Elgin's walls wrapped around him.

"Harder," said Elgin, arching his back as he tried to meet Annan's thrusts.

Annan shook his head, refusing without a word and slowing his pace so Elgin would feel every inch as he pressed his way inside. The next time he cried out, Annan paused before making a few short thrusts that nailed Elgin's prostate dead-on.

"Fuck, I'm gonna—" Elgin flexed, gritting his teeth as he grabbed for his cock. Annan was balanced on his hands, unable to reach for him to slap his hand away, even if he wanted to.

"Don't you dare touch yourself, Elgin," said Wallace, his voice deep with warning. His eyes were so dark, his hand moving fast on his own cock as he watched them.

"Please, baby. *Please.*" Elgin grabbed for the sheets as Annan nailed his prostate again, slipping deeper, only to readjust and start all over again. Elgin was going to ache for days, his prostate battered by the onslaught.

"Come."

At Wallace's voice, Elgin snapped taut, arching as his cock twitched. His cock spurted, dribbling over his groin and chest as he cried out, his body clamping down on Annan and trying to drag his orgasm from him. With a grunt, Annan slipped out just long enough to discard the cock ring before he pushed his way back inside.

Not yet.

Wallace was close, and Annan was too far gone to care if he had permission or not. Grasping Wallace by the hair, he pulled him in for a kiss as he continued to batter Elgin's spot, pushing him until his cries grew weak.

Wallace jolted, letting out a gasp at the kiss and jerking his hand faster. A moment passed before he slowed his pace, his cock erupting to paint his hand.

Fuck. Annan pushed himself deep one last time, letting himself go. He came like a freight train, emptying himself into the condom until there was nothing left. He heaved as he collapsed onto Elgin, the cum smearing on his chest as his cock slipped out.

Elgin winced, wiping his hand over his sweaty face. "You were right. You were the last one to come during your first threesome."

Chapter Six

Elgin

He slung his bag over his shoulder as the elevators opened for the top floor, strolling through and smiling at the receptionist. As soon as Derk saw him, he perked up, dropping his cell phone and pen.

"Mr. Bekker, it's so good to see you." Derk stood up, circling around the desk. He'd been the receptionist for the last three years and controlled every bit of information going in and out of the building, including the gossip. Luckily, Elgin has always landed on his good side.

Elgin gave him a smile, not slowing down as he made his way past the desk. "Good to see you, Derk. Sorry... I've got to talk to Wallace right away, and I'm sure you're super busy. I don't want to take up any of your time."

Derk's eyes sparkled as he smiled. "I always have time for you, Elgin."

That's what I'm afraid of. It had taken Elgin months to realize that if he paused at the front desk, he wasn't making it past for at least a good twenty minutes.

"Wallace is still in a meeting," called Derk as Elgin slipped by the desk, aiming for one of the largest offices in the building.

The whole thing had been redone from top to bottom two years prior, but Elgin had noticed very little difference. The walls were still the same beige, with offices highlighted with frosted glass and thin carpeting.

"I'll interrupt. It's important." Elgin sent him one last wave before he picked up the pace, hiking his bag up higher on his shoulder. Hopefully, Derk thought the bag was full of confidential documents or a laptop, when in reality it was his gym bag, lined with neatly folded clothes and a change of undies.

He'd been halfway to the gym before he'd realized that Wallace hadn't joined him on his last six runs. He needed to clear his head, and a run together was the ticket. A certain someone had been haunting his idle thoughts, memories of sweet laughter and smiles trickling in. *And abs – Those were some amazing abs.*

But he hadn't heard a word about Annan from Wallace in the last week. It was as if the man had never existed in their home, the sheets smelling of leather days after he'd left in the early hours when Elgin had barely roused at the sound of the front door closing. He knew Wallace had gotten his number. He'd said as much when he'd crawled back into bed, placing a kiss on Elgin's forehead.

It just wasn't like Wallace to avoid a topic or keep anything from Elgin. It was hard to keep secrets when

Elgin was borderline obsessed with his husband. *Maybe a bit more than borderline.*

"Hey." Elgin ducked through the door to Wallace's office, pulling the door shut behind him. Wallace looked up, a smile immediately on his lips. The droning mumbling of a conference call was going in the background, someone talking numbers that made Elgin's mind go numb.

The room itself was modest compared to what Wallace used to have. Once they'd moved to a real home, Wallace had taken out half of his space and the washroom, converting it into a second office. What was left was made up of mostly shelves and a few business awards, along with a single shuttered window that overlooked the city.

Elgin strolled to it, parting the thin slats of the blinds. With everything else of value in the office, these blinds were a cheaper plastic model. They were always open to let a touch of freedom in through the window, but today they were shut tight, the last glow from sunset dim in the office. Even the overhead fixture was off, the yellow lamp at Wallace's desk the sole source of proper light.

"Is it a pajama party?" asked Elgin quietly, just in case Wallace's mic was on for the conference. "Budgets, then s'mores in the dark?"

Wallace shook his head, tapping a key on his computer to presumably mute his microphone. "Just a headache, love. The sun was cutting right through the window and making it a lot worse."

"Oh." Elgin dropped the pull cord, smoothing the slats shut where they had rucked up. "Can I get you anything to help it? I've got a few painkillers in my bag, or I could ask Derk to grab you some coffee. Nothing like feeding the caffeine addiction."

Wallace shook his head. "I'll be fine." He tapped the button on his computer, chiming into the meeting as if he'd been paying attention the whole time. Elgin immediately zoned out, strolling to the opposite wall and running a finger over the nearest award.

Wallace had worked hard his entire life and had rocket-shipped to the top of the company fast enough that many took notice. So many others had tried to poach him, but Wallace was as loyal as they came, sticking with the company, even in the tough years when they didn't hit projections.

The commitment seemed to resonate throughout the staff. People like Derk and Wallace often worked long after regular business hours.

"Did you get off work early?" asked Wallace, tapping the same key.

Elgin furrowed his brow, checking his watch again. Occasionally he lost track of time, but he was usually pretty good about getting the fuck out of his office before the rest of the folks. After five, his give-a-shits officially expired. "It's seven o'clock."

"Oh." Wallace blinked, glancing back at the computer screen. The monitor was filled with squares of the others who were chiming in, some black squares and others with the most ridiculous backgrounds.

"I came to ask you to join me at the gym, but now I think I should take you home." Elgin crossed the space between them, meeting be damned. "You look tired, and you aren't feeling well. Come on. Let me take you home."

His heart ached whenever he saw Wallace like this. He had always been professional through and through and never bagged off work like Elgin did. Sometimes that meant sleepless nights, but he always made it home.

"I can't." Wallace winced, rubbing his temple. "It's quarter end, and I want to make sure everything is where it should be."

"Fuck quarter end." Elgin crossed his arms. "The numbers will be there next quarter, and the one after that." He leaned in close, whispering against Wallace's ear. "I'll let you top tonight."

Wallace spluttered, turning his camera off as he flushed bright. His eyes sparkled as he leaned up, kissing Elgin softly. "I can do that any time I want, and you know it."

I sure do.

"How about this?" Wallace closed the session, flicking the computer off. "I'll see myself home, but you still head to the gym. That way you'll be too tired out to fight much when I take your ass tonight, and I'll have a chance to take a nap."

"But—" Elgin started. It did sound like an awesome deal, except for the going alone part. "I'm feeling kind of lonely, baby. We haven't talked much about last week, and I know you've been busy, but I want to make sure we're okay." He let out a breath, scratching the back of his head. "Are we okay?"

"Of course," said Wallace, furrowing his forehead. "I love you more every day, and last weekend was amazing. I never thought I'd get to see that side of ourselves, and I really enjoyed it."

A grin broke out of Elgin's lips. "Thank Christ. I thought I was the only one. That was hot as fuck, am I right?" He motioned his hands down his own body.

"All this, and a bonus package for your viewing pleasure? It was like fucking Christmas."

"And Easter, all wrapped into one," said Wallace, rubbing at his forehead again as he leaned heavily into his chair. He looked so tired, his face gray in the low light. "New plan," said Wallace. "I'll send someone with you to the gym. I know it's not the same as me, but you can work out with them and talk shit for an hour before you come home."

"As long as it's not Derk," said Elgin, glancing toward the door just in case the assistant was listening in. "Anyone but that guy."

"Even your sister-in-law?" Wallace grinned as Elgin felt himself pale.

"Shit, is she in town?" He hadn't heard much from his brother in the last few months, which wasn't exactly odd. They'd been a lot closer in their younger years, but now they were nearly strangers. Part of their drifting apart had been directly related to Elgin's utter loathing of his brother's wife. She was one of the most racist and homophobic people he'd ever met.

"You can't back out now," said Wallace, grabbing a few things from his desk before he placed a kiss on Elgin's lips. "Have fun at the gym."

* * * *

The gym was fairly busy, which wasn't surprising for a weeknight, the smell of sweat and fifty kinds of deodorant, cologne and perfume striking him all at once as he went in the door. He took a deep breath of it, grinning as he waved at the front staff.

He was there often enough that they knew him by first and last name, and that if he ever went on holiday, they would always ask him about it when he came back. When he'd had a three-week business trip to Ireland, they'd apparently thought he'd died—or moved.

Elgin glanced at his cell phone as it buzzed.

I'll tell your gym buddy to meet you at the treadmills.

Wallace knew him way too well. He wasn't much for warming up, despite what every single personal coach had told him. A sprint on the treadmill until his heart was pounding was his idea of a good workout. Then a stretch, before the rest of his routine.

He stepped up to a free machine, wiping it down before starting it up. Giving himself a minute to get his balance, he upped the incline, ramping up the speed every few steps until he was in a jog. A few paces later, he was running, then pushing it faster, until he could barely keep up with the flying belt.

The first time he'd tried it, he'd slipped, flying off the machine and straight into a laughing Wallace. But that had been nearly fifteen years before, when he'd been trying to impress his future husband. He'd found something so much deeper that day.

The laughter would always be best.

"Holy shit."

Elgin would have ignored the words. It happened sometimes with people who didn't recognize him at the gym. He was there for a reason, and that was to push himself to the max, very often making a fool of himself. He didn't have the fastest run in the world, but he knew he was intimidating from the way others often moved away to the next machine over, giving him a wide berth.

But he couldn't ignore it this time, because he recognized that voice.

He stumbled, hitting the emergency stop, his legs trembling as he heaved in huge gulps of air. He'd only done a few hundred meters, but it was enough to have his heart pounding and sweat prickling over his skin.

"Annan?" he turned to the man who was paused a few steps away from the treadmills with his mouth hanging open.

He looked just as good as Elgin remembered—maybe even better. That nervous suit from their first night had been replaced with loose track pants and a black tank that left nothing to the imagination. The memory of touching and kissing Annan could never match to seeing him again in person.

"Yeah." Annan rubbed the back of his head, a grin on his lips. "What can I say? I got a text to meet you guys here, and I couldn't stop myself. I didn't run or anything." He shifted his gaze to the side, a flush on his cheeks.

Wallace. Elgin tilted his head back, breathing deep as he looked to the ceiling. He wasn't exactly sure what his husband was playing at, but he fucking loved this game. And that lie about Annan not running? His chest was heaving, the smell of sweat on his skin.

"Where's Wallace?" Annan turned his head, looking from the treadmills to the ellipticals on the other side of the room. Nearly every single one of them was occupied, each person in their own world as they worked up a sweat.

"Excellent question," said Elgin, resetting the machine as he motioned to the one next to him. "Do you usually run, or did you want to check out one of the other areas?" He glanced back when Annan didn't answer.

Annan had dropped his gaze, his cheeks pink as he eyed Elgin's ass. Elgin flexed in response. *Might as well show off.*

"Treadmill's good," said Annan, dragging his gaze away. When he started up his own machine, he kept his eyes locked on the settings, starting at an unsteady walk that had him clutching the handrails. He furrowed his forehead as he touched a few buttons, hiking the incline up, then back down to where it had started, his eyes flying wider as his speed jumped.

"Shit, shit." He jammed the 'down' button, nearly running into the front of the machine when it slowed too quickly. "Sorry." He lowered his voice, the flush extending down to his chest as he fiddled with the controls. His knuckles went white as the speed jumped again and he clutched the handrails.

"Come here often?" Elgin raised one brow before reaching across to slow down Annan's machine. "It takes a bit to respond, so give it a few seconds each time you push it." He put it to the speed of a medium walk, and Annan let out a soft sigh.

"The last gym I was at had one treadmill that was just for walking and a few weights," said Annan, chuckling as he eased his grip on the bars. "Thanks."

Elgin made a noise in the back of his throat, upping into a quick jog. He was still a bit out of breath, but energy bubbled under his skin, fueled by the adrenaline from seeing Annan again.

"That's a surprise." He panted between each word, getting back into the quick run that always came just before his sprint. "You're in fantastic shape."

A body like Annan's didn't come from sitting in an office chair or watching quarterly meetings. It took a lot of hard work, especially after the thirties loomed in. Elgin was nearing forty himself, and he remembered how much harder it had gotten for him after that birthday cake with the big three-o.

"This is all natural," said Annan, motioning to himself.

Elgin stumbled as he looked to the side. Annan's arms were bulging, even just from a walk with the way he gripped the handrails every few steps. Not to mention, he was fucking chiseled and rugged, like he spent his days out in the sun rock climbing.

"I'm a hands-on kind of guy," said Annan as he nearly tripped again. Those hands were wrapped so easily around the rails, veins straining against tanned skin.

I know that one for sure. Elgin slowed his machine before he could make a fool of himself. Track pants were usually his go-to for the gym, but maybe they'd been a poor choice for today. His memories of those hands were far too crisp to be reliving in a packed business that wasn't a club.

"I didn't mean it that way." Annan held up his hands, his entire face turning crimson. "Sorry. I'm not trying to hit on you. I don't really know what I'm doing here. Wallace was supposed to be here, but he's not, and I don't want to get you into any trouble. I know we've had sex, but he was there."

Elgin nodded, the same feeling tightening his gut. He'd never had a single doubt about his marriage or his husband, but this situation was strange. *Is it a test?* He couldn't see Wallace doing something like that. His husband knew how obsessed he was with him. There shouldn't have been any doubt.

Even if the sex had been *that* hot. But sex wasn't everything. Hell, despite how much he loved dirty jokes, sex was only a small part of his marriage — more like the lines of lust between the sweet pages and touches.

Pausing his machine, Elgin stepped off, wiping down the surfaces he'd touched. Annan followed suit with something akin to relief. Elgin watched him, following each movement with his gaze. Yes, he was turned on, but he was half the time, anyway.

Making up his mind, he slung his towel over his shoulder before holding out his hand. "Friends?"

A smile slid over Annan's lips. "Friends."

Their palms touched with a zing of heat, but Elgin forced himself not to respond. Maybe if Wallace had been there, he would have tugged Annan a little closer, tasting the sweat on his neck, but not like this.

"Can we *not* go on those ones?" asked Annan, casting a look at the other row of different machines. A few people had moved on, leaving more than enough space for them. "I will break something for sure."

"Sure." Elgin grabbed his water bottle, taking a few slow swallows to steady himself. "Let's go down a floor to the weights. I'll finish up my cardio, then I can spot you if you'd like."

The gym itself was comprised of three floors, with classes like yoga and pound up top, the more complicated machines in the middle, and mats and free weights on the bottom floor. It was one of the higher-end places in town, which suited Elgin just fine, but only because they had a shit-ton of equipment and space.

"This is so much better," said Annan as soon as they'd reached the lowest floor. He headed straight for the barbells, grabbing a size above the small ones with the plastic coating. After a moment's consideration, he placed it back on the rack, going for the one that was five kilograms heavier.

Elgin grabbed a skipping rope himself, setting himself up on a firm section of mats not too far from Annan. This time he took it slower, shifting from foot to foot with each hop so he didn't catch the rope and have it slice against his skin to leave a purple welt.

"So, what does a guy do that's so hands on that it leaves him as ripped as you are?" asked Elgin, flipping into a few double unders to get his blood pumping again, not that watching Annan lift weights wasn't doing that itself. Each move had Annan's biceps and shoulders flexing, even his pecs straining through his shirt.

"I work with horses," said Annan, shaking out his hand before lifting the weight into a curl again. "I'd rather harvest hay than hit the gym any day, which is saying something." He chuckled, letting out a huff as he shook his hand out again.

Does that mean you're just here for me? Elgin shook the thought away. He must've been horny as hell for Annan to be fucking with his head this much.

"Hay is brutal," said Annan. He wiped his hands on his track pants, looking at his palms. "It's heavy, awkward and it kills your back and hands. It's usually hot as hell any day you have to haul it, and everyone who promised to help mysteriously disappears." He glanced around at the mirrors and the line of various sizes of weights along with the heavier set ups on the opposite side of the room. "Still beats this."

Elgin paused, narrowing his eyes. *This is a nice gym.* He had some good friends here, and the staff were second to none.

"Sorry." Annan flushed. "I'm sure this is a nice place." He ran his hand through his hair. "I just keep fucking up today — not just today." He let out a long sigh. "Sorry."

Elgin knew a little about fucking up. He was cocky, obnoxious and turned everything into a joke most days, just to see people laugh. Hell, he was probably fucking up right now with his heart beating fast and his palms sweatier than they had ever been at the gym.

"Tell me about it." Elgin dropped the rope before taking a seat on the nearest bench. His muscles burned with unspent energy, but they would have to wait for now. Annan looked at him, startled.

"You want to know about hay?" It wasn't a question — more of a thinly veiled accusation, as if Elgin would dare to take an interest in something so terrible and menial.

"Nah." He took another swig of his water. It was metallic and stale, which probably meant he'd forgotten to refill his water bottle and was sipping on last week's leftovers. "Hay sounds awful. Tell me about the horses. I've never touched one before."

He'd been to petting zoos when he was a kid, but he'd been a tiny thing back then. Anything above three feet had been intimidating as hell, and his family had moved to the heart of the city long before he'd hit puberty.

"I can't even remember the last time I saw one...maybe when I was younger, and before I met Wallace."

There was a tour group who took carriages around the scenic parts of town, but he wondered now if they'd gone out of business. The rhythmic sound of those hooves on pavement had always turned his head, but he'd never had the desire to take that tour himself. His own two feet were reliable enough, thank you.

"You've never... *Jesus.*" Annan made a noise in his throat, shifting on the bench next to Elgin. "You can't be serious. A drive of thirty minutes in almost any direction puts you in horse country."

Elgin quirked his lips. "Wallace keeps me busy." *And the only way I usually leave the city is on a plane.*

The smell of Annan's sweat was thick, and Elgin could almost feel the heat from his body. He licked his lips, rubbing his thigh where the skipping rope had caught him a single time. The purple welt was already fading to red.

"It's hard to describe the horses," said Annan. He turned his head, his gaze catching Elgin's. "They're simple in a way. Sometimes, they're trying to kill you, and others just want to please, but it's the connection that really matters. No matter how many times I get bucked off, I still get back on, just for that chance that we're going to have a breakthrough and they finally understand what I'm asking them for."

Elgin clasped his hands, resting them over his thighs. He knew how to navigate the political minefield of the modern business world with intimidation and stubbornness, but he'd never come face to face with an animal ten times the size he was.

"You should come see them sometime."

Elgin jerked his head to the side, catching Annan's gaze. Annan gulped, looking away.

"I'm going to take off," said Annan. "Thanks for the workout...I think. I guess I'll see how sore I am tomorrow."

I should ask him for his number. Elgin opened his mouth, only to snap it shut a moment later. He grasped his hands together, scraping a nail over his palm. "I'd like that. To see them...I mean."

Annan nodded stiffly, busying his hands with his water bottle. He'd barely touched it, but he hadn't been there that long, either. He looked as out of place here as he had at the restaurant. *Is it bad if that makes me want him more?*

"I'll ask Wallace when he can go," said Elgin, his gut twinging with guilt. He wasn't this guy — the guy who went behind his husband's back — and he'd never had an unfaithful bone in his body. "He loves horses."

Annan's smile looked a little easier, and Christ, if that didn't make him even more beautiful. Elgin couldn't drag his gaze away, staring at the empty exit long after Annan had disappeared.

Chapter Seven

Wallace

They were perfect for each other—maybe not as good as he and Elgin were, but they'd had more than fifteen years of practice. Elgin was as snarky as Annan was shy, complementing each other with every nuance.

Even when Wallace had sent Annan a message to meet them in the gym, he could imagine the blush on his cheeks and maybe a stumble as he rushed for the door.

Everything was coming together.

Elgin was going to be okay.

Chapter Eight

Annan

"You have to tell me what's going on, Annan. I haven't seen you like this since what's-his-name."

Annan glanced through the metal bars into the neighboring stall. Milo was leaning on his fork, the plastic tines bowing from the strain, despite his slender build. His blond hair was currently dyed blue and held off his forehead by a ball cap that was twisted around backward. The look suited him, despite the wood shavings on his clothing and the sweat on his skin.

"Which one was what's-his-name?" asked Annan, shaking his head as he moved along to the corner of the stall, scooping what he could and putting it into the wheelbarrow.

Some horses spun in their stalls at night, and it took three times as long to clean the stalls, but Annan didn't mind. It was steady work where he could lose himself to his thoughts and pass the day by, his arms and back burning by the end.

The barn had grown progressively larger over the years, but the feel had stayed the same. The fire was the only thing that had put a wrench in that peace. Today was the first day that he couldn't smell the dark ash, despite the blackened and crumbled frame close by. The insurance companies had started their work, and the rain the night before had taken care of the rest.

That doesn't stop the memories, though. He shivered.

"Shit, I don't remember." Milo wiped his forehead on the back of his arm. He was a hard worker, even if he was skinny as a rail, and he was at the age where it seemed to be his goal to work a swear word into every sentence. *Oh, to be nineteen again.* "He had black hair, about yay high." He held his hand a few inches above his head. "When you brought him to the barn, he wouldn't even get out of his seat. And he freaked out when he got a fly in his car. I heard him screaming from the ring." He chuckled, leaning his fork against the side of the stall and stretching his arms over his head. "You seemed to like him, though."

"Oh." Annan racked his brain. Most of his boyfriends hadn't liked coming to the barn for some reason. A few of them seemed to like the *idea* of horses, but at the first whiff of manure, they ran back to the car. Many thought 'rich' and 'horse' often went together, which wasn't the case for Annan at all. "I think that was Jack."

"No." Milo scratched his chin. There was hay in his hair along with the shavings, a bit of dried slobber smeared on his arm. He looked like he'd rolled in one of the stalls, or he'd lain down for a nap, which wouldn't have been surprising. He'd barely been sleeping since the fire, the dark smudges under his eyes a testament to that.

"I remember Jack," said Milo. "He was the one who rolled in here with a Jag one day, only to bitch you out for being late or something."

Annan shook his head, shifting the wheelbarrow back to the entrance of the stall. It was nearly full, his arms straining as he pushed it, its nearly flat tire resisting every step. "That was Victor."

That was a relationship that he'd only realized was toxic after it had ended. Victor had been almost like a reverse stalker. If Annan wasn't thinking about him or in his presence at every moment, Victor would get upset. The final straw had been when Victor had almost gotten violent when he'd been out with his own friends, angry that Annan hadn't tried to track him down and interrupt his time away.

His car had been really nice, though.

"Anyone ever tell you that you have shitty taste in men?" asked Milo, snickering as Annan grabbed a handful of shavings and chucked it through the bars.

"Says the nineteen-year-old who told me how he puked when his boyfriend stuck his tongue in his mouth for the first time." Annan grabbed the full wheelbarrow, rolling down the aisle to the storage area at the end.

"That's a low blow, man!" Milo shouted after him. "I have a sensitive gag reflex."

"TMI," Annan called over his shoulder. He shuddered at the thought. Milo was sometimes like a little kid in a nineteen-year-old body, but he was also a little brother to him. Annan had been there for him in some of his roughest times, and that was never going to change.

Milo was slumped against the wall of the stall by the time he returned, his fork abandoned and his phone in hand, scrolling endlessly through an app.

"You never told me what has you all bothered," said Milo, looking up as Annan stepped into the stall with him, sifting through the areas Milo hadn't gotten to yet.

"Don't worry about it," said Annan, his grip going tight on the rake. He wished he could forget about it...and the two men who had somehow turned his life upside down within two brief meetings.

"Annan."

He looked up. Milo's gaze was steady, his lips set in a thin line. Sliding his phone into his back pocket, he grabbed the rake from Annan, tossing it across the stall. "Don't say that to me ever again."

Milo curled his hands into fists, bunching his shoulders as his face flushed red, the vein at his temple throbbing. He gritted his teeth, baring them in something akin to a snarl. His ball cap had twisted on his head, some of his messy hair escaping.

Annan almost took a step back, forcing himself to stay relaxed and casual. The way Milo could switch on and off was still shocking, even after all this time. "Okay."

The word seemed to give Milo pause, some of his rage visibly quelling.

The first time Annan had seen Milo at the barn, screaming his brains out and tossing rocks at the animals, he had been almost certain that the kid was a lost cause. He'd seen a few teens in the foster care system, but Milo had been so far gone — so fucked up from everything that had happened to him.

"I hear you, buddy," said Annan, keeping his hands at his sides. He'd seen someone lash out at Milo before, only to get beaten into a bloody pulp a few seconds later. He had no control of his rage, the smallest things setting him off, even though they'd come a long way.

He was tiny but fierce in the worst way. "Tell me what's going on."

"You're my best friend," said Milo, spitting the words through his teeth. "I get to worry about you if I want to."

He was still verbal, which was a good sign, and he could form sentences. It could have been so much worse. There were times when his brain seemed to switch off all together and he couldn't speak past the consuming wrath.

Those days were the hardest of all.

"I never thought of it like that," said Annan, grabbing for the fork. A plastic tine had snapped off it, but other than that, it was still intact. "You're right. I shouldn't be keeping any secrets from my best friend. It's not good for either of us." He focused on the shavings, keeping Milo in his periphery. "It is about a guy."

He ducked his head, getting back to scooping with his gaze focused on Milo. He was already winding down, his body not nearly as tense and some of the flush fading from his face.

Today's a good day.

There was a fine line between being manipulated into what Milo wanted and managing his overwhelming temper, and Annan still screwed up some days. He fucking tried, though. The kid deserved that, at least, and the validation for what he was feeling.

"You help me with the next stall, and I'll tell you about it," said Annan, finishing the side and rolling the wheelbarrow into the next stall. Milo followed behind him, jamming his fork into the wooden planks along the way. Another plastic tine broke free, skipping into the hallway.

That first day Milo had thrown rocks at the animals had also been the last day he'd ever raised his hand against them. Now Milo seemed to understand them better than he did people most days, and the horses bonded with him. Even the young ones, who were usually rascals, were always gentle with Milo.

"What's his name?" Milo stabbed the ground, flicking a pile of shavings into the wheelbarrow. Most of it missed, but it was the effort that counted.

"Elgin," said Annan, ducking his head and keeping his hands busy. He shouldn't be saying his name out loud. Thinking about him was one thing, but talking about him made him more real and tangible.

"Sounds fancy. He rich?" Milo let out a huff, his shoulders drooping a bit. His light freckles were visible again with his flush faded, sweat speckling his cheeks. The freckles always darkened once they moved outside in the morning for chores, seeming to go light again when they mucked stalls.

"Probably." That house had been fucking huge, especially in the city, where everything cost twice as much. It was a price that Annan would never be able to afford. "I got the feeling he works in business — a big hot shot or something. Ralph seemed to know him."

"That's not a good sign," said Milo.

Why did everyone seem to realize how shitty his boyfriends were except him? Milo seemed to be able to tell even better than most, but he'd been through absolute hell. He didn't trust anyone, save a few select people.

"Normally, I would agree," said Annan. His arms were aching, a cool cross breeze prickling against his skin. They only had a few stalls left to go before they could break for a snack. "But he was *different*. He was wearing a suit when I first met him, but he's the type of guy that would fit into anything. And he's funny as hell—and sweet in a backward kind of way."

"The opposite of Ralph, then."

Annan nodded. "Like Antarctica and Australia."

"So you're in love with him. What's next?" Milo quirked his lips, tossing another loaded forkful into the wheelbarrow. It was teetering, but they were nearly done with this one. The flies kept close, landing on the pile within.

"I'm not in love with him," said Annan, pointing his rake threateningly. "And besides, even if I was, it wouldn't matter. He's married."

Milo's mouth dropped into a wide 'o' before he quickly recovered. He'd stopped scooping, though, leaving the rest for Annan. "That's an all-time low, even for you. I guess it will stop you from proposing, though."

Annan grabbed a scoop of mostly clean shavings, tossing it toward Milo. It struck him in the side, absolutely coating him. The thing about wood was that even if you washed your clothes, it still managed to get stuck on everything. Milo's undies would be giving him splinters for a month.

"Don't be mean," said Annan.

"Who's being mean?"

Annan glanced up, grinning at the sight of Oliya leaning against the open door to the stall. Her dirty blonde hair was done up in a messy bun, a bit of pale skin poking from her shoulder strap that was otherwise surrounded by a tan.

"Not me," said Milo, ducking his head and setting straight back to work. He finished the stall in a few swipes before grabbing the wheelbarrow and hiking it down the aisle.

"I thought maybe he turned down one of your marriage proposals," said Oliya, grinning at Milo's retreating form. She was young but she still had all the sass of a mom, while being cool at the same time.

Annan let out a groan, stepping out of the stall and moving to the next one. Oliya followed along behind him, her hands on her hips as she giggled.

"Does everyone know about that?" Normally, Annan would be a little upset about everyone's teasing, but this time felt different somehow — more tolerable. That, and he knew they had his back. If he ever needed a good cry, Oliya would be the first one to hug him. Milo would stand back and wait for the tears to stop before he came in for a hug of his own.

After the fire had finally gone out when one of the barns had burned down, they had stood together in front of it, wrapped in an embrace that had lasted for hours. It was one of the only times Annan had seen Oliya cry.

"Yep." She glanced over her shoulder, lowering her voice. "Is Milo doing okay today? He was up most of the night with night terrors. You know how it is. He won't tell me a thing about them."

Even though she looked to be in her twenties, Oliya had fostered Milo a few years prior. After he'd turned eighteen, he'd stayed on at the farm with seemingly no desire to leave. Oliya was more of his mother than anyone else had been to him before, and she cared about the kid more than his own family did.

"About the fire or his past, I wonder?" Annan didn't keep his voice low. Milo was just a regular person, and he deserved to know if he was being talked about. "I'll chat with him. In exchange, you have to bring us lemonade. Not the fake crap—the one you make."

Milo chose that moment to return, pushing past them into the stall. "I'll take one, too, if it's not too much trouble."

Oliya smiled wide. "No problem, little dude. But you have to do me a favor."

Milo turned toward her, wiping off his hands on his pants. "Sure thing, ma'am."

Her eye twitched, and Annan could almost see the shudder from being called that. She'd told him before that being called 'ma'am' should be reserved for when she was a ripe eighty-five. Until then, she was just Oliya.

"I have a feeling this guy is going to propose to *me* next." She waved her hand toward Annan. "Be a dear and make him fall in love with you so I can avoid that awkward conversation."

Milo burst out into a laugh. "Really? You and this guy? You know he's gay, right?"

Annan let out another groan, rubbing his hand over his forehead. "Yes, Milo, she knows."

"Have fun, boys." She turned, flicking a bit of dirt off her shoulder as a sparrow flew past her head. Some of the boarders hated the birds in the barn, but Annan loved the little guys. Soon enough, the babies would be flying from the nests, making a fool of themselves for his amusement.

As soon as she was gone, Milo leaned back against the side of the stall, effectively giving up on his side. Oliya was right. Annan could see how tired the kid was, with dark marks under his bloodshot eyes and that faraway look.

"I've got a deal to make with you," said Annan, staring at Milo until their gazes met. "I'll tell you about my date with this guy, and you tell me about your dream."

Milo scrunched his nose before raising his foot and putting it flat on the wall behind him. The last horse to be in this stall was a bit of a kicker, with crescent markings all over the planks of wood as evidence.

"You first," said Milo, finally nodding. His T-shirt hung from his thin frame, his jeans cinched tight with a belt. "Then we have a deal."

"Sure." Annan let out an inner sigh of relief. "I proposed to Ralph—as everyone seems to know, but this Elgin guy stood up for me, basically kicking Ralph out of the restaurant." He set his fork against the wall. "Your turn."

"Jeez." Milo looked away, shrugging his shoulders. "The usual. Dad with a needle in his arm lying on the floor, and me trying to wake him up—only I can't. There was a fire this time, too."

"Shit." Annan crossed the space between them, holding his arms out in an offered hug. Milo only hesitated for a moment before he gave in, wrapping his arms around Annan's waist and stepping closer. "Sorry, kid. I hate that you have to go through that."

Milo shrugged again, even as he trembled. His voice was strained and cracking when he spoke again. "Like I said, just the usual." He squeezed Annan tighter, sniffing. "What happened next? After the guy kicked Ralph out—which is awesome, by the way."

"It was." Annan nodded, not letting go until Milo was ready. "Him and his husband—uh—invited me back to their place."

"Say *what*?" Milo pushed him back before grabbing at his shoulders with wide eyes. His cheeks were streaked with tears, dirty tracks amongst his freckles. "You had a three-way?"

This is way too much information for a nineteen-year-old. "Kind of."

Annan broke away, grabbing his fork. "Come on. The stalls are never going to get done if we keep up with story time."

"Hey, Annan?" Milo asked softly. "Don't tell Oliya about the dreams. She worries a lot, but I'm okay."

"All good, man," said Annan, his chest going tight. *She isn't the only one who is worried.*

Chapter Nine

Elgin

Elgin bent over the flower box, cursing the weeds that seemed to be overtaking the flowers already. "Try gardening. It will be easy, they said. It will be fun." He jabbed at the thistle with his small shovel, the little spines shaking as they tried to stab him.

Stinging nettle had gotten him a few days ago, and he was still a little on edge because of it. His hand had burned for days, the miniscule spikes working their terrible magic.

"It's good for you," said Wallace. He was lounging in a chair nearby with a book in his hand and a beer beside him. With the sun filtering through the awning, he looked like a siren, the sunglasses the only thing that didn't look out of this world.

"Good for me, my ass," said Elgin, tossing the shovel and going for the weed old fashion style. He yelped when a few spines scratched along his arm as he dove for the root, scraping the dirt away with his hands. "I put two layers of weed barrier and three feet of soil up, and the thistles and weeds still grew to the top. I bet I could cover them in a bit of tectonic plate, and they'd still grow. They're like the roaches of the plant family."

Wallace folded his book in his lap, shielding his eyes despite the sunglasses. "Then maybe it's just good for me. You're shirtless, sweaty and dirty—my three favorite things in the world."

"Your favorite thing should be me totally naked," said Elgin, swaying his hips a bit before groaning as he stood from his crouch, the thick-rooted weed clasped in his hand.

Wallace hummed, laying his head back against the top of the lounger. He'd tossed and turned all night, which was why Elgin had suggested they stick close to home and do a little gardening. A little had turned into a lot, and all he had to show for it so far was one very green tomato and two tiny pea pods that had lasted thirty minutes.

Maybe it's time for us to take that trip. They'd always wanted to see the mountains, and they'd been to so many places in the world, but they'd never made it to the Canadian Rockies. Hopefully, it would give Wallace the much-needed rest he seemed to be craving.

A ringtone cut through the sound of mid-day crickets, and Wallace furrowed his forehead, looking to his phone that was on the table next to his beer. It buzzed away as it rang again with the most boring ringtone available. That could only mean one thing.

Work.

Elgin looked away, digging for the next thistle. He brushed against a sad-looking sprig of basil, the leaves yellow and drooping with a few ominous brown spots that probably spelled the plant's demise.

Everything online made gardening look so simple, but reality was a hard thing to swallow.

"Are you going to answer?" asked Elgin when the ringing came again. Wallace had picked up the phone, but he was staring at the screen, his eyes scrunched.

"I don't recognize the number."

"Give it to me if it's the duct cleaners," said Elgin. "I'm pretty sure they almost called the cops on me last time when I told them I didn't have any ducks to clean, but I've got one hell of a big cock problem. They didn't understand I was talking about the neighbor's chickens."

Wallace chuckled, putting his phone to his ear as he accepted the call. A moment later he went tense, leaning halfway out of his chair before getting to his feet.

Dropping his shovel, Elgin took a few steps closer before Wallace waved him off, covering the mouthpiece with his hand. "It's okay, but I need to take this call. I just have to grab something from my office."

"Go for it," said Elgin, tossing his small shovel and wiping the dirt from his hands. Wallace's book had fallen to the ground, so he swooped down, plucking it from the dirt. The title caught his eye, and he shot a grin after Wallace's retreating form.

Here he was getting all hot and dirty, and Wallace was reading smut—and not just any smut, some real kinky shit. The cover was fairly discreet, but from the back page, it was all spice. He flipped to where the bookmark was, plopping down in the chair and taking a swig of the beer that was still half full.

That hits the spot.

The story took him away in seconds, throwing him into a world of werewolves and kink in moments. He shifted on the chair at a particularly spicy moment, flushing bright as he heard the patio door open again.

"This book is *hot*," said Elgin, glancing to his husband. "I honestly thought I'd figured out every way to fuck you, but I was just proven wrong...very wrong." He flipped the page, nearly dropping the book at the title of the next chapter. "We need to go shopping."

Something buzzed in the distance — a lawn mower or maybe a chainsaw cutting down one of the last trees in the city. Elgin glanced up when Wallace didn't respond. He was biting his lip, his face turned to the side as he stared into the backyard, his gaze distant and filled with something Elgin couldn't quite grasp.

"Everything okay? Was quarter end really that bad?"

Wallace let out a rough sigh, shaking his head slowly. "Yeah." He touched his lip, leaning heavily against the door frame. "Do you think we could get out of here? I need to go on a trip or something to get my mind off a few things."

Elgin dropped the book, crossing the space between them in a few strides before pulling Wallace into a hug. Wallace was shivering, his breath catching as he clutched Elgin tight.

The last time Wallace had been in this state was when one of his employees had lost their life in a car accident. *Who was it?*

"What do you need?" asked Elgin softly. "If you want to quit, I get it. We don't have to live in a place like this. We can go back to the apartment. I can get another job if we need to, or I can pull extra hours and convince the board to give me a raise. Anything."

"It's not as bad as you make it sound," said Wallace, letting out a wet chuckle. "But it would be pretty hard to quit my job when I'm the boss."

"We can make the impossible possible, baby."

"Just take me somewhere nice. I just need that, okay?"

He could smell the tears, the dampness of them soaking into his skin as Wallace broke down. Fuck, it killed him to see Wallace like this. Once or twice a year, people leaned on Wallace too much at work, and he started to take on more and more responsibility. Eventually, it got to a point where he shut down, those beautiful blue eyes going lifeless until Elgin kissed him better and snuck him away for a few weeks.

"Do you like horses?"

It was a stupid idea — maybe the stupidest he'd ever had. The last thing he wanted was for someone else to see Wallace during a moment of vulnerability, but in a way, Annan had already seen that and had taken it in stride.

Wallace leaned back, catching Elgin's gaze before he wiped his cheeks with the back of his hand. "Don't buy me one, if that's what you're asking. The last animal you brought home ran away, and we found out three weeks later that the neighbor had stolen him."

Elgin winced at the memory. That poor dog had been so tiny that it had slipped right between Elgin's legs when he'd opened the door. After days of searching and signs posted on every pole, they'd given up. Wallace had taken it surprisingly well, but Elgin had felt for the poor lost fella — at least, until he caught the neighbor walking him weeks later. Apparently, the dog had bolted straight to their house on that first morning, and he'd been theirs ever since.

"I just thought—maybe it was silly. Maybe you wanted to see Annan again? He works with horses. I read that they are supposed to help with stuff like this when you're upset."

"You want to see Annan again?" asked Wallace, something like relief passing over his features.

Elgin swallowed, ready to make any sort of excuse but he came up blank. He'd never lied to his husband before, and he wasn't going to start now. He nodded slowly, dropping his gaze.

Wallace smiled softly. "Let's go."

Chapter Ten

Wallace

How could he not tell him? His heart was broken—smashed to bits with the thought of losing his husband to something that was so far beyond his control.

Annan had to be the answer.

Please give me the strength to do this.

Chapter Eleven

Annan

This was the strangest day of his life.

He tucked his cell phone back into his pocket, blinking as he tried to comprehend what he'd just read. Wallace had texted him, and they were coming…to the barn.

It was the same place he'd had to literally drag every single one of his previous boyfriends to, but they were coming *willingly*. And they weren't even boyfriends. He wasn't sure what the hell they were.

What the fuck?

He wiped his forehead with the back of his arm, glancing at his clothes. There were bits of brown that weren't chocolate in patches on both his jeans and his T-shirt, and he was coated in shavings, hay and sweat. His deodorant had worn off halfway through the afternoon, and he reeked of hardworking man. He loved the smell of horses, but most people didn't, and mixed with body odor, it was an acquired scent.

Oh shit.

He dropped the hose that he'd been using to fill a bucket with water, dancing to the side as it sprayed his boots and legs. It was freezing cold, striking like ice where it caught his jeans. It took less than a moment to warm, dragging at his skin uncomfortably.

Grabbing for the tap, he shut off the water, his hands shaking as he jammed it all the way down. The hose was looped along the grass, but he left it, taking off at a run toward the house. Stones kicked up under his boots as he hit the main road on the property, dust marking his trail. It was too hot to run, but he pushed himself onward, his lungs screaming for cool air.

One of the yearlings in the paddock next to the road shot its head up, taking a few prancing steps as it eyed him. As it reached the electric cord that marked the fence, it bolted, letting out a whinny as it raced him, easily outpacing him in a few strides.

He couldn't stop his grin or his shout of 'get', as the yearling circled back to him, her ears pricked forward. She was a beauty and would probably end up in a Grand Prix some day if she ever got over her irrational fear of puddles and random rocks.

She'd reared up on him one day when she'd spotted a rock that the family dog had dug up, and she'd nearly pulled his arm out of his socket. After a few lessons in manners, she was doing much better, but beneath her loving veneer, she was chock full of crazy.

When he reached the house, he nearly keeled over, sucking in lungfuls of air as he stopped with his hands on his knees. Sweat stuck to every part of his shirt, turning the colors murky with filth.

The door to the main house creaked before he could open it, and he looked up, panting open-mouthed.

"Everything okay?"

Milo was in a dressy white shirt and shorts, a glass of water in his hand as he eyed Annan as if he'd gone mad. Thank God he had managed to keep his calm, especially with the memory of the fire still fresh in all their minds. The last thing the kid needed was fresh panic with Annan running around like a lunatic.

"Need...water." Annan grabbed the glass in Milo's hand, chugging it back as soon as it was in his hand. Ice clinked against his teeth, the cold going straight to the roof of his mouth. A moment later it felt like his skull was about to burst with the most wicked brain freeze of his life.

"I was going to drink that," said Milo, closing the door behind him before he made his way along the covered porch to one of the swinging chairs. "Please tell me you didn't just run all the way down the lane to get a glass of water. I thought you usually drank from the hose." He scrunched his face as he said it.

Because apparently people don't drink from hoses these days. Sometimes Milo made him worry. Any bugs that came out of the hose were just a little extra protein.

Annan cleared his throat once he was finally able to see straight again, his heart rate mostly back to normal. "I need to borrow your shower. It's an emergency. Those guys I told you about are coming to the barn...*now.*"

His gut clenched, and he looked over his shoulder at the sound of a car approaching, but it was just one of the boarders. He still flinched as they got out, slamming the door to their pickup.

"So?" Milo kicked his feet up, the swing groaning as it rocked. "What's wrong with what you look like right now?"

Annan let out an exasperated sigh, pointing to three separate kinds of stains on his shirt. He had work clothes for a reason, and most of his stuff was ratty as hell.

"The last time they saw me I was in a suit." He'd rented that suit for more than it was probably worth, but he hadn't thought to buy it at the time. *Or pack it in my car in case of emergency.* "Come on, Milo. Help me out."

"Nope." Milo slid his sunglasses from on top of his head to cover his eyes.

Of all the times to be stubborn.

"Fuck." Annan ran a hand through his hair, looking along the lane. It could be minutes or hours before they came, but he had a feeling it would be the former. Or maybe they would back out once they saw the place, and go straight past the driveway, claiming they couldn't find it.

"Have you ever wondered if maybe the reason you get dumped in epic proportions is because you're always trying to hide who you really are, letting them see only what you want them to see?"

Annan's breath caught in his throat. "That's…"

He couldn't even say it wasn't true. Over the years, he'd kept his passion for horses close to his chest for longer with each relationship, only dropping little hints to feel out the waters. There were so many misconceptions about people who loved horses – that they were crazy, rich or thought about nothing but their equine companions.

"Completely true," said Milo. He looked better than he had in the last few days, a new color to his cheeks with the dark lines mostly gone. Hopefully, his nightmares had gotten better. Sometimes they lasted for months.

"I want to make a good impression," said Annan. "Maybe I just want them to like this place." There was a beauty in the stillness of the air and the distant sound of traffic that was nothing more than an occasional whoosh or the bump of tires down the lane.

Every season was beautiful, even when the horses were confined to the barn or their dirt pens to wait out an ice storm. Once that storm passed, the trees glistened, and the horses kicked up their feet with the joy of being outside again.

"If you're that worried, just take off your shirt," said Milo, crossing his arms. "That will get rid of most of the dirt and maybe they have a cowboy fantasy or something to go along with the three-way."

"*Milo.*" Annan sent him a warning look. Sure, they talked about each other's dating lives, but Annan didn't like to go into too much detail, not when Milo had a type of innocence to him that could so easily be changed. That sweetness was worth holding on to.

"*Annan.*" Milo glared right back. "Get your ass back to work before I tell the boss lady that you're slacking. And lose the shirt."

Well, someone is feeling better.

A walk back to the barn had never felt like such a walk of shame before.

* * * *

Elgin

"This is gorgeous," said Elgin, opening the window all the way as he pulled into the driveway. Bits of gravel popped under his tires, the car rocking over the potholes. His Audi may not have been the best choice, but he didn't give a shit. Wallace was still looking pale in the passenger seat, his gaze locked on the window, but he let out a gasp as they passed a fenced-in area before rolling his own window down.

"I thought it was a cow," said Wallace, tugging at Elgin's sleeve. "But look! Oh my goodness, it's so cute."

Elgin craned his neck to watch the spotted horse trot along the fence line, only to kick out at another horse, who let out a squeal. It really did look like a cow, with massive black spots on a white background. Even the longer bits of its hair were multi-colored.

"This is nice." Wallace nodded, before pointing to the buildings that must've been the barns. There was a gap in between two of them, with a few massive trash containers heaped with charred wood. Whatever had happened, there were skids upon skids of building materials in front already, the construction site still at the moment.

Pulling close to another car, Elgin flipped the stick into park, taking a deep breath as he stepped outside.

Okay, so it's not the freshest smell in the world. Grass, a fresh breeze, a touch of ash and manure mixed together in the strangest way. But it was a barn, so he'd expected that. Slipping over to the other side of the car, he opened the door for his husband, taking his hand and helping him out.

"Oh, your hands are cold," he said, grasping Wallace's hands between his own. The sun was beating down on them harshly, sweat already prickling over his skin. He hadn't bothered washing up much from his gardening adventures, and he was starting to get itchy with dried sweat.

"I'm always cold lately," said Wallace, smiling softly as he turned his hand and threaded their fingers together. "I hope we get to see around this place." He glanced toward the fence again, grinning at the horses.

Elgin wasn't exactly sure what the fences were made of, but he spotted some sort of white tape. The horses seemed to know the flimsy-looking material wasn't to be messed with, keeping well clear as a rhythmic ticking noise sounded.

"Where do you think he is?" asked Wallace, tugging him along as he headed to one of the first barns. The whole end of the building had a large door that was open, showing off parallel rows of wooden boxes with metal bars. One horse inside let out a loud call, sticking its head over their door. There had to be room for dozens of them in that building alone, and there were multiple barns dotted around the massive property.

"A pond." Wallace pointed to where a grove of trees tapered off to a small pond with lily pads along the edges and a rickety-looking dock that stretched toward the center.

"I hope the tour includes skinny dipping," said Elgin, letting himself be dragged past the construction zone to the next building that had a massive sand area with jumping fences and a seating area off to the side. The lights were off, with no one in the massive arena. It wasn't long before Wallace dragged him onward.

Squinting against the bright summer light, he turned his head at the sound of water, squeezing Wallace's hand tight as his jaw dropped. His heart pounded in an instant, his mouth going dry. *Holy fuck.*

Annan was standing around the side of the barn, dousing himself with water from a long green hose. It poured over his head and down his skin, little droplets tracing every part of his naked upper body. Water soaked into the top of his jeans, coloring the denim darker.

"I *really* hope the tour includes skinny dipping." Elgin licked his lips, glancing to Wallace, who seemed to be in a similar state.

"I remember him being pretty, but not so...hot," said Wallace, his grip going slack. His blond hair sparkled in the sun, the small breeze sending the soft fluff bouncing.

"Must be all that *moisture*." Elgin chuckled, holding Wallace back so hopefully it would take longer for Annan to notice them. The guy must've been sweltering, because he was giving himself a true dousing, his pants getting more soaked by the minute. Jeans were awful when they got wet. *I'll just have to suggest he take them off.*

"Are we doing this?" asked Elgin softly, looking to Wallace again. His palms were sweaty like the first time he'd met Wallace and had seen him smile, knowing that he wanted to be with him for the rest of his life.

"If by 'this', you mean 'him', then I hope we find out soon. I wouldn't mind having him back in our bed." Wallace tucked a strand of hair behind his ear.

"Hey, hot stuff." This time Elgin did raise his voice, calling across the small space.

Annan jerked where he stood, dropping the hose and spinning toward them. A bit of water splattered over his boots before he reached to turn the water off. He looked from them, then down to himself, before screwing up his face. "I got dirty."

Think clean thoughts, think clean thoughts.

"This place is wonderful," said Wallace, releasing his hand and stepping onto the patch of thick grass between them.

Thank you, Wallace.

Elgin followed behind, his running shoes sinking into the soft foliage. It wasn't like his grass at home at all, which was thin and almost artificially green. This was lush, with thick blades that brought thoughts of a meadow or a plain. And despite the summer warmth, he could almost feel the coolness of it.

"You like it?" asked Annan, running a hand through his soaked hair. A few stray drops dragged down his chest, skipping over his nipples and going straight to his navel. *God, he looks good.*

Wallace nodded, pointing across the property to the horse he'd first noticed. It had gone back to chomping grass and flicking its tail, completely ignoring them. "I honestly thought that one was a cow. I didn't realize horses could be so many colors."

Elgin hid his smile behind his hand. He hadn't had any clue, either, but he wasn't going to admit it.

"Did you want to see them a little closer?" asked Annan, obviously brightening. He didn't seem to have a shirt anywhere, or a towel, but he was quickly drying. The wind must've been chilly with the way his nipples were peaked into little nubs.

" – Elgin?"

Elgin blinked, shaking his head as he heard his name. Annan and Wallace were both looking at him expectantly. *Shit.* "Sure. Sounds good."

Annan snickered, Wallace rolling his eyes before smacking Elgin's shoulder softly.

"You could at least pretend to be interested," said Wallace, giving him another poke. Elgin winced, forcibly keeping his gaze away from Annan.

"I am interested – very interested – but did you see those pecs?" He couldn't help it. There was still a bit of water left on Annan that was dripping from his hair, his chest hair looking a bit dryer. Letting out a soft groan, he slapped a hand over his eyes.

"Colors, horses, something else. It's all wonderful." He wasn't even trying to be sarcastic. It really was cool.

"I guess that makes Annan the hottest cowboy I've ever seen."

Annan let out a chuckle, rubbing the back of his head as Elgin dropped his hand. It may have just been the sun, but he looked flushed, his cheeks rose-colored. "I'm not much of a cowboy. I've got a mean belt buckle, but not the right boots."

He was wearing black rubber boots, but he still looked good.

"But you can ride a horse," said Elgin, tugging Wallace closer. His husband was going to have a sore neck from how intensely he was looking around. "Wallace was hoping for a tour."

A grin stretched across Annan's face. "Really? That's great." He glanced to their shoes. "You might get dirty."

Elgin shrugged. "It's a barn, so I figured. But I'm pretty sure these horses live better than we do." The barns were freaking snazzy and had far fewer spiderwebs than he'd expected.

"You're right about that one." Annan reached for the hose, coiling it up and hanging it on a small hook. A few drops trickled out as it moved. "Come on this way. We have two mares that foaled in the last few weeks, and they love visitors."

Following Annan was like touring a whole different world. The two tiny babies were the most adorable things Elgin had ever seen, and the other parts of the impromptu tour were just as good. There were over a hundred horses in the massive complex, with dozens of fenced areas with grass and smaller dirt pens. Anything from poles to huge natural jumps were in the multiple indoor and outdoor areas, and they even got to watch one of the ladies ride.

Her horse moved like it was something magical, prancing like it was swimming through molasses, then moving quickly, its legs flying a moment later. Elgin had never seen anything like it.

After she left the ring, Annan led them to one of the trees by the pond, leaning against the trunk and looking back at them. His chest had flushed red, presumably from the heat or the sun, his hair dry from the earlier dousing, but his jeans still dark.

Elgin could sympathize. His own shirt was soaked with sweat in a very unflattering way, and cologne only did so much against the natural smell of the area. He still didn't mind it, especially after being around it for the last few hours. In fact, mixed with the scent coming from Annan, he could get used to it very quickly.

"What's the verdict?" said Annan, shuffling so he was seated against the tree, the scratchy bark probably digging into his skin. Still, he seemed so relaxed, a fluidness to his movements that Elgin hadn't seen in the restaurant or at the gym.

"I'm trying to figure out which car I'm going to sell to afford one of them," said Elgin, sitting right next to Annan and patting his lap. Wallace dropped onto his lap a moment later, wrapping his arms around himself. He still felt cool to the touch, despite the heat, tugging his sleeves down to cover his hands. Elgin wrapped his arms around him, pulling him back to his chest.

When Wallace was overworked, he always managed to get the flu, and it seemed like he was headed straight there.

"Can't have just one horse," said Annan, chuckling. He reached for a rock next to the trunk, tossing it toward the pond. It skipped over the surface twice before slipping below the water and disappearing out of sight.

Annan was only a few inches away, but the distance had never felt greater.

"I don't want to leave," said Wallace, turning in Elgin's arms and squirming down so he could lay his head in his lap. He closed his eyes, letting out a soft sigh. Freckles were spotted over his nose and cheeks, standing out against his pale face. He looked so peaceful like that, the weight of the office finally retreating.

Money isn't worth this. Perhaps it was time to have that chat that he'd always dreaded. He knew Wallace loved his work, but...

"If we're bugging you, we can hit the road," said Elgin, running his fingers through Wallace's hair. "But it would be great if we could stay — even if it's just for a little."

"Yeah." Annan shook his head before shifting against the trunk. "I just can't believe you want to stay." He moved again, putting himself a touch closer to them.

Elgin couldn't resist any longer. With one hand in Wallace's hair, he reached for Annan with the other, touching his chin. Annan turned to look at him, blinking with what looked like surprise.

"Kiss me," said Elgin. He didn't pull Annan closer, or force him to move, but his mouth tingled as Annan stared, flicking his gaze between his eyes and his lips.

"Here?" He looked to the barn where a car was pulling out, leaving them in relative isolation. The construction crew had started up their work during their tour, but the music and sounds were easy to tune out.

"Anywhere," said Elgin. Wallace moved against his lap as he said it, watching from below with half-lidded eyes.

Annan touched his cheek, then a moment later their lips met, heat and pressure morphing into sweetness. He'd ached for this for two weeks, maybe even more.

Elgin parted his lips, inviting Annan inside with a whispered moan. Wallace moved against his leg, sliding a hand along his inner thigh as Annan deepened the kiss, tilting his head and cupping the back of Elgin's neck. It took a certain kind of man to make Elgin powerless, but right now, that was exactly what he was.

With one word, both of these men could have had him in any way they wanted. Something about that filled his chest to the brim, overflowing as Annan's tongue graced his in a slick slide that pushed him into absolute madness. Fuck, he wanted him.

"Can I?" Elgin asked as he pulled away for a breath, his chest heaving. "Please." His question was directed at the man in his lap—the owner of all but a sliver of his soul. That tiny sliver was reserved for himself, so frail and fragile that it wouldn't exist without Wallace there, supporting it with both hands. But it made him, *him*.

"I want you to," said Wallace, his voice barely above a whisper.

Annan let out a groan, hobbling closer and thrusting his hands into Elgin's hair. He pulled him in, his breath hot and heavy as their lips met again. This time there was no sweetness, the sound of the birds and the frog in the pond fading to the pounding of his heart and the whoosh of blood in his ears.

Wallace could probably feel him under his palm as he stroked the inside of his thighs, settling over his groin for a brief second with each pass. His movements were slow and steady, with no hurriedness to them, as if he had all the time in the world to kiss someone who wasn't his husband.

"Ow."

Elgin pulled back, his head swimming as his heart jumped. Wallace had a hand over his eyes, scrunching his forehead as he drew his knees to his chest. His cheeks had paled, his freckles standing out as stark dots on a snowy landscape.

"Wallace? Baby?" Elgin dropped his hand to his husband's. He was still freezing, his hands cold and clammy as his breathing picked up. His chest was rising and falling fast as he clenched his hand against Elgin's leg, digging into the broad strip of muscle there.

"Baby, talk to me." Elgin's heart picked up until it was pounding with panic, his vision narrowed to the one person who could change his world for the better or worse. "Tell me what I can do. Let me help."

They never should have come. Wallace was obviously too tired. He should have insisted they stay home and lounge in bed with the air conditioning whispering over their skin.

"Here." Something touched his arm, and Elgin flinched, staring at the proffered soda. "I brought it for my lunch. He looks like he might be dehydrated or has heat stroke. It happens in the sun sometimes."

How was Annan so calm? His face was steady, even with his lips swollen and bruised from the kiss they'd shared moments before.

"Just a headache," said Wallace, his grip finally loosening even as he spoke through gritted teeth. "Too much sun."

Elgin cracked the can, helping Wallace sit up before pressing it to his lips. He took a small swallow before closing his lips tight. "No more. My head made me a bit queasy."

"You should try." Annan knelt next to them, placing a hand on Wallace's forehead. "You feel cool, which could mean heat stroke. Sometimes you won't feel thirsty either, but you need to try to drink, anyway."

Elgin lifted the can again, and Wallace took a small sip, wrinkling his nose. "I can't fight when two of you gang up on me, but it's root beer. Gross."

Thank Christ. Elgin looped an arm around Wallace's waist, tugging him closer with a trembling arm. He'd thought— He wasn't sure what he'd thought. He wasn't sure what he would do if Wallace somehow got hurt.

"I'm fine, Elgin." Wallace patted his arm, taking one more sip, which was enough to soothe Elgin's fear. "Just a headache."

Chapter Twelve

Wallace

How long could he keep up the lies before Elgin figured him out? His husband had always believed him implicitly, but he could already feel himself slipping as he lost bits and pieces.

He couldn't remember what he'd had for breakfast or what the weather had been like the week before, but he hoped he'd never forget what it was like to lie with his head in Elgin's lap, with them kissing above him like that.

He hadn't expected to *feel* quite as much as he did. It was strange looking at someone who wasn't his husband and trying to list the reasons that he shouldn't like them when he already knew the answer.

Annan was for Elgin, even if he didn't know it yet.

Chapter Thirteen

Elgin

"Thanks for inviting me along," said Annan. He was two paces behind, but Elgin could almost hear the spring in his step. "It's too bad Wallace couldn't make it."

It hadn't been Elgin's idea. Wallace had been all for it — the whole 'sunshine and sexy men' vibe.

Whoever had invented hiking should be shot. Elgin grumbled under his breath, barely avoiding a tree root that took that moment to make an attempt at executing him. There were no less than five mosquito bites on his ass alone, and something itchy on his legs that had started to turn red.

That, and his heart felt like it was about to beat out of his chest. He was panting as subtly as he could, especially since Annan seemed to have enough breath to chat away about everything they passed.

He reached for his leg, scratching the bit that was more painful than itchy now. The tips of his fingers seemed to have the same thing, tingling away like they had a mild burn.

"Stop scratching," said Annan, touching Elgin's elbow. He knelt beside him on the narrow path that was mostly overgrowth with a carpet of green leaves. "Looks like poison ivy. The more that you scratch, the more the oil will spread. Where else did you touch?"

"Great." Elgin took a few deep breaths. "I didn't realize I was going to be poisoned on this trip, but I guess it's a good way to go." He glanced along the way they had come. What had felt like a sheer climb looked more like a gentle rise to the naked eye.

Annan chuckled, shifting his legs to straddle the path before pointing to one of the plants that was stamped with his footprint. Identical leaves were everywhere along the edges of the blazed path, and between most of the trees in sight, filling up the brown spaces with shades of green and red, speckled with tiny green berries. "All this stuff is poison ivy. You should have worn long pants."

It was hotter than all hell, even in the trees where it was mostly shaded. Wallace had told him the exact same thing, but there was no way Elgin was going to torture himself with long pants on top of the impromptu outdoor adventure.

What was the problem with a treadmill? A nice, flat, beautiful treadmill with a safety switch and the ability to stop immediately when he was done was the perfect piece of equipment.

Elgin narrowed his eyes, pointing to Annan's bare legs. It was the first time he'd seen his calves and thighs on display and the same reason he'd offered to lead the way. They would have gotten nowhere with him drooling over Annan the whole trip. "It will all be worth it when you get this rash."

"You're grouchy this morning," Annan stood, passing him by to take the lead. Elgin let out a sigh, running a hand through his hair before immediately wincing. "And I hate to break it to you, but I'm one of the few people who aren't allergic to poison ivy. I can roll around in the stuff naked and be totally fine."

That was an image he could live with any day.

"Sorry." Elgin took a moment to admire Annan's ass as he jogged a few steps ahead. Fuck jeans... Annan should have lived in loose shorts, preferably ones like he was wearing now that cupped his ass with stretchy fabric. "Haven't slept well the last few nights."

Nighttime had always been like something out of a dream for him, where people's lives were displayed through the little windows of their houses. The air was always calmer and cooler, and he could sit in his garden for hours and listen to the crickets with a clear head, Wallace beside him with his beer and book.

But lately he'd been searching for and failing to find that same calm, even with Wallace there. There was something missing.

"Worried about Wallace? That headache of his came on pretty suddenly the other day. I was hoping I would get to ask how he was feeling today."

Elgin shook his head at the memory. For just a headache, he'd been terrified for those few seconds. Luckily, it hadn't lasted long, and Wallace had been back to himself by the time they'd gotten home, even if he had been a touch quiet.

"He had to go in to work today for a few hours. He knew we were going together, though." Elgin stumbled as a rock shifted beneath his foot, throwing his arm out to catch a nearby tree trunk. The path to their left dropped away to a sheer cliff where even many of the trees seemed to struggle to hold on. He wouldn't stand a chance. He didn't have roots to hold him to jagged rock, even if the poison ivy didn't seem to mind.

"He doesn't have an issue with it? I mean, us being here without him?" asked Annan, looking over his shoulder. He wasn't even out of breath, his strides eating up the path so much faster than Elgin's.

"Nope. And he's not upset that you've been keeping me up every night, either. Some nights, you're all we talk about." He snapped his mouth shut before scratching at his arm where another bug had just taken a bite out of him. "Sorry. I didn't mean to freak you out. I know I can come on strong—according to Wallace, at least."

A sparrow flitted by his face, calling an alarm before it soared into the treetops. Despite the bug bites and the spreading rash, it really was peaceful out here. There was no traffic, and they had yet to see another soul. *They were the sane ones who decided to stay at home in the heat.*

Annan paused, bracing himself against a nearby trunk. He blocked the path with his foot, crossing his arms. His chest was rising and falling a touch faster now, a flush to his face that hadn't been there before.

"I don't know what you mean," said Annan, his throat bobbing as he swallowed. "You don't have to think of me like that. I'm not trying to come between you guys."

"I know." Elgin glanced down the sheer hill, shifting to a safer side of the path as he took the much-needed break Annan was offering. "But maybe we want you to?" *Fuck, I'm not good at this.* He grabbed for his pack, pulling his water bottle out. The ice cold of it shocked him as he took a swig.

"Wallace asked me if I was going to kiss you again today — if I could take a picture for him because he couldn't be here himself." He twisted the cap back on, trying not to wilt under Annan's unsure gaze. It had sounded so hot at the time — enough that Elgin had agreed to the hike against his better judgment.

Annan took a step back, shaking his head slightly as he turned back to the path. His steps were quick, and Elgin struggled to keep up, pine needles shifting under his feet as he hit a dry patch where all the mud had evaporated away. A mosquito buzzed past his ear, circling just out of reach when he tried to swat it.

"Annan?" Elgin asked softly, scratching at his arm where an itch had sharpened. "It's okay if you don't want it. There's no pressure here. I would love it if we could still be best friends."

That joke he'd told during their first hour together in the restaurant of Annan being his best friend, still seemed truer than most things in his life. In business, everything was cloak and dagger, but Wallace had always been truthful. Annan seemed to make sense, too.

"Don't waste your time," said Annan, shouting over his shoulder as he picked up his pace.

Elgin stumbled over a rock, ivy slapping against his leg as he nearly fell. His throat was burning despite his recent drink, his legs close to jelly. *Christ, even riding a horse has to be easier than this.*

"I'm not," said Elgin, hoping the truth came through in his words. "If you aren't available, that's fine, but I'd still like us to be friends. I'll try not to stare at your ass, but no promises."

He had to keep it realistic. He hadn't looked away from Annan's ass since they'd switched places. It was the ass of every cowboy fantasy he'd never admit to.

"Oh, I'm available," said Annan. He slowed his pace for a few steps, finally seeming to notice Elgin's struggles. "And that's the issue. I'm not worth your time, Elgin. You and Wallace are amazing and I'm…just me."

Reaching for Annan's arm, Elgin dragged him to a stop. His heart was pounding, his lungs burning, but he wasn't sure how much of that was because of the hike and how much was pure exhaustion. "I don't see the problem."

"Then you're blind." Annan tried to shrug him off, but Elgin resisted. He was strong — stronger than Annan, and more stubborn than Annan gave him credit for. There was a reason Wallace hadn't been able to get rid of him early in their relationship.

"I wouldn't drag my ass up this hill of perpetual punishment for no reason." A bit of dirt rolled over the side of the hill as he shifted, tinkling as it dropped toward the bottom.

"Then you just want to get fucked," said Annan, his lips twisting into a frown. "I get it. I'm easy, I'm available and it couldn't have been more convenient for you. There aren't a lot of options for me, and if you guys text me to come over for a good time, I'll probably show up. Hell, I already did once."

Elgin dropped his hand. His fingers tingled from the warmth of Annan's skin, but his chest ached in that spot right beneath his sternum. It fucking hurt to see that look in Annan's eyes — that betrayal that he'd never expected. "I'm sorry."

He'd taken so many missteps, and he hadn't even realized. Wallace had been his focus over the last few days, and he'd forgotten that Annan was probably worried, too. What must that silence have felt like? That wondering if Wallace was okay and what the kiss at the pond had meant.

Blue blazes marked his way back to the car, but Annan had helped him so many times when he'd almost lost the trail. He would most likely be able to make it back without taking a wrong turn. Even if he did get lost, he was already covered in poison ivy rash, so what did a bit more matter?

"I'll head back to the car," said Elgin, keeping his gaze on the ground. *It was too much to ask — too soon.* Wallace and he had fallen hard and fast when they'd first met. He couldn't expect everyone to be on the same wavelength. "You're welcome to finish your hike, then I'll drive you home. I'll wait for you."

"No way." Annan shook his head, grabbing a handful of Elgin's T-shirt. To his credit, he didn't even wince when he no doubt felt the amount of sweat soaked into the fabric. "You promised me that you'd make it to the top."

Elgin swallowed, a touch of hope seeping into his chest. If Annan had really been against them, Elgin had to trust he would tell them outright. "What am I to you?"

Do I know the answer to that question? A month ago, everything in his life had been so certain, but now he was surrounded by forest and uncomfortable as hell in multiple ways. He was outside of his usual zone, and completely loving it.

Annan let out a long sigh before looking off into the bush. A small bird took off, its wings humming against the underbrush. "I don't know."

Elgin nodded, holding his hand at his side to keep from reaching out. That uncertainty—he couldn't bear it. "Fair enough. We don't know each other all that well yet and maybe I gave you the wrong impression, but Wallace and I don't fuck around."

Annan scoffed. "You had a threesome with me when I was a random stranger who you picked up in a restaurant after I'd just got my ass dumped."

"Nope." Elgin shook his head, scratching his chin. "We had a threesome with my future best friend. I knew within thirty seconds that you were one of the good ones. Every moment since has just been proof."

"I don't—" Annan snapped his mouth shut, letting his hand drop back to his side. He clenched and unclenched his fist and three beats passed before he gave the tiniest nod. "We're almost to the lookout. Five more minutes and we can head back."

Annan turned away, each footstep a thud that resounded along the path that seemed almost hollow with the amount of crisscrossing tree roots and pitted rock. A pull in Elgin's gut dragged his feet forward, following Annan just a few paces behind.

What am I supposed to think?

Elgin was a happily married man—the happiest. He'd never even dreamt of having a mid-life crisis, but maybe that was what Annan was. He was smart, funny and down to earth in an infuriating way that made Elgin regret every second of buying hiking boots.

When Wallace had told him to go, he hadn't hesitated, but maybe he should have. For a gut-wrenching moment, he wondered if he would ruin everything they had built together.

Annan glanced back, relaxing his shoulders as he did. "I thought maybe you were going to head back."

"Nah." Elgin shrugged, dragging his arm across his forehead. He was soaked with sweat everywhere from his head to his ass crack. The drive back was going to be windows closed with full air conditioning and quiet music that would calm his heart. "I can't let you start thinking I'm an old man."

He certainly felt old with how much his muscles were protesting. He was a sprinter through and through.

"How long can you hold your breath?" asked Annan, dropping back so he was only a pace ahead. Turning to the side, he bounced on his toes.

He has way too much energy. "Maybe a minute?" Elgin scratched the back of his head where there was probably another bug bite. How did people like hiking and find it relaxing? "I can swim, but it's not one of my strengths."

"One minute is a long time," said Annan, slowly nodding. He pinched his lips together as a smile attempted to escape. "One might say that length of time is completely average and okay."

"Wait." Elgin stopped, leaning his hands on his knees. "Are you making a sex joke right now?"

Annan snickered. "Maybe. But seriously, one minute is a *long* time. You shouldn't be upset about it—totally average."

"You know, I've never had that problem." Elgin narrowed his eyes in mock seriousness, chuckling when Annan laughed.

"Don't I know it. Fucking you was like running two back-to-back marathons."

"One-minute marathons?" asked Elgin, raising one brow.

"Hey." Reaching out, Annan poked Elgin's shoulder. "I'll have you know I can hold my breath for five minutes…in thirty-second intervals."

Laughing, Elgin squinted as the forest thinned, the ground peaking sharply before leveling out. Annan followed his gaze, going quiet at the sight.

The ragged earth ended abruptly, transitioning into light gray rock that jutted out between the tree roots that were like spider webs over the surface. The horizon disappeared, plunging straight down a cliff where the bottom was so far away that it was slightly hazy. Blue water stretched below them seemingly forever, the waves sparkling in the sun that was perched straight above them.

"Oh, the breeze." Elgin raised his arms, letting the wind take away the oppressive heat on his body. There was no car exhaust or scents from the city on the wind — only water, trees and the saltiness of sweat.

"Was it worth the struggle?" asked Annan quietly, moving in behind him. One hand was moved to each of Elgin's hips as Annan put his chin on his shoulder.

"Wallace has always wanted to see the mountains. Did I tell you that?" asked Elgin, feeling the last of his tension drain away with Annan's hands on him. In the back of his mind, he knew what Annan was trying to do. There was nothing like a distraction and a joke to avoid the big issues. *Too bad I can't let it go.*

"But for me, the view isn't worth that hell," said Elgin, skimming over the distant treeline on the far side of the water. He'd known they were close to the lake, but from within the forest, it had seemed impossible. Now he could see it for real, and the water stretched so far it was seemingly endless. "This is, though."

When Annan tried to move away, Elgin covered his hands with his own, holding him close as the wind continued to whisper against him. Annan's hands were hot but not sweaty like his own, the warmth sinking straight through him. It was the type of warmth that could heal anything and melt away his uncertainty.

"We should take that picture," said Annan, tugging one hand free. A moment later he produced his cell phone, sliding his face closer as he held it out in front of them.

On the screen, Elgin watched as his own forehead crinkled as he smiled, unconsciously leaning closer to Annan. His face was flushed, his hair in complete disarray and the red welt of a bug bite on his cheek, but Annan looked completely calm and at ease. *Beautiful.*

Elgin turned his face as Annan took the picture, pressing his lips to Annan's cheek. The screen froze as the picture took, Annan's eyes wide.

"I was going to send the picture to Wallace," said Annan, fumbling with his phone.

"Well, in that case." Elgin turned, grasping Annan's chin and guiding their lips together. Annan gasped, moving his hands to Elgin's neck and digging his nails into the aching muscle there. The coldness of the phone in Annan's hand pressed against his skin as Elgin groaned, deepening the kiss and slipping into Annan's welcoming mouth.

Hell. Every kiss was just like the first one—new but familiar, turning him harder than steel between breaths. When his lungs started to crave air, he pulled back, but only enough that he could speak. "Take the picture."

Fuck air. I don't need it. Kissing Annan again was nourishing enough that he could have lived for years on it alone.

As he bit Annan's lip, feeling more than hearing the whimper, he heard the click of the phone.

Turning toward the sound, he inspected the screen. Annan's eyes were closed, so he'd obviously taken the picture blind, but he'd done a decent job. There was only one problem besides the slight blurriness.

"Here. Turn around so the water and sky are in the background." Elgin spun them, barely letting their lips separate as he did. When he finally stopped and caught the sound of the camera again, he kept kissing until he was throbbing and ready to push Annan against the nearest tree.

Annan pushed at his shoulders, turning his head away. His chest was rising and falling fast, his lips glowing and bruised. "We should stop."

"Hmm." Elgin dragged his nose over the column of Annan's throat, sucking in a breath of saltiness. "Why? I feel like this would be really romantic."

Annan let out a groan, gripping Elgin's shirt and keeping him close. "Did you bring lube?"

"Don't need it. I'll eat you out," said Elgin, trailing a hand to Annan's ass and squeezing each cheek.

"Condom?" Annan tilted his head, shivering as Elgin dragged his lips over his neck. He tasted so good.

Always so practical. "I assumed you had one in your hiking bag. You said you'd pack everything we'd need." He sucked a mark into Annan's skin, licking over the blush. "This is so much more important than a compass."

"We're not—*fuck*—without a condom." Annan groaned as Elgin bit down, tugging the collar of Annan's shirt to give him more room to work.

"There's more than one way to get fucked."

On the edge of the rocks, with the wind buffeting against them, Elgin dropped to his knees. He braced Annan's hips as he nearly stumbled, leery of how close they were to the teetering over. He wanted a fun time, not a fall.

"What?"

Elgin cut off Annan by tugging his zipper down, reaching inside and bringing his cock out into the open. He was already fully hard, the vein along the underside throbbing. Licking his lips, Elgin took his fill.

"I can't believe we're doing this," said Annan, glancing toward the spot where they had emerged from between the trees. "Anyone could see us."

Like anyone is crazy enough to scale that fucking hill in this heat. "I'll be quick. One minute, to be exact." Elgin chuckled, licking his lips.

"Wallace."

Elgin paused, staring at Annan through half-lidded eyes. "I told you we don't fuck around." He glanced to the phone in Annan's hand, something sinful passing through his brain. "Film it. We'll send him the video instead of the picture."

"*Jesus.*"

Annan did stumble as Elgin licked him, so Elgin grabbed him by the ass, tugging him close. They were so near the cliff that when the wind changed, it tugged at them, urging them close to the precipice.

"I'm gonna fall." Annan gripped Elgin's hair, easing him so the tip of his cock rubbed against Elgin's lips.

"I've got you." Elgin opened wide, nudging until Annan's cock slid over his tongue, coating it with his taste. He was strong with the edge of sweat from their hike mixed with pine and sunshine and the thrill of adrenaline that was slowly building. He hit the back of Elgin's throat, but he didn't stop, swallowing to let him all the way inside.

"*Jesus. Please.*" Annan tugged at Elgin's hair with both hands, gripping tight but not urging him off or deeper. "Just like that."

Elgin swallowed again, sucking softly as he bobbed his head a few inches. Annan's cock dragged right over his gag reflex, his eyes watering as he fought the urge to gag or try to breathe. His lungs burned as he forced himself longer, his head spinning.

Pulling back with a gasp, Elgin wiped his lips with the back of his hand, staring at the phone that was pointed at his face. He grinned, flicking his tongue against Annan's cockhead and reveling in the fresh saltiness that greeted him.

"Wish you were here, baby," said Elgin, circling his tongue over the head as he stared at the camera. Annan's mouth was open wide as he dragged in huge lungfuls of air. "I'll bring him home so you can taste him. He's so good that I want to keep him for myself for a while longer yet, but he would be perfect between us."

This time he licked the head into his mouth, sucking hard enough to hollow his cheeks before he eased up and flicked his tongue along the lower vein.

"I'm not going to last," said Annan. His hands were shaking, which probably wasn't the greatest for the video, but it sure was an ego boost. "I'm gonna come."

"Hear that, Wallace? Can he come, baby? Will you let him?" He popped on and off the head of Annan's cock, focusing all his attention there. It must've been infuriating from the way Annan tried to thrust his hips, whining the whole time.

"Call him," said Elgin, palming his own cock when the pressure became too great.

"Wha—?"

"Call and ask him if you can come." Elgin squeezed himself. *Whoever said three is a crowd was completely uneducated.* "I told you we were a little kinky."

Annan fumbled with his phone, the sound of a ring cutting through the air a moment later. It rang three times before there was a click, and Wallace answered, his voice on the speakerphone instantly making Elgin's heart beat faster. *Some things never change.*

"Hello? Annan, is everything okay?" Wallace's honeyed voice was soft in the quiet air, a bit of it swept away on the breeze.

"C—can I?" asked Annan.

Fuck, he sounded so broken and depraved, as if he would have done anything in that moment to come. Elgin palmed himself again, loudly sucking Annan into his mouth until he was probing the back of his throat.

"Please, Wallace. Can I come?" Annan gripped his hair, the sting of it sending Elgin's thoughts into the clouds.

"You... Send me a picture," said Wallace, his voice losing every bit of concern as it dropped into a gravelly tone.

Annan whined, tapping the screen as Elgin watched him through watery eyes, staying down as long as he could.

"*Wow.* You look so good, Elgin, but you're hiding that pretty cock from me. Let me see it."

Elgin throbbed at his husband's voice, his head swimming as he pulled back, opening wide and sticking out his tongue to hold the very tip so it was heavy against him. Annan let out a groan, his hands visibly trembling.

Wallace let out a long moan over the speakerphone as he presumably got the picture. "Hell." There was a pause and muffled voices in the background. "Elgin, make him come. Annan, I'll see you at home. Don't think we're done with you."

The phone went dead a moment later, and Elgin went to work, bobbing his head and flicking his tongue in every effort to get Annan off. Seconds later, Annan's grip on his hair went tight, and he groaned long and low as he coated Elgin's tongue and thrust against him in tiny, aborted movements.

With the saltiness heavy on his tongue and Annan still panting, Elgin stiffly rose to his feet, brushing off his knees where a fresh rash was already spreading its itchy tendrils. He would have to shower or something before he touched Wallace so his husband didn't break out, too.

"I changed my mind," said Elgin, adjusting himself as his cock gave a painful throb. Annan fluttered his eyelashes, giving a questioning grunt. "The sight of you was absolutely worth the trek."

Chapter Fourteen

Annan

The drive back to the house was silent except for the low hum of the radio and the wind from the open windows. Elgin was staring ahead at the traffic that slowly thickened as they drew closer to the big city again, a small smile on his lips.

One thing passed through his mind on repeat, resonating every time he tried to relax into the leather.

Should I be guilty?

He'd let a married man suck his cock while begging the husband to let him come over the phone. Hell, he should probably go to church at this point and find out if there was anything left of his soul worth saving. *I doubt it.*

"How long have you been with Wallace?" asked Annan, his guilty conscience starting to wear thin. He stared at the spotless dash of the car before inhaling the deep scent of leather.

"That depends on which one of us you ask," said Elgin, sending him a grin as he adjusted his grip on the steering wheel. Placing his arm on the frame of the open window, he held his palm out into the wind, surfing over the buffeting air.

"For me, it was when I first saw him twenty years ago." Elgin let out a wistful sigh. "I was mostly an errand boy at that time and had popped by a local shop to get coffee, and there he was."

"A barista?" Annan tilted his head. "I never would have guessed that."

"Nope." Elgin chuckled. "He was waiting in line, his head buried so far into a textbook that he didn't notice my staring until it was his turn to order. I made a joke, he laughed, and I asked him out on the spot."

"I can picture it," said Annan, holding up his hands as he lowered his voice to imitate Elgin. "Is it just me or did you want some cream in your coffee? It's fresh and vegan."

Elgin chuckled, flipping his visor down as they made a turn, the sun cutting straight through the flimsy tint of the windshield. "Close enough, yeah. I don't remember exactly now, but something about 'I can grind your coffee, then grind with you' type of thing."

They really are in love. Elgin's eyes crinkled at the corners every time he spoke about his husband, and his shoulders relaxed at the mention of his name. *They're meant to be together. I can't fuck this up.*

"What does Wallace count from? The first date?" Annan ran his hand over the edge of his seat, tracing the stitching with his fingertip. "Or when you got married? He seems like an official paperwork kind of guy."

"Usually he is," said Elgin, his lips going thin for a moment before he relaxed again. "But technically, we never got married."

What? Annan turned in shock, his lips parting.

"It was something that didn't really make sense for us," said Elgin, turning the radio down as he merged into traffic. "Neither of us are religious, and we knew how much we meant to each other and that was all that really mattered to us. I bought Wallace a ring and we had a honeymoon, but no big wedding or anything."

"Oh. That actually makes me feel a little better." He scratched his chin where it tingled. He hadn't been lying when he'd said that he didn't break out in a rash from poison ivy, but it did make his skin feel tight. Elgin was practically covered in the stuff from his hands to his legs and a bit on his neck that he probably didn't realize.

"What are your thoughts? Is it okay to have two boyfriends, but not be a boyfriend to two married men?" asked Elgin, his voice surprisingly light.

Boyfriend? Annan rolled the term around in his head. "You're the strangest boyfriend I've ever had—and that's saying something."

"I've met one," said Elgin. "I can only hope it goes uphill from there."

Annan shook his head, pinching his lips together as they pulled up to the familiar house before rolling into the garage. Elgin moved the car into park and stepped out as soon as the engine cut out. Before Annan could react, Elgin was holding his door open for him and offering his hand.

"Unfortunately not," said Annan, staring at Elgin's proffered hand. "Is this like valet services? Do I have to tip?" He grinned as Elgin furrowed his brow before dropping his hand back to his side.

"Sorry," said Elgin, glancing at his own hand. "I guess it's automatic. I always open the door for Wallace, but I can try to stop if it's not something you want."

"It's nice—sweet." He went to step by, but Elgin grasped his elbow, forcing him to a stop. His lips were pressed into a line, his eyes narrow and focused.

"I want you to know that if you decide to be with us, we will do our best to treat you right," said Elgin, stroking his thumb over Annan's skin. "We aren't perfect, but Wallace is pretty close. I'm a near second, not that I want to brag about it."

"I hadn't…" Annan stopped himself before he could say anymore. *I'd forgotten I had the choice.* Through every minute, he'd never thought of the concept of saying no, even when things had gone differently than expected.

"I'll try, too." Annan ducked his head, looking to Elgin's hand against his. Elgin was lighter, most likely from his extended bouts in the office, even if he did get out into the garden. "Don't judge me too harshly. I've never been with two men before, and it will probably be different than what I'm used to." *Hopefully, in a good way.*

"If the last few weeks have taught me anything—it's exhausting." Elgin broke out into a laugh. "I'm kidding. You guys are great—both of you."

"Aren't we?"

Annan looked up at Wallace's voice. He was in a sweater despite the heat, the gray fabric tight to his neck. Maybe it was because of the color of the sweater, but his face looked pale, his eyes more tired than Annan had seen them last time. *But he's been working all day.* He didn't know how Wallace could keep such a strict schedule. He loved the horses, but even *he* took his weekends off.

"You bet." Elgin rushed ahead, wrapping his arms around Wallace's waist and bringing him close for a kiss. Annan would have felt like an outsider if Wallace hadn't been looking at him the whole time, a soft smile on his face.

"Did you have fun?" Wallace kissed Elgin's cheek once before he crinkled his nose. "Oh wow, you stink like bug spray and body odor. And what happened to your legs?" He glanced down, his eyes going wide as he spotted the red rash that looked like it was sprouting little dots between the irritation.

"Oh crap." Elgin drew his hands to his sides, taking a step back. "I need to shower before I touch you. I guess poison ivy spreads." He looked back to Annan for confirmation. "And, it was terrible, except for the top. The top was great."

Wallace chuckled, stepping aside as Elgin slipped past him. Elgin shouted as he pulled his shirt over his head. "We should all shower together. That would make up for the three blisters on my heel and the nineteen bug bites."

"We'll meet you there." Wallace hesitated until Elgin disappeared before he turned back to Annan. All joking from moments before disappeared, his shoulders tight and stiff. "We need to talk."

This is it. It was a great run. God, I'm going to miss these guys.

"I didn't mean it like that," said Wallace, holding out his hand. "It's something…serious, but not what you're thinking." He stepped out of the door, closing it behind him before lowering himself onto the top step. He slumped his shoulders right away, lowering his face into his hands.

Wallace sniffed, shaking his head before he dropped his hands. A tear rolled down his cheek, tracking over his pale skin and the faded freckles from the summer sun. In seconds, he seemed to age a decade.

Annan dropped to his knees, holding his hand out awkwardly before he settled a palm on Wallace's shoulder. His heart pounded, his chest going tight as he flushed hot and cold. Even through his sweater, Annan could feel the cold and the shiver that seemed to vibrate along Wallace's skin.

Is he okay? He could ask, but of course, he couldn't. Wallace was a grown man who had just broken down in front of the most likely cause. He'd obviously been putting on a brave front for Elgin. *I should go.*

"I'm sorry if I hurt you," said Annan. The hike had been uncertainty mixed with the guilt of the ride back. Now it was all coming to a head. Wallace was crying because of *him.*

Wallace shook his head again, the corners of his eyes crinkling as a shaky sob escaped him. "No. You didn't, trust me. I'm—" He took a deep breath, clearing his throat. "You can't tell Elgin. Promise me."

"I promise," said Annan, his knees aching from kneeling after such a long hike. "Whatever it is, I'll take it to my grave." There was a thin thread of trust between them, and he knew one false move would send it all tumbling into nothingness. He tightened his grip, stroking over Wallace's trembling shoulder.

"I'm sick." Wallace looked at him with his eyes wet and bloodshot, his voice shaking as he said it. "It's nothing good, but I can't tell him." He rubbed his face, bringing a flush to his cheeks as he let out a strained sound. "Elgin means everything to me—everything—but he needs something I can't give him."

Cold shocked straight through Annan's gut.

The headache, the pale skin and the tears all made sense. "I... *Shit...* What do you need? I can take you to the doctor, or, did you need medication? We can drive to the pharmacy. Or I can just pick up your meds or run errands for you. I can help you until you're feeling better."

Whatever it was, Wallace wouldn't be able to keep it a secret for long if he continued looking like this. Remembering back, it all seemed so obvious. It was only a matter of time before Elgin figured it out.

Annan had come down with pneumonia once and it had taken him six months to recover. Without Milo and Oliya's help, he would have ended up in the hospital...or worse.

"They can't fix it." Wallace cleared his throat. His blond curls were wild as he brushed them back, his blue eyes stained red. "It's not operable."

Annan dropped his hand, standing to take a step back as his throat went tight. *No, no, no.*

He couldn't have heard that right. If Wallace was talking about surgery then... He couldn't bear to think it.

Wallace was so fucking sweet and good. Why the hell was this happening to him? Blood roared through his ears.

"H-how long?" Annan barely managed to get the words out. *Is that what people usually ask in these situations? Tell me I'm wrong. Tell me I misheard you.* This couldn't happen. Elgin loved Wallace so much.

"A couple of months—maybe a year, if I'm lucky." Wallace shrugged, dropping his gaze to the ground.

"Or maybe not so lucky. There are times right now that it's really bad, but it's only going to get worse."

He couldn't fucking do this. Annan shook his head. There were no tears on his own face, but Wallace was still crying. Tears were far out of his reach—an all-consuming numbness smashing into him. *He's wrong.*

Sure, Wallace was pale, but some fresh air and a good meal would solve that, no problem. Elgin had mentioned how much Wallace worked, and Annan had seen it with his own eyes. All he needed was rest. *But.*

Annan looked at him—really looked at him. There was a darkness in Wallace's eyes that Annan had seen before. It was the look of someone who had given up on life, and there was no changing his mind.

His heart was breaking. Going to his knees again, Annan wrapped his arms around Wallace's shoulder, tugging him in close. "I'm so sorry. Christ, I can't imagine what you're going through."

"I-I need to know," said Wallace, burying his face in Annan's neck as he choked on another round of sobs. "Can you love Elgin? Can you be there for him when I can't anymore? He won't make it alone."

You can't ask me to do this.

Wallace trembled, his grip weak on Annan's T-shirt. "You have to promise me that you'll be there for him, even if he tries to pull away from you. Don't listen to him when he says he wants to be alone. *Promise me.*"

Fuck, fuck, fuck. It's all falling apart. How could he hold the key to breaking the hearts of two men when he couldn't be trusted with his own?

"I promise."

Chapter Fifteen

Wallace

Telling someone was the strangest sensation he'd ever had. There was a sudden emptiness after a steady grind of tension that had built for so many months, along with a gut-wrenching fear of what was next. It was so real — a sickness that he didn't want to ever say out loud.

He could feel it, like a bug squirming behind his temple, waiting for the opportune moment to buzz and render his limbs numb while shooting pain like none other through his skull.

He'd hoped for relief and assurance, but Annan's watery eyes looking back at him with confusion and desolation was of no comfort.

It was just too real.

Chapter Sixteen

Annan

He patted his cheeks, trying to dry his tears before he could start all over again. Wallace had calmed himself surprisingly quickly, with only a bit of redness about his eyes and cheeks that could have been easily explained away.

"He'll come looking for us soon," said Wallace, leaning against the door frame with his eyes only open in slits. There was a furrow on his forehead, and he winced when he turned his head.

Tilting his head back, Wallace let his eyes fall shut, slumping against the wood as if he couldn't keep himself upright. The smile he'd had for Elgin when they'd arrived was long gone. "Don't think about it. It's easier that way."

"No can do." Annan shook his head, biting at his lip as he fanned his face. His nose was swollen and clogged, his eyes aching as he held back fresh tears. "Do you think he'll notice?" His cheeks burned.

Annan had cried for two weeks when they'd lost one of the foals on the farm, and this was something else entirely. Everything around him had purpose and meaning, and Wallace was such a big part of his life now.

It wasn't just that, either. *Elgin... He doesn't even know.*

Peeking one eye open, Wallace looked him up and down with tired eyes. "You look fine—maybe like you're having an allergic reaction or something. If you hop into the shower, Elgin won't notice a thing. My husband is a wonderful man, and he's observant as hell, but sometimes he sees what he wants to see."

Which is why you've been able to hide this for so long.

It was all wrong, leaving an acidic taste in his mouth that threatened bile.

"Okay." There was nothing else he could say. He was relatively trapped here—chained with the knowledge and the powerlessness that he couldn't do anything at all to change.

The house felt so empty, their footsteps echoing off the walls in the big rooms. There were a few bits of artwork with a canvas streaked with green paint and dotted with thick petals to make up some very unrealistic flowers, but it was dead and lifeless. Even the flowers at the closed window were a pale, gaunt pink.

Steam was pouring out of the bathroom door when they approached, the thickness of soap in the air already making him feel a little fresher. Beyond that was Elgin, who was so strong that Annan knew he would somehow fix this.

I can do this. Maybe Wallace wasn't telling him the whole story? There was so much that had changed in medicine that 'inoperable' was barely a thing anymore. *He has to be wrong.*

"That you, baby?" called Elgin, his voice echoing from within the shower. The stall was sheer glass, the inside lined with water droplets and steam, but he could still see straight through it. The sight almost made him forget that he'd been crying moments before.

"We came to get an eyeful," said Wallace, turning to the sink and glancing into the mirror. His voice was steady as he looked at his own reflection, his fluffy hair bouncing as he ran his hand through the wild strands.

Annan was caught. *I can't do this.* When Elgin grinned, looking over his shoulder, Annan grabbed for the wall to support himself. Water was streaming down Elgin's body, dipping and falling over every perfect inch. As Elgin turned, he flexed his thigh and Annan couldn't tear his gaze away.

"You okay?" asked Elgin, looking between the two of them.

Annan swallowed the lump in his throat, trying to meet Elgin's gaze. *It can't be true. Elgin would know.*

"He got something in his eye in the garage," said Wallace, leaning closer to the mirror and fluffing his hair. "I tried to get it, but I accidentally poked him."

"Ouch." Elgin winced, bending to grab for a bottle of soap and squirting some onto his palm. "I'm almost done in here, then we can *fuck.*"

Annan looked to Wallace as Elgin slid his eyes shut against the suds running over his scalp as he worked his fingers through the strands. Wallace was steady, giving a slight shaking of his head.

"I'm pretty filthy," said Annan, brushing his pants where a few burrs and bits of debris had clung to him on the walk. His muscles were pleasantly warm from the exercise, but he doubted he'd be sore tomorrow. He was more likely to be curled up in bed, denying that the last few minutes had ever happened. "Is it okay if I jump in after you?"

"Sure," said Elgin, scrubbing at his head beneath the water. "Hell, jump in here *with* me. There's lots of room."

Wallace tugged at his own sweater before pulling it over his head. He didn't *look* overly thin, at least not from what Annan could remember to compare. He was pale, though, with no tan on his skin that should have been exposed to the summer sun. The only bit of color was over the bridge of his nose where those pale freckles were threatening to fade away.

"Too bad, Elgin," said Wallace, tossing his shirt and going for his pants next. "I already called dibs. Annan is showering with me, and you're going to meet us in bed like a good boy."

How the fuck can he do this? How can he pretend when his world is falling apart?

"Why can't I watch?" Elgin whipped around, drawing his finger across the glass as he went. He wasn't soft anymore.

"You had your turn," said Wallace, dropping his pants and boxers to the ground. Annan fought the urge to look away, doing his best to act normal, even if he wasn't sure what that was supposed to look like. He hadn't been worried to look before, but now he wondered if things had changed so much that he shouldn't. Wallace was a delicate piece of glass that his gaze could shatter to bits.

"I earned it," said Elgin, grabbing the shower door and sliding it open. "I had to climb a mountain to give that blow job, and I'm exhausted." He let out a dramatic sigh.

"Then you'll be too tired to scrub my back." Wallace squeezed past Elgin, taking a step into the shower and sighing as the stream hit him. "Annan, be a dear and join me."

"Uh...yeah." Annan tugged at his shirt, tossing it with the rest of the dirty clothes in a pile on the ground. His pants went next, thunking hard when his keys struck the tile.

"Oh, ouch." Elgin ducked closer, looking into Annan's eyes. He could almost taste the sweetness of his skin carried on the steam. "He must have poked your eye really hard. It's pretty bloodshot. Does it still hurt?"

"No—no, I'm good." Annan scrambled toward the shower, ducking through the glass before Elgin could see through his terrible façade. He'd never been a good liar, and Wallace was right. Elgin saw everything.

Giving them a lingering wave, Elgin ducked through the bathroom door, water still dripping down his skin and steam billowing after him. Annan was so focused that he jolted when warm, wet arms encircled his waist.

"I didn't mean to scare you," said Wallace, pressing his chest to Annan's back. He was shorter, but Annan felt dwarfed beneath the weight of his limbs, his chest twisting as his heart pounded. Wallace had barely touched him—always watching and waiting and taking that step back for Elgin to be his hands.

"I'm sorry. I shouldn't have told you," said Wallace, laying his head against Annan's back. "It's too much of a burden."

"No." Annan turned, gently coaxing Wallace's arms wider so he could move without one of them slipping. "I'm glad you told me. It feels like a bit of a lie, though, doesn't it?" *Stop trying to pretend it's okay.*

The fancy house, the nice car and the dinner dates. What was the fucking point?

"No." Wallace shook his head, wrapping his arms tighter and resting his cheek against Annan's chest. His skin was naked and warm, flushed from the shower so he appeared perfectly normal. "I'm alive now, and that's all that matters. Elgin and you are the most precious things in the world to me, and I'm not going to waste a single moment."

"But—" Annan dipped his head, placing a kiss on the top of Wallace's curls that were slowly staining darker. His hair was wet, but still soft, droplets clinging to his locks. "You need to tell him. This isn't right, Wallace. I'm a stranger compared to him, and he deserves to know."

Tilting his head back, Wallace stared up at him. There was something so heartbreaking in his gaze. Annan could see the strength and the stubborn edge that he liked so much, but Wallace looked so tired.

"Not yet," said Wallace, digging his fingernails into Annan's skin. "Please don't make me." He dropped his voice, whispering against the pounding water. "I want things to be good for as long as they can be. I can't see him as helpless as I've become."

"*Fuck.*" Annan gave in to the tears that clawed to escape, wrapping Wallace in a tight hug as he broke down. "I'm sorry. I wouldn't."

This sweet man, who didn't ask for anything himself, was keeping it together even as Annan was breaking. Annan had to be able to give him one thing in this world, even if it killed him. And even though he didn't know Elgin all that well, Wallace was right. His husband was obsessed with him. His world would be turned upside down at the first hint of a new unidentified medication in the cabinet.

"Thank you." Wallace rubbed at his cheeks before tilting his head toward the spray of water. His limbs were trembling, a paleness to him even beneath the flush of his skin. The fierce grip he had on Annan faded to almost nothing.

"Are you okay?" asked Annan, trying to support Wallace as he reached for the shower wall, his small hands leaving a blank stain against the condensation.

"Just feeling a little shaky," said Wallace. His fingertips were trembling as he touched the glass, a wobbly breath leaving his lungs.

I can't do this. His eyes burned at the delicate man in his arms.

"You guys are so rich." Annan took a deep breath, forcing his own grief back. Wallace needed someone to be strong in the broken moments when he couldn't be himself. "I would have figured you could afford to put a bench in your shower, at the very least."

Wallace paused, his lips parting a moment before a smile touched his lips. That tiny movement lit up his whole face, banishing the dark lines and ghostly shadows.

"Why, you little— I thought you were sweet, but you've got just as much attitude as Elgin." Wallace softened, sinking into Annan's touch.

"I don't make nearly as many innuendos as he does," said Annan, shaking his head. He wasn't sure if *anyone* did. "But I like to see you smile." *Please keep smiling. I won't be able to bear it if you cry again.*

Wallace nodded, carefully turning away while keeping one hand on the wall. Annan dropped his hands, ready to catch Wallace if he started to fall. The floor was textured, but it would only take one drop of shampoo to send someone tumbling if they lost their balance.

"You're in luck then—because I love smiling." Wallace grabbed for the soap, passing it back to Annan. "Now I believe you promised to wash my back."

"I did." Annan's bravery disappeared the instant the soap was in his hands. It was one thing to joke to try to break an ominous mood, but it was another to lay his hands on someone else's partner when the lies were thick and fresh. "Is Elgin okay with this? I mean, if we touch like this?"

He held out the container of soap, squinting to read the label that he didn't recognize. It smelled fantastic, settling deep in his lungs as he poured a drop onto his palm. It was cold and slick, trying to disappear between his fingers so it could trickle down the drain.

Wallace turned, leveling him with a look that brooked no question. "Let me make something abundantly clear. I like you. I like you more than I ever thought I could like another person besides Elgin. No matter what happens, I hope that feeling continues to grow."

That hurt more than it should, settling in the wounded spot beneath his ribs.

But it was all the answer he needed. Warming up the suds in his hands, he placed his palms on Wallace's back, gently skimming the soap over his skin. Wallace jolted at the initial touch, letting out a small gasp.

"You okay?" asked Annan, his question like a broken record.

"Yeah, I just...didn't expect you to feel so good." Wallace lowered his head into the warm stream, his fluffy hair plastering to his head. "I've never been touched by anyone but Elgin. I was a virgin when we first got together, and before you, I never wanted anyone else but him."

Annan swallowed, but it stuck in his throat, nearly choking him. He was being torn apart, somehow falling into a spiral of lust while grief still tugged at his belly. But Wallace was here now, in his arms. *Don't waste it.*

"So you learned all your tricks from him?" asked Annan, digging his fingertips in a bit. Wallace let out another gasp, leaning into the touch and flexing the muscles in his back. Water dripped along the middle seam where his spine lay, dipping low to disappear between his cheeks.

Annan followed the next drop with his finger, pausing just above the rise of Wallace's ass. His breathing was coming faster, his thoughts spinning. *Was it possible to love two men, even when one of them just hurt you deeply?*

"We should get out before the water gets cold," said Annan, giving himself a very quick scrub without taking his eyes off Wallace.

Wallace cracked a yawn, stifling it with his palm as he made to lean against the shower wall. "Yeah. Elgin's probably got his video of choice playing and his ass in the air."

"If you're too tired you can say that," said Annan, touching Wallace's wrist before shutting the water off. "We don't need to."

"I want to," said Wallace, crossing his arms and narrowing his eyes. "I can sleep in tomorrow."

A moment later, his stubbornness disappeared. His knees buckled and Annan barely managed to catch him before he sprawled against the soapy floor. Wallace was so light in his arms, fitting perfectly as he tried to gather his feet.

"Don't ask me if I'm okay," said Wallace, clutching at Annan's chest as he heaved in deep breaths. "*Don't.*" He was trembling, his teeth chattering as he finally seemed to give in, slumping against Annan completely.

I can't do this. "Warn a guy," he said softly, combing Wallace's hair away from his face with his fingers. "If you wanted me to catch you like Prince Charming, you only had to ask." He swallowed the lump in his throat, using his foot to open the shower door and slowly half-carry Wallace out.

His trembling worsened in the cooler air of the bathroom, and he grew heavier as he seemed to lose more strength. Annan did his best not to slip on the wet floor, aiming them for the counter where the towels lay. When they reached it, Wallace slumped against the black surface, the color of his skin a stark contrast.

That furrow in his forehead had deepened, his face so pale that even his freckles appeared bleached.

Annan went to his knees, reaching for a towel and bringing it against Wallace's skin. It was the softest towel he'd ever touched in his life, but it still felt like it would scrape too harshly against the delicate skin before him.

"Is this too rough?" asked Annan, letting the cloth whisper over Wallace's leg. Water droplets sluggishly made their way from above, streaming over the expanse he'd just wiped dry. He repeated the action, unable to look up and face him.

On one hand, he wanted to wrap the fluffy towel around Wallace's neck and punish him for ever daring to get sick. How could he have the audacity to even think of leaving Elgin behind? On the other hand, he wanted to cradle him softly, brushing each part of his flesh until he was vibrant and new — *healed.*

He looked up when Wallace didn't answer. His eyes were closed, his head tilted back and his mouth parted. He could have been sleeping if not for the trembling and the way his arms shook as he tried to hold himself up.

Standing, Annan wrapped the towel around Wallace's shoulders, stopping the water at the source. Some of his hair had already started to dry, springing up and defying gravity in clumpy waves.

"I can carry you to bed," said Annan, combing Wallace's hair back over and over just to watch it spring free. It was so light and delicate, the thin strands slipping straight through his fingers.

"Elgin—"

"I'll tell him I tired you out. You need to rest, Wallace." Annan fought a sob as Wallace opened his eyes, tears caught in his lashes. "It's okay. I won't tell him."

Wallace went slack, defeat in every line.

"Okay."

It was harder to carry a grown man than most people made it sound. Wallace was small, but Annan still grunted as he lifted him bridal style, trying to make sure that the towel remained fixed in place against Wallace's chilled body. His muscles burned as the water on the floor threatened to sweep his feet out from under him and send them both sprawling. It barely registered that he was still dripping wet, his own skin prickling against the cold.

Wallace was shaking hard by the time they stepped out of the bathroom, and Annan moved faster, blinking to clear the water from his eyes. Tile turned to hardwood, a touch more warmth in the material.

Elgin was on the bed with the sound of a seedy movie playing on the television that took up a good chunk of space on the far side of the bedroom. His eyes were closed, his mouth open as he let out a huge snore, a drop of drool hovering close to the edge of his lip.

There was a bottle of lube in Elgin's hand, and the sheets were wrapped around his ankles, but he was dead to the world.

"Well, you were mostly right," said Annan, gently lowering Wallace to the bed. Wallace let out a sigh as his head hit the pillow and he turned to look at Elgin, a sweet smile on his lips.

"What a dope," said Wallace, letting out a soft laugh. "This is how half of our sex life ends. Did you know that?" He reached out, running a hand over Elgin's arm. Elgin didn't even twitch. "If I'm not in the mood, I just have a shower or grab a snack, and he's out like a light. I think he likes sleep more than sex."

Annan shook his head, helping Wallace get rid of the towel before pulling the blankets over him. He left the lube in Elgin's hand, tugging up the blankets to keep the cool at bay.

He turned from the bed, but Wallace reached for him, clasping his wrist. "You're staying."

Annan swallowed the lump in his throat, unable to pull his arm away. "I shouldn't."

I shouldn't be here in the first place. Without him, Elgin and Wallace probably would have been fine. Hell, this was all his fault.

"Get in the bed, Annan," said Wallace, his grip surprisingly strong. "I didn't tell you I like you just for you to wander off."

"I have to…" Annan bit his tongue, trying to muster up an excuse. Nothing was forthcoming. "Why do you even want me here? I'm just a guy that gets along better with horses than I do with people, and you two are way out of my league. I should go."

"I'm not going to fight with you," said Wallace, releasing his grip and relaxing against the pillow. He closed his eyes, but the furrow on his forehead remained like it always seemed to. "But know that you're right."

What? Annan took a step back, his feet sticky from the moisture that remained on his skin.

"You're just a man." Wallace took a shuddering breath. "And we're just men."

That hurts.

Annan slipped between the sheets, settling himself between them. His skin prickled as Wallace wrapped an arm around his waist, pressing them together. There were tears on Annan's cheeks as he closed his eyes, pleading for sleep to take him.

Chapter Seventeen

Annan

He'd often wondered how long he could hold his hand on an electric fence before he was forced to pull away, the little ticks growing stronger with every beat until his entire arm tingled, each jolt causing his body to twitch uncontrollably.

Or maybe there was a different form of torture that was just as painful that would suit what he needed right now.

There were a few green horses that needed exercise, and his particular favorite was a blue roan who loved to buck. He spent more time in the mud than on the back of that horse, but it was worth it when the horse finally dropped his head, chewing as he settled.

Casting a gaze at the house, he turned away from the fence. "Fuck it."

He spat at the ground before scuffing his boot, dust rising into the air. He'd been pissed for days, and the horses didn't deserve that. There was only one person who had been with him through the roughest patches, and he seemed to be hiding as well.

The burned remains of the barn were gone, the new frame fully constructed and grander than he could have imagined. Things should have been better, but the claws of guilt and regret refused to leave him be. Wallace was haunting his every thought.

I can't take this anymore.

"Milo!" Annan shouted at the house that he'd been slowly making his way to, stomping closer when he didn't get a response. He lowered his voice, grumbling under his breath. "You better not be holed up in your room." It was a beautiful day, even if he wasn't enjoying it himself.

He hovered at the door, holding his hand ready to reach for the screen. He'd been told countless times that he was family and to walk straight on in, but he still knocked every time.

There was nowhere in the world where he was *truly* family. At the barn, he was still an employee, even if he happened to be close to the owner. And with Elgin and Wallace...? He didn't want to think about them anymore.

Pulling the screen wide, he grabbed the doorknob, flinching as it turned easily under his hand. He kicked his boots off, wiping a few stray bits of hay from his clothes on the porch before toeing his way inside.

It smelled of cookies with a distant hint of lemons from the no-doubt homemade lemonade that was probably ready in the fridge. It was powerful stuff, with just as much tang as sugar, and every time it hit his lips on a hot day, it was like a profound awakening.

"Hello?" Annan called softly — probably too softly in the large house. On second thought, he hadn't looked to the far side of the house to see if there was a car in the garage or not. For all he knew, they could have taken a run to the store, and they'd come home to find him standing in the front hall covered in dust and dirt and looking guilty enough that they'd probably think he robbed them.

He turned back to the door, pausing when he caught the sound of a distant shuffle. Holding his breath, he treaded toward the sound, taking the same steps he would if he were approaching a mare who was ready to run him over.

When he stepped around the corner, he couldn't take a breath, everything in his mind grinding to an absolute halt. His heart pounded, sweat breaking out over his skin as he flashed hot and cold in an instant.

No.

Milo had a black hoodie pulled over his head, one white drawstring caught between his teeth. At least, it had probably been white at some point. He must've been chewing and gnawing at it for a while, catching his lip a few times. Pink soaked the fabric, his lips bright red, even as he bit down again, one of his teeth cutting into his flesh.

His eyes were bloodshot, his hand trembling as he plunged it into Oliya's purse that had been thrown over the back of one of the kitchen chairs. She'd probably left it there the last time they'd come back from town, or maybe they were planning to go out again sometime soon.

Milo lifted the wallet from within, pinching his tongue between his teeth as he slowly zipped it open. The drawstring dropped from his mouth as he snagged a few bills, stuffing them into the pouch of his hoodie. The pouch already looked full, the corner of another bill peeking from the other side.

"What are you doing?" asked Annan, clutching the wall for support. "Milo…"

Milo jumped, flinching back violently. He caught the edge of the chair with his elbow, and it crashed to the ground, the purse thudding against the floor and keeling over. A tube of lipstick rolled out in two pieces as the cap broke free.

"Fuck." Milo took a step back, shoving his hands into his pouch. There were deep shadows under his eyes, the skin smudged nearly black.

"Milo." Annan swallowed, forcing himself to stay where he was. Milo looked ready to run, his body and jaw tensed as he retreated again. He blinked slowly, wiping at the corner of his bloody mouth.

"Don't fucking yell at me, old man." Milo bumped the wall as he retreated harshly, missing the doorway by a few feet. He looked over his shoulder, narrowing his eyes when he must've realized there was nowhere to run. "What are you even doing in here? No one is supposed to be here."

Annan held up his hands, biting back every curse that sprang to mind. "I'm not here to yell." He swallowed, taking a slow breath as he glanced around the room. It was spotless except for the overturned chair and purse, the other three chairs at the kitchen island still standing. In the middle was a plastic goose, nearly bursting with napkins from a dozen different take-out restaurants.

"And I was hoping to grab a cup of lemonade. It's a great day to drink a glass on the porch, and I was hoping you could join me." Annan cleared his throat, his mouth suddenly bone-dry.

Milo jerked his head side to side, the shadow of his hands bulging in the pouch. "I'm leaving."

"Okay." Annan nodded, slowly lowering his hands before walking to the fridge. He trained a glance over his shoulder, keeping an eye on Milo's every move. "Another time then?"

"I'm not fucking coming back." Milo spat, a glob landing against the hardwood floor. It was worse than the purse or the chair, its presence an insult to whoever had put so much work into the house. Oliya had always been proud of the place, doing the majority of the work with her own hands.

"That works out great," said Annan, his hand shaking as he grabbed the jug of lemonade from the fridge before setting it on the counter. "I've been hoping for a road trip for months, and there's no time like the present. Which way are we headed? Down south to the border, or maybe out east to the coast? I've always wanted to see the mountains, so maybe I can convince you to head west. We can take your car or my truck. Either way there's lots of room." *Wallace wants to see the mountains, not me.*

He shook his head, banishing the thought as he poured a second glass, placing the pitcher back in the fridge.

"N-north." Milo's voice trembled. His face had paled, blood welling on his lower lip as he finally stopped chewing at it. He looked so tired — so defeated.

And I've been so focused on myself that I didn't even notice. Guilt gripped him harder, slashing across his gut.

"Oh." Annan scrunched his face, strolling to the island and sliding into one of the stools. It was rigid and uncomfortable, his back protesting immediately as his clothes shifted over his sweaty skin. He placed the second glass across from him in the spot where the chair had fallen, a ring of condensation already forming. "North is okay."

Milo furrowed his forehead, pulling his hands from the pouch. A few bills escaped, and he quickly bent over to grab them. They weren't the same bills Annan had watched him lift from the purse. "What's wrong with north?"

"Nothing. It's just..." Annan took a sip, hoping the sweet juice would calm his racing heart. He'd never been an actor, and he was barely holding himself back from launching himself at Milo and hugging the kid. "The bears."

Milo slowly blinked, his eyes going wide. He looked so small in his hoodie, his face pale against his blue hair. The color had faded over the last few weeks, blond poking through at the roots.

"They are always out this time of year," said Annan. "First comes black flies, the mosquitoes, then the bears come out. They should still be frisky, and you know what that means for the boys. They're worse than stallions. Once it *really* warms up, the rattlesnakes are everywhere, so we'll have to make sure to pack our boots."

Summer had them within its grasp, but spring had been a recent memory only a few weeks ago. Far enough north there was probably still snow piled in the deepest parts of the woods.

"I don't want to see snakes." Milo took an unsteady breath, his eyes going glassy. "I just want to go somewhere cold, where there are no fires and no memories to haunt me. I don't want to see them anymore." A tear spilled over onto his cheek. "Are there dangerous things like that out west? Let's go see the mountains like you said."

"That's the spirit," said Annan, forcing a grin on his face even with his own eyes prickling. "There are bears out there—bigger ones, too—but the snakes aren't as bad. There's only the prairie rattlesnake to worry about there, not the massasauga."

Annan had never been himself, but one of his exes had grown up in Calgary, and they'd told him about the animals out there. Annan had always thought that the view of the mountains would be worth a few predators.

"No bigger bears— I don't want any bears. East?" Milo perked up, not even attempting to wipe his tears. They tracked down his cheeks, dirty and soaking into his clothes.

"Sorry." Annan shrugged. "Black bears out that way."

"Fuck." Milo's voice caught, a sob in his throat. "Where the fuck am I gonna go? I just—I don't want to be afraid anymore."

"There's only one place I know without bears," said Annan, scratching at his chin. "It also has some of the best fire protection I've ever seen." He pointed to the ceiling.

After the fire, Oliya had installed some state-of-the-art equipment all around the barns and house. There were built in sprinkler systems, fire suppression and enough alarms to wake the dead. It had probably cost her more than the house, but as far as Annan was concerned, every penny was worth it.

"You're gonna say here," said Milo, shaking his head as he let out a sob. "But here is where the memories are the worst. It's when I feel safest that everything goes to shit." He clutched at his shirt, the fabric bunching under his hands. "My boyfriend told me he loved me. He wants to go out again tonight." Milo ducked his head. "I don't understand how he can say something like that. He doesn't even know who I am—*what* I am. I can't drag him into this mess, too."

Oh, Milo. This kid always managed to rip his heart out. Today, he could barely take it.

"You could always live with me," said Annan. Standing, he grabbed his empty glass before setting it in the sink. His stomach churned, ready to empty itself at a moment's notice, but he bit down on his tongue, waiting for the sensation to pass.

"Ew." Milo scrunched his nose. "You—you're...no." He wiped at his cheeks with both sleeves, sniffing hard. There was dirt clinging to parts of his shirt that made Annan wonder how long he'd been wearing it. "I feel so fucking stupid."

He could see the cracks forming as logic started to sink in. Milo had such a sensitive trigger that it took a long time for his rational thoughts to catch up most times, but keeping him talking was the best therapy.

"Don't belittle yourself," said Annan. "I was in that fire, too. Remember?" He remembered the smell of smoke with that terrible undertone before he'd heard the first horse scream. That sound would be with him forever, along with the memory of how slow his legs had gone as he'd run for the barn, his hands shaking as he'd grabbed the nearest bucket of water that had proved useless against the flames. The wall of heat had battered him back and he'd been paralyzed until the fire trucks had arrived, the sirens piercing louder than the screams.

They'd managed to get all but two mares out, the poor creatures burned beyond recognition. He'd lost it when he saw their bodies, Oliya and Milo in a similar state as they'd hugged each other on the lawn. A few horses had gotten loose, their hooves thundering on the ground as they'd galloped around the property. One had taken a day for Annan to catch, the poor thing shivering with exhaustion when he brought her to water.

His hands were shaking, tears rolling down his own cheeks. "Can I give you a hug?"

Milo nodded and Annan crossed the kitchen in a few strides, hugging him tight. He was so tiny and frail, his body nearly feeling weightless against him. He was young, but he'd suffered too much for one person. Hell, he'd suffered more than three should.

"You gonna run?" asked Annan, patting Milo on the head in the way he knew he secretly loved. Annan was shaking, too, despite how hard he was trying to calm his own fears. "I'll have to do all the chores. I'll be camping out at the barn every night to get them all done, and I'll have to ride Folly when he gets too energetic."

"You keep your calloused paws off Folly," said Milo, narrowing his eyes as he tugged himself free. "You don't know how to handle him. He's delicate, and you have heavy hands."

Annan forced a smile on his face, his chest still raw and open. He probably had some of the lightest hands at the barn, but Milo had always had a connection with Folly that no one else had managed. The horse liked and listened to one person in the world. "The money..."

"Most of it's mine," said Milo, reaching for the chair and righting it. "I only took a hundred bucks from her purse. Figured I would need it for the road." Even as he said it, he plucked the bills from his pouch, sliding them back into the wallet before putting the purse back in its place.

Annan nodded. *Thank God.* "So if you're all done robbing, then we should hang out and have that drink I was talking about. It's been days since I've heard about that boyfriend of yours, and I've got to hear about this confession."

Milo shook his head, turning away. "I'm going to bed. Don't touch Folly. I was serious about that."

As Milo disappeared up the steps, Annan turned away, rushing from the house. The door slammed behind him, and he bent over as soon as he reached the grass, his hands braced on his knees. "Fuck."

That kid. That poor fucking kid. If he could take it away, he would, but he was powerless. Helplessness sank into him, slipping over his skin and threatening to swallow him whole.

I could have saved those horses if I'd been faster. I could have stopped Milo's nightmares if only I'd known him sooner. His breath came in short bursts, his head swimming. *I could save Wallace if only I loved him enough.*

A soft nicker caught his attention. When he looked up, he saw Thelma standing there just on the other side of the thin fence, her ears pricked toward him and her head as high as she could probably lift it. She was an older mare that had come to the barn on accident. From what little they knew, she had been a broodmare almost all her life, popping out babies until her back was bowed and her teeth were almost gone.

Somehow, she still managed to graze, and her legs had never given her any issues. When Oliya had talked about selling her a few years before, Annan had put his foot down. If she went, they both went. Since then, she'd been kept in one of the paddocks close to the house with the yearlings, who she was happy to show the ropes. Maybe she missed her own babies, or maybe she just enjoyed how ridiculous the young horses could be.

"Hey, girl." He reached for her, careful to avoid the thin wire of the electric fence. She snorted, nosing at his fingers before lowering her head toward his palm. She moved her tail constantly as flies buzzed around her, flicking her skin every time they landed. As a young colt approached, she pinned her ears, giving him a look until he backed off.

"Be nice," said Annan, grinning as she turned her head back to him. "I'm here to see you."

She tossed her head, stomping in the grass as more bugs flew around her. Even on days with a bit of wind, they'd been awful all season. There were little yellow spots on her front legs where the flies had started to lay, the irritation probably worse than the flies themselves.

"Wanna go for a spin?" He gave her one more pet before ducking between the wires of the fence, wincing as he grazed the top wire. "Stand, girl."

She perked up, curling her head toward him as he walked next to her, placing one hand on her withers, which was the highest point of her back. She was a massive horse, her shoulder nearly at his eye level. It was another reason she was one of his favorites.

Hopping a few times, he grasped a chunk of her mane, launching himself onto her back. It had taken him a hell of a lot of practice before he could do the move smoothly, so he didn't land too hard and risk hurting her back. He grunted, squinting as he adjusted himself so his balls didn't get squashed.

"You good?" he asked, holding onto her mane as he patted her shoulder. He was always careful with her, sitting lightly so he didn't strain her back. She didn't seem to mind, flicking her tail to strike another fly from her side.

She arched her neck, taking a few steps as he clicked to her. Her stride was smooth, carrying them over the ground with ease as she avoided the few thistles spotted around the field. Whatever her real age was, she had enough stubbornness in her bones that Annan didn't doubt she would live into her late thirties. She tossed her head, grunting as she picked up the pace.

"Go for it, girl. *Get.*"

With a tiny buck, she launched herself into a gallop, tearing along the fence line. Annan let out a yell, grabbing her mane with a second hand and arching over her neck as she picked up speed. The bugs were left behind as the wind buffeted against them, her body moving like a well-oiled machine beneath him. She let out a snort, bucking a second time.

"Whoa there, big girl. Try not to kill me." Even if he liked to pretend, he was not a real cowboy, and the way he barely recovered his balance after her buck was a testament to that. He rocked back, tensing his abdomen and relaxing his thighs to regain his seat as she took a wide turn, picking up her pace.

She slowed as they reached the other end of the field that was far away from the house, trotting a few steps before dropping her head to graze. The yearlings followed a few strides behind, their tails held high as they played. Two of them broke off from the small group, racing back toward the house while bucking and rearing like a bunch of idiots.

"You're teaching them bad habits," said Annan, his heart pounding as he leaned against her neck. He was covered in sweat, and the sun was beating on them from above, but this was the only place where no one could touch him. Not sickness, or the pure guilt of Milo trying to run from his demons and the helplessness when he realized there was nothing he could do.

"Shit." He wiped at his cheek as fresh tears rolled down his face. "What the hell am I going to do?"

Thelma didn't answer him, swatting rhythmically with her tail as she chomped away, somehow managing to eat despite her lack of teeth. One of the yearlings came right up beside them, her palomino coat almost shimmering in the sunlight. She was nearly perfect except for the small crescent scar on her side that was no-doubt from one of her herd mates.

Letting his mind wander, he stroked Thelma's shoulder until his back was aching from the position, flies buzzing around them both and landing on his exposed arms, tickling as they moved over his skin.

"I'm not sure how much more I can take, girl." He took a shuddering breath. "I don't care about Ralph—fuck Ralph. He was always an asshole. But these two guys? They've got me so wrapped up I don't know what to think. And Milo... You gotta keep an eye on him when I'm not here."

Chapter Eighteen

Elgin

He pulled into the driveway at the ranch, the car jolting as he hit a pothole. Slowing, he cranked the windows all the way down, letting a few flies in through the cracks. It was another sunny day, the greenery soaking up every ray.

He wasn't sure if 'ranch' was the right word, but he didn't have another. All he knew was that Annan was sure to be here, and he had to give the guy a hard time after not answering his last three text messages.

Their last night together had been wonderful, even if Elgin had slept through all of it. At first, he hadn't been sure if Annan had stayed at all, but the sheets had smelled like him, and Wallace had assured him that Annan had played little spoon all night between the two of them.

I can't believe I missed it. He'd been ready to rock, lube in hand and his favorite movie playing, and the next thing he'd known, he'd been half lying on the bottle with Wallace snoring beside him. His husband had laughed when Elgin grumbled about being cheated out of playtime.

Pulling up to the same spot where he'd parked before, he glanced around, shielding his eyes with his hand. It had been warm at home, but out here it was roasting, the sun beating straight down at him. He peeled his T-shirt off, tossing it back in the car and leaving him in just a tank and jeans.

The smell of fresh wood was overpowering but the construction site was quiet today, only a pile of gravel and tools left behind at the new build. When he'd asked Annan about the building before, he'd gone oddly silent before moving on to the next topic. Elgin hadn't pressed.

There was no sign of Annan when he peered toward the little pond, and the barns were hushed except for the sound of horses and one chicken that was crowing repeatedly. He was about to give up when he caught the sound of thundering hooves.

His jaw dropped as he caught sight of horses running inside one of the fenced areas, a huge one in the lead and trailed by four others that were tiny in comparison. It took him a moment to recognize the man on the back of the leader, leaning forward as they raced along the ground.

"He *is* a cowboy." His heart picked up as they got closer, not slowing at all as they neared the thin fence. Maybe they didn't even see it. It was only a tiny wire after all, and the horse was massive.

"Wait," he shouted, darting toward the fence while waving his arms. "You're gonna crash!" He ran right up to fence, flinching as the horses pounded closer. They were so loud, dirt kicking up beneath their feet as their tails trailed behind them. From what he saw the last time he was at the barn, he'd thought horses were calm creatures, with soft noses and kind eyes, but this group appeared almost wild.

At the last moment, the big mare dug her heels in, dropping her backend low as she skidded over the earth. The smaller following horses acted with much more agility, turning and darting back along the fence and tearing away as fast as they could.

As the mare came to a stop, Annan hunched forward, letting out a groan as he slid from her back. He tripped as his feet touched the ground, falling back with a grunt. He thudded against the earth, air rushing from his lungs. "Ow."

"Oh my God." Elgin scrambled between the fence lines, flinching as he was shocked twice in a way that wasn't nearly as pleasant as when Wallace did it with that little tool he'd bought them. "Are you okay? Are you still alive?"

Annan raised one arm, waving at him before he dropped it back to the ground. His hair was stuck to his face, his shirt plastered to his skin with dark stains. The massive horse snuffled around his prone body, hovering near Annan's face. *She's going to bite him.*

Granted, Elgin had never been an animal person, but he charged at the horse with every bit of confidence he had, yelling and waving his arms as he screamed at her to get away. She snorted once, kicking up her heels as she darted away, those massive hooves barely missing Annan. He chased her for a few steps, making as much noise as he could to scare her on, and only stopping when she showed no sign of turning back.

When he looked over his shoulder at Annan, he was sitting up and leaning on his hands, his head thrown back as he laughed. His eyes sparkled as he wiped his cheek, a chunk of dirt smearing across the surface.

"I would pay to see that again," said Annan, grunting as he rose to his feet. With his legs wide, he adjusted himself with a wince, hair and sweat coating the inside of his thighs.

"She was eating you," said Elgin, slouching his shoulders as he huffed. "I thought you were hurt."

For some reason that made Annan laugh harder, the corner of his eyes crinkling. He threw an arm around Elgin's shoulders, leaning against him. "My brave rescuer." His body shook with laughter. He smelled of sweat, horses and leather, which wasn't that bad of a combination. But he was filthy and not only from his roll on the ground.

"We were just playing," said Annan, patting Elgin's back. "She's a horse, not a lion, so I'm not really for her palate." He winced again as he brushed some grass from his leg. The strands fell to the ground, leaving a green imprint behind.

"But you fell." Elgin pointed to the spot of squashed earth, still dazed. Annan's grin only widened. "You're just making fun of me."

"The fall was real," said Annan, rubbing the back of his neck. "I can usually ride bareback with no problem, but that last buck she did threw me forward and pretty much crushed my balls. You rescued me." He threw his other arm around Elgin's front, giving him a brief squeeze before pulling back.

Bareback? That brought too many dirty images to process in a few quick minutes.

"What are you doing here, though?" Annan suddenly seemed to sober. "Are you okay? Is Wallace okay?"

Why wouldn't we be?

"I came to give you a hard time," said Elgin, rounding on Annan and poking him in the chest. The thundering of hooves slowed as the horses all settled on the far side of the fence. *Thank goodness.* "You snuck out like a college one-night stand, and I haven't heard from you since." Elgin put the back of his hand to his head, pretending to swoon. "No note, no kiss, just empty sheets and an unused bottle of lube."

Annan ran a hand through his hair, his lips quirking. It may just have been the light, but his eyes looked dark, streaks along his cheeks that were tracks through the dirt. There were still a few bits of grass stuck between the strands of his dark hair, but it only made him seem more adorable. Elgin leaned in, brushing some of it free. He didn't mind the sweat that soaked his fingertips, smoothing it over his own hand.

"I didn't sneak," said Annan, sinking into the touch and closing his eyes briefly. "There was work to be done, and I hadn't been home all day. I didn't want to kiss you awake just to say goodbye, but I can next time."

"Next time…" Elgin let out a hum. "I like the sound of that. Or, you can skip the kiss and go straight to a morning fuck. I would also be amenable to a blow job."

"You won't say that at four o'clock in the morning," said Annan.

Elgin grimaced. "You're probably right. Stick with the kiss, and come straight to us after you've been here."

Annan bent over, reaching for a piece of blue twine that had been hidden in the grass. He curled it up and shoved it into his pocket. "I'll smell — probably more than I do now." He took a whiff of himself. "Maybe not."

Elgin stretched out, wrapping an arm around Annan's shoulders again. "I think you smell manly." He took his own deep whiff. Beneath a very distant cologne there were a lot of smells, and they were ripening under the sun. "Maybe just a quick shower."

Annan snorted, starting toward the fence and slipping through the wires without letting them touch him. Elgin made to follow, eyeing up the strands, but Annan was already opening a small gap in the fence that Elgin hadn't noticed.

"Did you want a ride?" asked Annan, nodding to the horses back out in the field, "Or did you want to take me for a ride?" He turned his gaze back to Elgin, his eyes sparkling. "There are a lot of places in this barn where no one goes."

"We could go for a roll in the hay," said Elgin, grasping Annan by his hips and pulling him close. The fence snapped rhythmically beside them, but otherwise, it was quiet, the breeze barely rustling the leaves of the nearby trees.

"Wouldn't recommend that," said Annan, sliding his hands up Elgin's arms to rest on his shoulders. "Hay is itchy as hell, and you'd be pulling it out of every crevice for days. There's a breeding pen at the back, though. It won't be used for a few weeks at least, and the name fits."

Elgin chuckled, leaning his forehead against Annan's. *As tempting as that sounds...* "How did it take us so long to find you?" He took a deep breath, trying to memorize every bit of the man before him. He was hot to the touch, his muscles hard, no doubt from the amount of work he did. And it was true—he did smell like a man, pure and simple.

"I guess I've been hiding behind other men," said Annan, looping his arms around Elgin's neck. "Where have you been hiding all my life? I can't remember the last time I was so relaxed and confused and sad."

Elgin drew a hand down Annan's back, digging his fingers gently into the muscle. "Don't be sad, baby. We just want you to be happy."

Annan instantly went tense, tightening his grip. "Sorry. I didn't mean it like that. I'm not sad like *that*…" He cleared his throat.

"I understand," said Elgin. "We are the most amazing people ever—I've met me, so I get it—and you're sad that you didn't slip into our lives sooner." He tilted his head, placing a kiss on Annan's forehead. "I get upset that I didn't meet Wallace sooner. I mean, I want to spend every minute of my life with him, but there were times before I even knew him. It's hard to come to terms with that sometimes."

Annan didn't relax, and if anything, he grew tenser, but Elgin held him tight, placing another kiss on his scruffy cheek. There was no one around, and even if there were, it wouldn't have mattered.

"Where is Wallace?" asked Annan softly. His blue eyes were so gentle and sweet, a bit of redness in them that must've come from too much sun. It wasn't a surprise that the horses seemed to love him.

"Work." Elgin relaxed his grip, letting Annan have a touch of room. "I thought I could pick you up, and we could both take him lunch. Unless you have more work to do?"

"I'm good," said Annan, suddenly seeming calmer. "All my chores are done, and I was just going to brush out a few horses yet, but that can wait." Maybe he wasn't the only one happy at the idea of seeing Wallace. Elgin saw him every day, but he still looked forward to the moments when he would see his husband. "I should shower."

"Nah." Elgin looked him up and down. From the scuffs on his pants to the bits of suspect brown, he was gorgeous. "I want you to go just like this. We just want to see *you*, and I know he won't care if you were covered head to toe in shit or if you were in a suit. Hell, I would take you naked coated in jelly and those glitter sprinkles that get everywhere." Whoever had invented that glitter was a terrible, terrible person.

Annan looked toward the fence before brushing his legs again. A few strands of grass filtered to the ground, rolling away on the breeze as it picked up. His face was flushed, more dirt than freckles on his cheeks, but he was still one of the most beautiful people Elgin had ever seen. It was more than attraction that swelled in his chest.

"Annan?"

Annan looked toward him, squinting his eyes against the sun. "Hmm?"

"Why didn't you answer my texts?" Elgin bit his lower lip. Reaching for Annan's hand, he traced the lines of his palm, bumping over softness and callus. It had killed him while he waited for a reply, no new lines of writing appearing on his screen.

"I guess I was trying to figure something out," said Annan, staring at where they were connected.

Elgin gnawed harder, almost breaking skin before he released his lip. He wasn't sure if he believed in reading palms, but Annan's lifeline looked thick and steady, as if nothing could break it.

"Did you?"

Annan nodded, a smile touching his lips. "I think so."

* * * *

The office was unsurprisingly packed for a Thursday afternoon, people in dress shirts, slacks or skirts and heels. Elgin fit right in since he'd pulled his T-shirt back on in the air conditioning in the car. It was Annan who stuck out like a strand of wheat in a perfectly mowed lawn. *I should bag off work early every day if this is my reward.*

Tanned was an understatement when it came to Annan, but it was the pure caramel that someone only got when they spent almost all their time outside. Even Elgin couldn't claim that from his time in his garden, and Wallace's colleagues were the epitome of an office worker with few freckles but many artificial spray tans between them.

But the biggest jolt was watching the way he moved through the crowded environment, repeatedly dusting off his clothing and trying to hide from people while simultaneously being as nice as possible. He'd blushed a half-dozen times so far and had nodded at nearly every person in greeting, which was so cute it had a warm feeling stretching through his chest.

People weren't too obvious about the smell of horses, only one man scrunching his nose and taking a step away as they rose skyward in the elevator. Elgin slunk closer at Annan's dejected look, looping an arm around his back and tucking his chin on Annan's shoulder.

"You okay?" asked Elgin, keeping his voice low as the elevator emptied, and they started to rise to the final floor. Annan shifted, glancing at Elgin through the surrounding mirrors.

"I had a nightmare like this once." He sniffed himself, crinkling his nose.

"You don't have to worry about what they think of you—not when you already belong to us," said Elgin. He hoped it wasn't too much, because he needed Annan to know exactly how he felt.

The elevator pinged open, and Elgin winced as he caught sight of Derk, releasing Annan. He'd forgotten to warn Annan about Derk and the rumors that would spread if he saw Elgin with another man. *On second thought.* Grinning, Elgin slid his hand into Annan's, weaving their fingers together.

Let them talk. The sooner people got over their gossip, the better.

Derk zoned in on their clasped hands immediately, but he managed to school his expression after his initial shocked gaze.

"Mr. Bekker, how nice to see you again," said Derk, leaning forward and narrowing his eyes slightly as Elgin squeezed Annan's hand. "How can I help you?"

Now that's just cold. If Elgin had known that he could have shaken Derk off his back just by holding another man's hand, he would have done it years ago.

"We're just here to see Wallace," said Elgin, sending a grin Annan's way. Annan was still caught looking around the office building, probably getting whiplash from how fast he was moving his head around.

He made to move past like he always did, but Derk circled around his desk, heading them off. "He's not available at the moment."

Like that's ever stopped me. Elgin just nodded. "Is he in a meeting? We'll wait in his office until he's done."

"He's not in the building at the moment," said Derk, a frown tugging at his lips. "I can't let you in his office if he's not here."

"Oh." Elgin faltered. Images of secret office liaisons flickered through his mind before he could immediately squash them. Wallace had been so busy lately that he'd probably forgotten to mention an appointment or something. Or maybe he'd finally booked that massage that Elgin had been pestering him to get.

"You're right," said Elgin, plastering a smile on his face. "I completely forgot that he had that appointment today." Releasing Annan's hand, he scratched his chin and leaned against the desk. Derk took a small step back, looking confused that he was willingly staying there to chat.

"Annan, do you remember where he told us to meet him? The address completely slipped my mind," said Elgin. *Please let it be a spa.* Spas were *the* best place to fuck in.

It took Annan a moment before he caught on, nodding as he darted his gaze around. "I don't remember."

Oh, come on. Be more convincing. "Was it King Street?" asked Elgin, sliding his hand over Derk's desk as he got more comfortable. It hadn't been as easy to tell before, but the smell of horse was stronger within the paint and paper of the office building, something Derk seemed to be taking great offense to if his scrunched nose was anything to go by.

"Maybe?" said Annan, biting his lip.

Just a little longer, baby.

"Well, we could just wait here for him to get back, since we can't remember," said Elgin. Reaching for Annan, he pulled him closer, until that sweat and sunshine was right against his nose.

The smell of animals had never appealed to him before, but now it was almost a Pavlovian response. Or maybe it had been watching Annan fly around a field on the back of a giant horse.

"It's on Erb Street," said Derk, holding a hand to his nose and glaring at Annan as if he were a personal offense. "Three Fifty-two. There's a medical office there."

The massage wouldn't be nearly as fun if it were a registered one.

"I know the place," said Annan, his entire being tensing. "I took my father there a few years ago." He chewed his lip, darting his gaze to the side. "We should just go back to the house and wait for him there. I wouldn't want to bug him."

"Oh, come on," said Elgin, tugging at Annan's hand. "It will be fun. Wallace loves it when I show up during meetings and appointments."

"I don't think he does," said Derk, sending him a mild glare. "But you can't stay here."

Maybe I should remind him whose husband owns the building?

"Then it's settled," said Elgin, clapping one hand against his leg. He smiled softly at Annan, who looked more nervous now than when he'd first stared at the tall office building when they'd pulled up.

"I really don't think we should," said Annan as Elgin tugged him back into the elevator. He met Elgin's eyes through the reflective glass of the elevator, and there was a touch of fear there that made Elgin want to kiss him better.

"You're beautiful," said Elgin, quirking his lips in a smile. "Don't let anyone make you feel less than perfect, no matter where you are. I don't care if Wallace is on the moon. We're going to go there."

Chapter Nineteen

Annan

His heart was pounding, fresh sweat prickling over his skin and turning his stomach until he was breathing deep through his nose, just to keep from throwing up. He couldn't remember the last time he'd had something to eat that wasn't the sugary sweetness of the glass of lemonade or his breakfast that seemed like a lifetime before, but everything in his stomach was ready to eject.

He knew their destination deep within his very soul, the name of the street enough to conjure the wicked ghosts of his past. When he'd taken his father to the clinic, he had been convinced that he would never see him again, walking through the doors like they were death row themselves with the doctor as the executioner.

His father had come out of that appointment with a smile on his lips. Sure, he'd been missing his prostate by then, but the tests had come back benign. He had been cancer free and had been ever since.

But Wallace…wasn't.

Annan started at the frosted glass window of the doctor's office, the lettering on it striking fear into anyone who happened to pass through. *'Oncology'*. He shuddered.

Surely, it should have been buried within the realms of the hospital where people screamed when you tried to help them, and where the smell of death was an ominous force. But instead, it was in a cute strip mall with free parking and a nail salon next door where you could have a mani-pedi before they put you into the ground.

Elgin was staring at the same words through the tinted glass of the car's window, so many emotions passing over his face that Annan could merely tremble at the strength of them.

"Oncology."

God, it even sounded like a final destination where you went in whole and were shuffled out the back door in a plastic bag. It echoed in his head over and over, sharpening to a pickaxe as he flushed hot and cold.

Elgin squinted at the door, tilting his head as his gaze seemed to settle on confusion. He reached for the button for his window, rolling it down. The warmth and light of summer streamed into the car, coating them instantly in heat that only made Annan shake worse.

"Derk must've given us the wrong address," said Elgin, leaning one arm against the open windowpane. Annan wasn't sure what he was looking for when he gazed up and down the strip, his tongue between his teeth.

"Or maybe I took a wrong turn," said Elgin, his gaze settling on the door again with its wicked lettering of broken lives. "Is there a Erb Street West?" He craned his neck back before scrolling the window up. It took a moment for the heat to settle before the air conditioning caught up again.

"No." Annan ducked his head, staring at the cracked dirt and mud on his hands. He hadn't had a chance to wash up yet, and he was still sticky and filthy from the barn. Normally, he wouldn't mind, but the unforgiving leather seats beneath him were making it so much worse than normal. *Or maybe that's just the guilt.*

"Weird." Elgin's voice wavered as he stared straight ahead, throwing the car into reverse and tucking back along another row of cars. Annan recognized the car they parked beside with a jolt—the memories from their night at the restaurant still fresh. Elgin turned his head, staring at Wallace's car before turning his gaze back to the door.

He tightened his hands on the steering wheel, rolling all the windows down before shutting the car off. Reaching across his body, Elgin unbuckled the seatbelt before settling back against his seat, his expression unchanging.

"What are you doing?" asked Annan, his voice cracking and weak.

Elgin didn't answer.

A small bell clanged as the door of the medical office opened and Wallace stepped out into the sunlight. He stumbled at the first step before he paused, shielding his eyes from the sun with both hands, despite his sunglasses. The dark sweater he wore made him look even paler than he was, parts of it hanging off his body in places that had probably fit perfectly before.

Annan bit his lip, tasting blood as Wallace slowly walked to his car, gripping the edge of the fender as he drew close. Annan longed to get up and help — to carry Wallace and gently set him in the passenger seat, but his limbs were glued in place. Wallace hadn't noticed them yet, seemingly lost in his head as he grappled with his door handle and tugged it open after three tries.

Elgin's face was hard — unchanging, not even as Wallace sat in his car, letting his head fall back against the seat. His chest was heaving, his cheeks wet with tears, even as he wiped them away. In the car that cost hundreds of thousands of dollars, he looked completely helpless.

Annan wasn't sure if Wallace felt their eyes on them or if he heard the crunch of leather beneath Elgin's hand, but he suddenly turned toward them, his head lolling to the side. His eyes were hidden behind the thick sunglasses, but his lips were pressed together. He didn't move — didn't twitch — just stared, his expression hidden.

Slowly, Wallace reached for his keys, putting his car in gear and pulling away with tears still fresh on his cheeks. The sound of his AM radio washed away as he disappeared from the lot, pulling into afternoon traffic without pause.

"You knew," said Elgin, breaking the silence of the car. He watched the spot where Wallace had disappeared, his expression blank. "You *knew*."

Annan shook. He felt as if it were his own secret that had been revealed — his own cancer gnawing away at his life force and draining him dry. He could barely raise his hand to run through his hair, sweat clinging to the strands.

"Yes." The word was dirty — filthy in his mouth. He shuddered in revulsion, bile burning his throat. What was he supposed to say? *Sorry? We were only trying to protect you?*

"Get out."

He didn't hesitate, unbuckling the strap and flying out of his seat. He'd barely slammed the door shut before Elgin pulled away, booking it out of the parking lot. His car was so much louder than Wallace's, the engine revving as he shot out into traffic. A honk sounded, someone shouting after him.

This is not how I imagined my day would go. He was with Elgin one hundred percent, though. Hell, he should have thrown himself out of the window on the way here to save Elgin the trouble of kicking him out. A friend didn't hide something like this and neither did a lover.

He'd betrayed them both. Elgin's trust was shattered under a layer of treachery, and Wallace would probably never tell Annan anything again. Not only that, but Annan had been lying to himself this whole time if he thought he was anything more to them than a way to fight the loneliness in a doomed situation.

The real trick was going to be getting back to the barn. His car was comfortably parked in the employee parking section, his keys in the ignition and his wallet with every credit card on the dash. He'd left his phone in the cupholder during chores like he always did, so he couldn't exactly call in a favor and ask someone to pick him up.

Annan kicked at the pavement, watching a rock roll toward the nearest car. It was busier than the average lot, with three medical centers with different specialties along with a chocolate shop, the salon and a pharmacy.

Sweat clung to his filthy jeans and shirt, the layer of fabric well and truly stuck to him. It was funny. Usually he went most of his summer working outdoors without air conditioning, but it really seemed to hit home today. He was getting too used to the little things that made some people's lives more comfortable. That, and holding back tears was taking up most of his energy over the last few days.

He glanced at the ominous door where a nurse was walking through in bright pink scrubs, her purse slung over her shoulder. She was probably headed for lunch...or maybe it was the end of her day. Her day was probably going even worse than his, so he wasn't about to stop her and ask to borrow her phone.

He moved to a shady spot under a stunted tree that had bent the edges of the pavement. Its branches were barely green, with thick grooves in its bark, probably from baking in the sun day after day.

What am I gonna do? He didn't care about the long walk home or back to the barn, but he couldn't imagine not seeing Elgin and Wallace again. They occupied every moment of his thoughts, slipping deeper into his heart at every opportunity. *Love?* He wasn't sure. It was a different kind of longing than he'd had before.

Sex wasn't the first thing on his mind. He'd rather be close to them, soaking up their presence for as long as it lasted. The little things were all he needed to keep going.

A flash of black had him looking up as a familiar car rolled into the parking lot. The engine was quiet as it coasted closer, the locks clicking as the driver threw it into park right in front of him. It wasn't a spot, but blocked off an exit that would surely piss someone off when they tried to get into the strip mall.

He didn't move toward the car, even when the window rolled down and the door unlocked a second time.

"Get in," said Elgin, his voice thick but soft. "I'm not going to just leave you here, so get in."

Annan looked toward the salon. A lady was stepping out, admiring her bright pink nails that were long enough to be considered daggers. She winced as she tucked her hair behind her ear, accidentally scraping herself.

"I'm good," said Annan. His chest was numb all the way to his fingertips, but he knew for sure that the last place he wanted to be was in that car. He couldn't face Elgin after betraying him so severely. He wasn't sure if he could ever face him again.

"I'm not asking," said Elgin, his voice a touch louder. "Do you even have a way of getting home?"

Annan swallowed. He wasn't some helpless kid who needed a sponsor to get through school and a friend to keep the bullies off his back. Those days were long gone. "I'll figure it out."

The door slammed after Elgin stepped out, circling around the car and marching toward him. His eyes were bloodshot and wet as he approached, rage in every step. Annan couldn't stop himself from shrinking back. He was a big guy himself, and no lover had ever laid a mean hand on him before, but he'd pushed Elgin past his control.

Elgin stopped dead, his face going pale. "I'm not…" He dropped his gaze, running a hand through his hair. "Please, just get in. I want to take you home."

"I'm good," said Annan. His voice was shaking along with his limbs. "I can take care of myself."

"I know." Elgin turned back to the car before opening the passenger door. "And I realized I don't have the right to be angry with you. You haven't just been taking care of yourself — you've been taking care of Wallace, too. You've been there for him when he thought I couldn't be. I should be thanking you."

That's not true. He'd done nothing but run and lie since Wallace had confided in him. Annan wasn't even sure if he was the real *him* anymore. He'd always been a straight shooter — an open book — and he hated how much that had changed.

But I don't have a choice. Annan slipped into the car, closing his eyes as Elgin shut the door. When Elgin got back into the driver's seat, he reached over to squeeze Annan's leg once. Annan fought not to curl into himself.

"Thank you," said Elgin, his voice taking on more roughness.

Fuck, I'm a terrible person.

Chapter Twenty

Elgin

Something was wrong with him. The moment he saw the clinic doors with '*Oncologist*' scrolled across them like some kind of award, he'd gone numb. There had been other places in the strip of stores — brighter places with pink and yellow hues. But those words were the only thing that mattered.

Tears seeped through the cracks of his lashes, and he could barely see the traffic as he shifted through it automatically, getting closer to home with every turn. He'd been driving the streets long enough to know his turns, and the traffic seemed to part for him, avoiding the car that seemed to have lost its mind.

He glanced at Annan, his chest going tight. He'd never felt rage so pure and thick as when Annan had looked at him with those beautiful eyes, so full of guilt and remorse. It had only taken Elgin a few seconds and one loop around the block before he'd realized that Annan wasn't the one he was angry at.

Wallace.

He'd been angry at his husband exactly once in his life. Years before, Wallace had worked himself to the bone, staying at the office overnight for nearly a week and avoiding Elgin's calls around dinner each night. On the fifth night, Elgin had stormed into Wallace's office, slamming the advertisement for their future home down on the desk.

"If you don't want to come home now, then you're going to buy us something that you can't bear to be away from."

Elgin had ended up loving the house more than Wallace seemed to, building a few gardens and making his own spaces in the vast rooms. But Wallace had been at home every night since. Sometimes he missed dinner, but he was always in bed next to Elgin by the time the night turned cool and dew gathered on the tips of the grass outside.

Because Wallace had never lied to him — he'd never had a reason to — Elgin accepted everything about his husband, from his workaholic tendencies to the sweet smiles and the tiny moments they shared together that made his days so much bigger. If Wallace had ever had the inclination to cheat on him, Elgin would have accepted that, too, just so he wouldn't risk losing the person he was so in love with.

But not this.

"You're going the wrong way," said Annan softly, still staring out the window with his cheeks damp and eyelashes clumped. He hadn't turned his head once, his jaw set and clenched.

"I'm taking you to our place," said Elgin, gripping the steering wheel tight. "You're going to have a shower, then we are going to talk to Wallace."

Annan seemed to shrink, slouching in his chair as if to disappear amongst the leather and fibers. Elgin's heart thudded and he hit the brake a touch too hard at the next light.

"I need to clear my head," said Elgin, running a hand through his hair. The scent of horse was so strong it nearly clouded the vehicle, but all he could think about was the antiseptic bleach of a doctor's office. Wallace had sat alone in there, suffering, and Elgin hadn't even known.

How could I? He bit his lip. There had been so many signs for months, and little excuses about work and budgets that Elgin had taken at face value. All along, he'd been lied to.

"How long have you known?" He reached for Annan's knee, squeezing through the fabric, only to snatch his hand away when Annan flinched. "I'm not going to— Hell, I'm sorry."

Pulling onto the main road, he blinked through the tears. He did *not* cry.

"I wondered if something was going on almost as soon as I met you," said Annan, his voice soft. "But Wallace told me that day when we went hiking."

"Oh." Elgin glared at the road, thinking back to that day. Annan and Wallace had both seemed so happy, even if Elgin had fallen asleep before they'd returned from the shower. The hike had drained him nearly completely, and there had been no way he would have been able to stay awake.

"Not long, then." It may have felt like weeks ago, but it had only been days.

"No," said Annan softly. When Elgin glanced over, he caught the tears on Annan's lashes. A few of them had escaped, trailing down his cheeks and leaving smudges of dirt in their wake.

"What gave it away?" asked Elgin. *How could I be so blind?* He thought he'd known everything about Wallace from his shoe size to the exact number of moles on his body. He could barely look away from him most days, so enthralled by the person he'd fallen so deeply for.

"At the restaurant, he didn't eat any dinner," said Annan, scraping his nails over his dirty jeans. A few flecks of dust sprinkled onto the leather seat. "First I wondered if he had an eating disorder, but then the headache at the barn made me start to think."

Elgin nodded. *I'm so fucking stupid.*

As he slowed to turn into the driveway, he had to suck in a deep breath. Wallace's car was sitting in the garage, the door still open as if he'd known that Elgin would race home after him. His gut fluttered, clenching tight at the idea of facing him. If he didn't go home, maybe it wouldn't be true. Wallace could still be in his office, and they'd simply missed him and mistaken a stranger for him.

No. Wallace deserved better than that. He deserved the world, no matter how lost he'd found himself.

"This isn't home," said Annan, rubbing a hand over his face and smearing filth across his cheek. He must've been so uncomfortable in his jeans and dirty T-shirt, but Elgin hadn't even thought about it. "You need to take me home."

Elgin swallowed, pushing every bit of mixed emotions aside. "No matter what happens between Wallace and me, it doesn't change how I feel about you, Annan. Your home should be with us."

"But, my car—"

"Please." Elgin took an unsteady breath before reaching across the center console. "I can't do this alone."

Annan grasped his hand, his grip firm against his own trembling one. His calluses scraped over Elgin's palm, more calming than a symphony of birdsong. "I don't think I can, either." His grip went tighter, and he squeezed until the point of pain. "Wallace is alone right now. I think he's trying to keep it that way."

"He'd rather burn than let the world help him." The words were bitter in his mouth and filled with a rage that he couldn't quite comprehend.

"I think you'd burn the world down, just to help," said Annan.

The anger drained from him in an instant, leaving him so empty that it nearly shocked him to the bone. Parking his car next to Wallace's, he squeezed Annan's hand once before letting go and getting out of the car. He was around the vehicle before Annan had even moved, opening the door and letting him out.

He didn't care about the smell of horse as he dragged Annan into a hug, or the sweat against his palm as he pulled him along.

Wallace was waiting for them just inside the kitchen, the drawers and a few cupboards open and a kettle with tea packets strewn on the counter. His face was pale, his eyes red as he stared at the electric kettle, the sound of rolling water filling the room.

Elgin crossed the space in three big strides, releasing Annan when he tugged at their connection. Wallace looked up a moment before Elgin threw his arms around his shoulders, pulling him close in the most delicate hug he could manage.

He wanted to squeeze so tight that Wallace would never escape him, and they could stay in this moment together, but the man in his arms was a thin shadow to what he should have been.

Annan was right. There was a time when Wallace was soft with a weight that was a comforting shield when he lay across Elgin's chest. But now he felt thin and frail, trembling under Elgin's arms. This was the same man who owned companies and could have Elgin do anything if only he asked. Now he was a wisp of that — a dream ready to waken.

How didn't I notice this?

Looking back, he realized Wallace had been getting thinner, but he hadn't focused on it. He worshiped every bit of him, no matter what shape or size, and it had simply not registered.

"I'm sorry," whispered Wallace, shaking as he started to cry. Elgin's eyes burned, but he held the tears back. He'd never been the strong one. Wallace had always been invincible, dragging Elgin through the clouds and showing him greatness.

"I love you," said Elgin, his chest squeezing tight at the overwhelming fierceness of it. "I love you so much."

Wallace broke down in his arms, sagging until Elgin had to grunt as he caught nearly his entire weight.

"Annan?" Wallace asked, his voice barely a whisper.

"I'm here."

He was close by, but not close enough, still hovering paces away with his hands clasped before him.

"I—" Wallace seemed to falter, the last of his strength draining away.

"Wallace?" Elgin tensed, staring at Wallace's face as his eyes fluttered shut, his body going limp in Elgin's arms. There was such an unnatural paleness to him, like a diabetic deprived of food.

"Baby. Wallace, *baby*." His voice rose, his limbs going tight. There was no response, not even the fluttering of lashes or a small smile. Panic seized him, slapping him across the face.

"Get him to the bed," said Annan, suddenly close. His face was stricken, but there were no tears, only worry and concentration. "It happened before. I think he gets really weak when his adrenalin crashes. Last time he could barely stand."

But Elgin couldn't move. His limbs were locked tight, his heart pounding fast. *Wallace, Wallace, Wallace.* Was it time already? He couldn't say goodbye—not now—not ever. His breathing picked up, his heart squeezing. "Wallace!"

Wallace flinched, furrowing his forehead before he relaxed again, peace passing over him.

"Elgin," said Annan. He appeared in front of them, supporting Wallace's head with his hand where it had flopped back. Crouching down, he slid one arm under Wallace's knees, moving the other to wrap around his shoulders and slowly lift him from Elgin's numb hands. "I'll get him to the bed."

Annan seemed so steady as he walked to the bedroom with Wallace in his arms before laying him out on the bed and dragging the blankets up to his chest. He placed one hand on Wallace's head, smoothing the hair back from his face as Elgin stared on, his throat closing.

"I'll grab him some water," said Annan, touching Wallace's cheek before he turned away.

Elgin grabbed his arm as he tried to squeeze by, the doorway too tight for two men of their stature. Annan flinched, but Elgin dragged him closer, burying his face in Annan's neck.

"Stay." He took a shuddering breath, closing his eyes as he breathed Annan in. He was terrified of looking toward the bed — terrified of what he would see. "Please don't leave me."

Annan brought his arms up, resting his palms on the dip of Elgin's back. "I won't leave."

Chapter Twenty-One

Wallace

Was it possible to be so happy while he was as close to death as he'd ever been? Wallace turned his head into Annan's shoulder, taking a deep breath of fresh shampoo that smelled of Elgin with undertones of leather. A smile was on his lips, and it had been there for the last hour as they lay together.

Relief.

He was light, almost floating, the tingling in his fingers from more than just the spike in stress and the migraine that had dropped him into Elgin's arms. They knew—both of them—and they were still here.

He'd wondered if perhaps Elgin would withdraw from him when he finally found out, struggling to stand on his own and grasp his new reality. But he was still strong, pressing into Wallace's back and humming under his breath as he stroked up and down his body.

"What can I do, baby?" asked Elgin, his heart steady under Wallace's ear. "I can be there for your next treatment. Whatever is it. Let me help you."

Wallace swallowed hard, blinking back a few tears that tried to threaten his peace. He'd made his decision almost as soon as he'd been given a diagnosis. He'd seen others go through treatment and chemotherapy, only to fade away. Some of them beat it, but none of them were ever the same after.

"No meds," said Wallace, balling his hand in Elgin's shirt. "I have stuff for pain, but nothing else."

He expected a fight, or at least an argument. The meds would have made him last longer so he could be with Elgin, but he couldn't be turned into something dependent and *frail*.

"We should go somewhere," said Elgin, reaching across Wallace before trailing his fingers along Annan's shoulder. Annan was spooning Wallace from the other side, his heat just as soothing as Elgin's. "All of us. You've always wanted to see the mountains."

Annan didn't respond and neither did Wallace. Instead, Wallace buried his face deeper, inhaling cologne, man and the saltiness of tears. "I'm sorry I didn't tell you, Elgin."

It was the only thing he regretted. He'd never lied to his husband — not about anything. Being sick had changed a lot about him, including the clean slate between them. It had also opened up his heart to another man. Annan completed him in the same strange way that Elgin did.

Elgin hummed, wrapping an arm around Wallace's waist and squeezing tight. "Somewhere tropical, maybe. There are beautiful mountains in Mexico. Annan, have you ever been to New Zealand? I went there five years ago for a business trip, and we keep talking about going together."

New Zealand sounded perfect except for one very important thing. He couldn't imagine facing the high pressure of the plane pounding against his skull for the extended flight. Even first class would be a nightmare.

"I don't think I can go on a plane anymore," said Wallace. Between the two of them, he'd never felt warmer. He snuggled deeper, letting out a sigh.

"H—how long?" asked Elgin, his voice shaking.

Wallace had had the number looming over him for months. He knew now it wasn't right, either—months made little sense when his brain flipped a switch and he was rendered powerless. The next migraine might put him in the hospital, and he couldn't see himself leaving if he ever went into those white-washed rooms with the sound of slow beeping haunting his every movement.

"Not long," said Wallace, taking a slow breath. There was a wall of terror that had been slowly chipping away at his mortality, but he couldn't let it take him too soon. As long as he could keep his moments like this, then what came after wouldn't matter.

"Years?"

Wallace let the question wash over him, listening to the steady thud of Elgin's heart. If he turned his head, he could hear Annan's matching every beat.

If it were years of these little moments, then he could see it. It was what came between them that he couldn't bear for much longer.

"No." He tried to say it softly, but he could feel it strike Elgin hard with the way he tensed, a shuddering breath the only sign that he was breaking.

"We should go somewhere before…" Elgin trailed off. "I guess I don't know what's going to happen. I don't want to give it a name."

Elgin stroked down his back, pausing at the dip of his spine. "I want you to be happy."

"I am happy," said Wallace. Sure, he was almost constantly cold, tired and some days he thought his brain was going to explode, but he had Elgin, and Elgin would have Annan. *I have Annan, too, even if he's not for me.*

"Is there anything we can do?"

It was almost the first time Annan had spoken since they'd arrived home, his voice rumbling under his ear. He was wrapped in only a towel, fresh from the shower and smelling like them. Wallace honestly preferred the horses and leather, along with the fresh breeze that usually clung to Annan's skin.

"Don't change." He turned and moved his hand across Annan's chest, resting a palm on his pec. "No matter what happens, never change." If their laughter ever died, his life and memory would blink out of existence. "I love you both for who you are. The only thing I need is for that to stay the same."

Annan sucked in a breath, and Wallace realized it was the first time he'd said those words to him. They were true. He may not have known Annan for long, but he was sure that it was love that flowed through his veins. *You aren't mine, but I love you.*

"Promise me," said Wallace, his eyes fluttering shut on their own. He could sleep for days with the weight of the lies lifted from him.

If they answered him, he didn't hear it.

Chapter Twenty-Two

Annan

Annan entered the password Elgin had given him into the borrowed phone, bringing up his text messages and adding in his boss' number.

It's Annan. I won't be in today and I probably won't be in tomorrow. Long story.

He rarely took sick days or even days off, so it wasn't shocking when three dots appeared as Oliya texted him back right away.

You okay?

He looked over his shoulder, but the coast was still clear. Elgin had barely been awake when Annan had shaken him, asking to borrow his phone. It was only three o'clock in the morning, but he was wired. There was so much for him to do at the barn, but he knew Milo would be able to take over for him for just one day or two. Not all the horses would get their treats, but they would live, and Milo would have his hands busy instead of his mind.

He couldn't leave this house — the place that Elgin and Wallace insisted was home. Not until he figured out what the hell he was going to do.

Not really. I'll be back soon.

He sent the text before closing the phone and sliding it across the countertop. It buzzed with what must've been an answer, but he didn't look. Instead, he moved to the kitchen island, leaning his elbows against the surface and putting his head in his hands.

"Hey."

He looked up at Elgin's voice. His eyes were shadowed and red, sleep clinging to his eyelashes. He looked so human and soft — more than he ever had. Annan never would have thought to see this side of him without Wallace in the room.

"Hey," said Annan, straightening. "Can't sleep?"

Elgin shook his head, pressing his lips together. "Do you need a ride to your car? You must have to go to work soon."

Annan glanced out through the window. It was in the perfect spot to watch the street while washing the dishes, the neighbor's houses in view as they spread any gossip. It was so different to his own apartment that overlooked a thin strip of grass and a brick wall.

It was pitch black outside, a few street lamps lighting the way for a scampering raccoon. Beyond that, people were still asleep in their beds, their dreams flitting behind closed eyelids. Most of the horses were probably down in their stalls, shavings clinging to their coats as they slept.

"I called in. That's why I needed to borrow your phone," said Annan, pointing to the phone that vibrated on the counter again. Elgin reached for it, squinting at the screen as soon as he unlocked it.

"Whoever you texted is asking if you proposed," said Elgin, a smile playing over his lips. "And not to worry about today or tomorrow."

Annan let out a chuckle, even if there was very little feeling in it. He was glad to find anything to laugh at, so he didn't have to face what was ahead of him. Wallace had asked him to be there for Elgin, and he could do that, but he couldn't promise not to change.

"I feel like there's a story there," said Elgin, sliding into one of the chairs at the island. He reached for Annan, stroking his bare arm with the back of his hand. "I knew about the one guy — whatever his name was — Frank or something. I didn't realize there were more."

Shaking his head, Annan let out a huff. "It's a bit of a running joke at the barn. I'm sure they have bets on it, too. Boyfriends very quickly become exes in my life when I propose to so many of them. I have a shitty taste in men."

"Hey," said Elgin, crossing his arms. "I take offense to that. I'm fantastic and tasty."

Annan grinned. His heart was beating slow and soft, even with Elgin so close and the expensive house wrapped around him. He wore Elgin's boxers and no shirt, but he didn't need anything more.

"I think this is what he meant," said Annan, closing the space between them to stand in front of Elgin's chair. Elgin turned, settling his hands on Annan's hips

193

and squeezing. "You always make me laugh, and I feel like he needs that more than ever now."

Elgin dropped his gaze to Annan's chest, his lips going thin. "It's hard to tell a joke when I just found out that the love of my life is dying." He blinked slowly, shaking his head. There was disbelief on his face, along with something else, as if Elgin hoped he was still wrapped in that nightmare and ready to wake up.

His throat constricted, tears prickling. "I know." He sniffed, carding his fingers through Elgin's hair. "I can't imagine what you're going through. I don't even know what to say. Nothing in my head sounds right."

"You don't have to say anything," said Elgin, looping his arms around Annan's neck. "He looked so peaceful when I left the bedroom. I keep wondering if he's lying about it—that there's really nothing wrong and we'll grow old together. I'd always hoped that he would outlive me, and maybe that's selfish."

Tears trickled over Annan's skin, soaking the hair on his chest as Elgin leaned into him. It took everything in him not to break down. He'd made a promise to Wallace, and he was going to be strong for Elgin, no matter what happened.

"I can't do this without him—without you," said Elgin, "but I feel like I'm trapping you. We just met, and you shouldn't have to deal with this." Elgin gripped harder, his fingers digging bruises into Annan's skin. There was salt in the air, his breaths coming fast. "You can go now, and I won't hold it against you. Get out while you can."

Fuck, that hurts. These two men were the best thing that had ever happened to him, and he wouldn't trade that for anything. He wasn't good enough for them, but he was going to give them everything he had. He had to — for Wallace — for *him.*

"I'm not leaving." He squeezed back, trying to convey the truth of it with the strength of his grip. "You could kick me out of the house and lock all the windows and doors, and I'd just stand out on the lawn, waiting for you to let me back in." He took a deep breath, stopping the tears in their tracks. "You've fed me, so you'll never get rid of me now. I'm like a stray cat, and sometimes I smell just as bad."

Elgin huffed out a laugh, a puff of air over Annan's skin. "Stop making me laugh. I'm having a crisis here."

One moment, Annan was holding Elgin in his arms, and the next, Elgin had moved until their lips were almost close enough to touch. The heat of his breath flowed over Annan's lips, the taste of him already in his senses. Elgin sighed, his fingers harsh before he shifted his hands to Annan's ass, tugging him the last of the distance.

The kiss was soft and gentle, barely there compared to the way they were usually so hungry. He kissed like he had all the time in the world, and there wasn't a timer over their heads, slowly counting to extinction.

Annan let out a soft gasp as Elgin teased him with his tongue, hardly able to breathe with how much he craved to deepen the kiss and take Elgin right here. He could reassure him by showing him, if that's what it took.

"We should check on Wallace," said Annan, tilting his head for one moment before their lips were sealed together again. His head was swimming, the room flickering in and out of existence as he focused on the two things of utmost importance to him.

"I'm here."

Maybe Elgin had known all along that Wallace was standing at the entryway to the kitchen, leaning against the frame but not looking like he needed the support simply to stay upright. There was a touch of color in his cheeks again, even if he looked more tired than the two of them combined.

Annan tried to pull away and apologize, anything to keep from kissing in front of Wallace, but Elgin wouldn't let him escape, grabbing the hair at the back of his neck and holding him firm. When he finally let Annan breathe, he whispered into his ear, his breath tickling over his earlobe.

"He wants this," said Elgin, his voice low and soft. "He wants this even more than I do."

Annan gave in, letting himself sink into the feeling with all his being. *So do I.* "Let's go back to bed. We're all exhausted."

Chapter Twenty-Three

Annan

He still smelled like their sheets, Elgin's jeans belted around his waist as they pulled into the lane at the barn, the sun just peeking over the horizon. It was an hour or so after he would normally be there, but he'd only ended up taking one day off. He could only spend so much time indoors before it started to wear on him, especially when they'd all gone through several bouts of tears.

His eyes were itchy and strained, a headache at the base of his nose that had been aching for hours. But every time the helplessness sank in, he pictured the sweet relief on Wallace's face as they'd lain in bed together, doing nothing more than snuggle and swap stories.

Annan had delved deep into his past, revealing some things that he never thought he would say aloud while Wallace listened in and Elgin snoozed next to them. A few times, Wallace's phone had rung, but he never reached to answer, eventually turning the ringer off.

"I'm not going back," he'd said, shutting his phone down completely before he'd lain back on the bed. *"They'll manage without me. They're stronger than I give them credit for."*

"Are you sure you're going to be okay today?" asked Elgin as he pulled up to the barn that was deep in the midst of construction. A few main beams had been erected in the last day, the frame nearly complete. With tools strewn about and the smell of fresh wood, it didn't even appear that it was a rebuild, seemingly fresh like it just sprung from the earth.

Elgin paused, taking a long look at it. "That's the barn that burnt down, isn't it?"

Annan nodded before glancing away. If he didn't look at it for too long, then he could almost forget about its past. It was bigger than the old barn, the frame wider and longer since they'd expanded the foundation. It was difficult to even remember exactly what the old one had looked like anymore.

"Show it to me?"

Annan's heart stuttered, claws digging into his gut. *No way.* That building was cursed and terrifying, and he hadn't quite figured out how he was going to muck the future stalls in there once they were erected.

"I-I," Annan stuttered, grasping for the car door handle.

"It will take my mind off things." Elgin blinked long and slow like he could barely stay awake. His handsome face was unshaven, a bit of something clinging to his lips. His world had effectively changed forever but he looked mostly the same — tired, but still alive, just like Annan.

"Okay."

He wasn't sure why he agreed, but as they stood in front of the barn, Annan's hand clasped in Elgin's, his heart pounded. His palms were slicked with sweat, some of it beading on his forehead and tumbling toward the collar of his borrowed T-shirt. It dwarfed him, the shoulders broader than he could ever imagine.

Elgin stared at the beams, tracing his gaze along the peaks of wood to the tools that lay strewn about the area. There were nails and bits of debris scattered around that would no doubt be a disaster to clean up in the near future.

"You're terrified," said Elgin, squeezing Annan's hand. He turned his wrist, threading their fingers together until his nails scraped against Annan's knuckles. "Me, too."

Elgin let out a heavy sigh, before taking one step back, their hands still connected. "Do you think we're going to make it?"

Yes. I hope so. Please don't leave me.

"I love you," said Elgin, tugging Annan's hand so he could cradle it between his own. He traced over his palm, following the lifeline with his fingertip before circling the calluses. "I won't ever compare you to Wallace, but fuck, I love you."

There was something buried in Annan's chest, but he wasn't quite sure what it was. He never wanted to be away from Elgin again, but Wallace was like a wedge of grief, weighing him down and forcing him closer. It would be easy to walk away now and never look back, but he wasn't sure if his heart would ever recover. It certainly wouldn't recover if he stayed.

"You don't have to say it back," said Elgin, releasing Annan's hand to run his fingers through his hair. "I wanted you to know before things...changed. I loved you yesterday and the day before and I think I loved you that first night when you agreed to tea bagging. We were basically soulmates at that point."

A smile tugged at Annan's lips, and he shook his head. There was no one in the world like this man before him, and there was no one like his husband. They were two unique souls, and he'd been caught in their gravity field.

"I should get back," said Elgin. He leaned in close, placing a kiss on Annan's cheek. The scruff of his unshaven chin scraped against Annan's cheek, soothing some of his frayed soul.

Annan turned, cupping Elgin's cheek and tilting his chin. Lining their lips up, he brought them together, letting out a sigh as they finally made contact.

He'd never thought much of kisses before. They were nice, soft and wet, but he'd never longed for them. With Elgin, he never wanted it to end. Oxygen wasn't important and neither was the car that was bouncing down the lane and creeping past them.

Wrapping his arms around Elgin's neck, he pulled him in — tighter, closer — giving everything up. Even if it wasn't love, he never wanted this moment to end.

"I don't know," said Annan as he turned his head, burying his face against Elgin's neck. "I don't know if I love you. I really don't. So many men before you have heard those words, and I'd been certain I meant them then. I don't want to say it now and find out that it's just another lie."

Elgin slid his hands to Annan's hips, holding him tight. "I want you to be sure. Things are going to be rough. If you're with us, I want it to be because you want to be."

Does he know? Wallace's plan wasn't exactly subtle, but Elgin was effectively blind when it came to him. But Annan could never be a replacement for a lifetime of love and memories — Wallace had to know that.

"I'll call you after work," said Annan, refusing to lift his head. "I could make dinner, then maybe we can talk about that trip some more."

Elgin pulled him in for one last long kiss before he got into his car, bouncing his way back up the lane.

"Well, well, well."

Annan spun toward the sound of Milo's voice. The kid was seated next to the new build, his back pressed to one of the beams and his legs kicked out in front of him. Annan hadn't even noticed him — then again, he was wearing gray which had allowed him to be effectively blended in with the gravel strewn almost everywhere.

"Let me see the ring." Milo tucked his phone into his pocket, heaving himself to his feet. Crossing the space between them, Milo grasped one of Annan's hands, then the other, dragging his gaze over his naked fingers. "Hmm. Maybe he's more of a new-age kind of guy. Are you getting tattoos?"

This kid. Annan couldn't help the smile that dragged his lips upward. Throwing one arm around Milo's shoulders, he chuckled. "It's good to see you too, kid."

Milo tried to side-step the hug, wrinkling his nose. "You smell like perfume. *Yuck.*"

"That would be cologne. You'll find out about it when you're older," said Annan. "Now are you going to help me with chores, or are you going to tell me about the date you had planned last night? I didn't forget."

Normally, he texted Milo right after every date. On the outside, he said it was because he wanted to make sure Milo got home safe, but really, he was worried about the kid. Emotions were a touchy subject, especially if confessions were involved.

Milo flushed, red sprouting over the bridge of his nose. "Nothing happened." He crossed his arms, pouting as Annan tugged him toward the largest barn where he was sure the stalls were begging to be cleaned.

"Uh-huh." *My little guy is all grown up.* "How was it?"

Reaching for the nearest wheelbarrow, Annan pushed it toward the first stall. A few of the horses were already out in the fields, but others were on very strict indoor board. One stallion in particular broke out in hives every time he hit the pasture, so they had custom-built a massive stall for him. He still made a habit of pawing at the ground, dragging his metal shoes across the padded floor.

"I told you nothing happened," said Milo, ducking to grab a fork and heading into the first stall. His face was tinted red, the tips of his ears nearly vibrant.

"That good?" Annan nodded with a grin. "I'm happy for you, buddy. This guy seems like a keeper." He pushed the wheelbarrow into the stall after Milo. "I mean, he says he loves you and stayed with you after you puked on him. That alone is a big green flag."

"You always have to bring that up," mumbled Milo. "How was I supposed to react when his tongue ended up in my mouth? It was wet and slimy. There was no way I could not gag." Milo scrunched up his nose. "He doesn't do that anymore."

"Cute," said Annan, hauling the first full fork up and dumping it. Milo had already cleared one corner of the stall and was putting him to shame. "You should bring him around some time when I'm here so I can meet him. Oliya has met him already. It's my turn."

Milo paused, his fork hovering in the air. "You have got to be kidding me. You'll see what a good guy he is and propose on the spot. I have to save him from you."

Annan snorted. *I missed this kid.* It didn't seem to matter what was going on in his life. Milo always made him feel better...eventually. Sometimes they had to wade through some emotional trauma to get there.

"I knew there was a reason I was keeping that ring in my car," said Annan. "Let me just practice. Hold on a sec." He leaned the fork against the wall before dropping to one knee. Elgin probably hadn't realized just how dirty his pants were going to get when he'd offered them to Annan for the day.

"Milo, I know we've been through a lot, and I love you, but can I marry your boyfriend?" Annan could hardly make it through without laughing, a grin splitting his lips.

Milo had backed himself into a corner, hiding behind his fork as he giggled. He winced as he pressed himself against the wall before immediately taking a step forward.

"Oh-ho-ho," said Annan, grunting as he got back to his feet. "I knew it! You can't hide that wince from me, buddy. Congrats. I hope it was everything you'd hoped for."

Milo ducked his head. His face probably couldn't get any redder by now. He bit his lip, apparently trying to cover up his smile. "It was amazing."

And if that didn't make Annan's heart sore. Milo deserved everything, including a kick-ass boyfriend.

They cleaned the next two stalls in near-silence, until Annan had to take a break to grab a drink. His water bottle was still roasting in his car from two days before, so he bent down, drinking directly from the nearest hose. He only had to spit out one earwig when it landed in his mouth, causing him to gag as it squiggled over his tongue.

Gross.

"You're out of shape," called Milo, already two stalls ahead of him. The kid was acting like he was on speed and not sore from a night of fun. After Annan's first time, he'd been ready to crawl back into bed with an ice pack and a heating pad. *It wasn't that great, either.* He certainly hadn't *glowed* the next day.

"Too much of the good life," said Annan, leaning heavily against the nearest post as he lowered the handle to shut the water off. "I had cheesecake yesterday. I haven't had cheesecake in years." He ran a hand over his belly. His muscles were still there and proud, but they were protesting like he'd taken a month off and not a day.

"Are you going to move in with them?" asked Milo, shouting so his voice projected. "You seem pretty serious, and I think they are actually nice guys this time. I was spying on you when you gave them a tour the other day."

Milo kept scooping as Annan took a break, leaning against the side of the stall. He may have sounded nonchalant, but there was tension in every move. They were both on the precipice of something new, but hopefully, Milo's prospects were cheerier than his own.

"I don't know," said Annan, wiping his arm across his forehead. Sweat coated his limbs, Elgin's clothes already filthy and stained.

"That's weird." Milo grabbed the wheelbarrow, taking another trip to the back. He shouted over his shoulder as he went, his voice so loud that a few sparrows took off from their roosts. "You always know. Even when it's a huge mistake, you always know exactly what you're going to do."

Annan narrowed his eyes before getting back to work. "You're too perceptive for your own good, kid. But there's a difference between being desperate and not knowing."

Milo started spreading fresh shavings two doors down, the smell instantly brightening the entire row of stalls. "Not really. I think you've finally figured out that sometimes you need to slow down."

Since when is this kid a counselor?

"You love these guys?"

Annan looked away, jamming the fork hard into the padded ground. His stomach grumbled as he longed for the late breakfast he'd eaten in bed with Wallace and Elgin the morning before. The sheets had been a mess after, and Elgin had dutifully changed them, Wallace giggling as he'd played statue.

"The fact that you aren't denying it tells me you do," said Milo. He paused, grasping his phone from his pocket. He flushed when he saw the screen, a smile touching his lips.

Now this kid can read my mind?

Annan's gut clenched, butterflies writhing in his belly.

"Is that the boyfriend?" asked Annan, already knowing the answer.

"Yeah."

"Tell him I want to marry him." Annan shook his head, a laugh in his throat. It wasn't so strained when he came to terms with the warmth spreading through his chest. "Send him my picture and tell him what I said."

Without hesitation, Milo brought his phone up, snapping a picture of Annan through the bars before typing rapidly. His phone pinged a moment later and he giggled.

"He says you're hot but he'll pass, because he's already got a beautiful man of his own."

Annan grinned. "I told you he was a keeper."

Chapter Twenty-Four

Elgin

He'd gone all out. Pouring his heart and soul into the idea, he'd made the call to the dealership as soon as Annan had told him he had gotten the time off. And the price tag didn't matter — not when it came to Wallace.

The dealership hadn't seemed surprised when he'd rushed over, signing the paperwork and paying in cash. After looking at a few other models, he'd gone with the best, adding every available option that they could get to him immediately.

"This doesn't seem like an authentic road trip," said Annan as he eyed up the RV that was shining in the driveway. He had a worn bag thrown over his shoulder and his sunglasses perched on top of his head, freshly shaven and showered if his damp hair was anything to go by. His jeans were torn and soft blue, matching the T-shirt that clung to his upper body to show off every moment of hard work.

"What?" Elgin turned, eyeing up the vehicle. The sun caught the glimmering gold and black paint, and he had to squint against the light. Without a speck of dust or paint chip to its name, it was full of gas and ready to roll across the country. The fridge inside was packed with snacks, and he'd made up the beds out back while he'd waited for Wallace to finish his breakfast in the kitchen.

As long as Wallace took it slow, he seemed able to eat a little more and have enough energy to make it until early afternoon. Elgin would often find him in the reading nook after lunch, a book on his lap and the sun filtering through the window to caress his skin.

The first time, he'd carried Wallace back to bed and he'd hardly stirred, only protesting later when he awoke with his book gone, along with his view. *I want to wake up and look outside to see the birds in your garden.*

The next time Elgin had found him there, he'd simply grabbed a blanket, pulling it over his husband's sleeping form and carefully setting his book on the floor beside him. Wallace had smiled as soon as he'd woken up, Elgin hovering close by to watch his reactions to the visiting cardinal.

The unfamiliar medications were the first real hit to their daily life. They seemed to make Wallace more comfortable but drained what very little energy he had. Their bedroom had become the prime spot for date night, cookie crumbs mingling in their sheets. Annan would find them there after work, sometimes joining them with the smell of horse still pressed on his skin.

Those are the best days.

"If we're taking this trip, we have to go soon," Annan had said as he'd kissed Elgin one night, Wallace sleeping peacefully next to them. There had been an

urgency to their touches that night, Annan thrusting fast and biting his lip to keep quiet. Wallace had only stirred for a moment to smile at them before drifting off again.

"I was expecting a beat-up station wagon with a used mattress in the back and a cooler that leaks everywhere jammed into the back seat." Annan looked between the vehicle and the house. "Or maybe a tiny Toyota with no mattress at all."

What the fuck? Elgin screwed up his face. "Who the hell would take a road trip like that?"

Annan chuckled, shaking his head. "Such was my childhood. It's not a trip until someone is screaming and there's tuna in the glove box."

I don't think I want to know. "That sounds terrible."

Annan only shrugged before heaving his bag and setting it on the ground next to one of the tires. "Where's Wallace?" He leaned against the side, looking toward the house again.

"Eating breakfast." Elgin grabbed the bag, tossing it inside with the accumulating pile of stuff he'd picked up at various camping stores. He wasn't sure why he'd thought they would need a dozen electric lanterns, but he was not returning them. "He said I was hovering, so he ordered me outside."

"That doesn't sound like him at all," said Annan, a smile on his lips. "It's a good day, then."

Elgin nodded, quirking the corner of his lips. It wasn't as hard as it had been to smile and act naturally again, especially with Annan by his side at seemingly every step. It was still terrifying to see Wallace on the bad days, with his forehead furrowed and the pain medication barely helping, but the good days made it worth it.

"You might just get laid," said Wallace. He was standing at the door to the garage wearing a large pair of sunglasses that were much too large for his face. They helped him with some of the migraines that were caused by too-bright lights and had the side effect of looking extremely cute.

"Hey, handsome," said Wallace, grinning toward Annan. He turned a look on Elgin. "Hey, horny."

Elgin sputtered, crossing his arms. "You guys are ganging up on me today...hopefully." He snickered as Annan turned away, covering his mouth as his cheeks flushed bright.

"You did good, baby," said Wallace, taking a few steps before he paused with his hands on his hips. "It looks great."

"I'll give you the grand tour," said Elgin, patiently waiting for Wallace to reach the vehicle before offering his hand to help him up the steps. There was nothing that his husband hated more than feeling weak, even if Elgin had told him he wouldn't think less of him if he had to carry him everywhere.

"Driver up front," said Elgin, pointing to the empty padded seat. There was a pair of red-rimmed sunglasses with the tag still on set against the dash, and a plastic dancing sunflower that wiggled back and forth in the sun.

There was one passenger seat up front with a snack bag currently resting on it, but the rest of the vehicle was like stepping into a cottage.

"I figured Annan and I could trade off for driving duties." Annan nodded, whisking off his own sunglasses and dropping them in the passenger seat. "Then we have the kitchen."

It was a small area with four cupboards total and a beige countertop that had an insert to go over the sink. He opened one drawer, showing off the dishes inside before shutting it tight. It held strong, locking unless he turned the handle just right. It was the one very smart feature that would keep all their dishes and utensils from flying about.

Annan followed behind him, grabbing his bag from where Elgin had set it on the walkway to the driver's seat. It was a touch cramped with the three of them jammed into the same spot, but he wouldn't have changed it. He wouldn't have cared if they really were stacked on top of each other in that station wagon.

The rest was spacious. With two closets, there was ample room for all their stuff and extra space for the things he probably shouldn't have purchased. A dining table folded down to give them more square footage, and there were a few extra seats that were tucked away to give them room to walk and relax. He'd switched out the couch for a recliner and had upgraded the television, too.

"Bathroom here," He motioned to the closet-type enclosure with a tiny toilet and shower that had no way of fitting them. "And my personal favorite — the bedrooms." Taking up most of the space was a master bedroom with a queen bed, but before that was a spot where a set of bunk beds was sectioned off with a curtain. The queen and the lower bunk were both made up with new sheets and pillows, a few fluffy blankets pulled on top.

"Who gets to be the third wheel?" asked Annan softly, already placing his bag on the lower bunk. Elgin could see him swallow, dropping his gaze.

Even with everything they had been through, he was still so fragile. In his heart, Elgin still hadn't been certain that he would agree to the trip. Hell, he wasn't sure if Annan realized how much he loved him, even though he said it every time they were together.

"It's for Wallace if he's not feeling up to sleeping next to us," said Elgin, grabbing Annan's bag and tossing it right in the middle of the queen. "I know sometimes you prefer to be alone." He touched Wallace's cheek with his thumb, skimming over the freckles there. They had paled with his infrequent visits in the sun, his pallor reduced to someone who hibernated their summer away.

"Perfect," said Wallace, an edge to his voice that sounded forced. "If I'm trying to sleep and you two can't keep your hands off each other, then I'll crash in here."

"It was more the curtain," said Elgin, sliding it across. There was no window in the bottom bunk, which had probably been a design flaw, but it worked perfectly for them. Between that and the thick curtain, it cast the lower bunk into almost-perfect darkness.

Wallace beamed, touching the curtain between his fingertips. "That's wonderful."

Elgin couldn't see his eyes behind the thick, dark glasses, but he could imagine them sparkling. "Did you think I was kicking you out?" Elgin moved in close, kissing Wallace's neck in a spot he knew he was most sensitive. "Annan hasn't seen me fuck you yet. There's no way you're getting off that easy."

Wallace chuckled, placing a hand on Elgin's chest but not pushing away. "You're terrible."

"No, you pegged me perfectly before," said Elgin. "I'm just horny."

Wallace giggled, running his hands through Elgin's hair. Even though he was paler than usual, and his touch was weak, he was still the same man. It was something Elgin had to remind himself every day so he didn't slip up. He couldn't think about the alternative that was looming closer.

Hospital beds, the smell of antiseptic and the despair of helplessness. He shook his head. "This trip is going to be amazing. My two favorite men, and the empty roads of the countryside."

"You can't say 'empty roads' until we're out of the city," said Annan, sitting on the edge of the bed. His jeans stretched over his thighs as he moved, the fabric straining. Elgin could imagine them in use at work, clinging to his thick thighs as he broke a green horse — or whatever cowboys did.

"It took me almost half an hour to get here this morning," said Annan. "Traffic was brutal."

Elgin could barely hear him, too stuck on his thighs. It had been too long since he'd kissed them — or Wallace's, for that matter. He had the sudden desire to lay them side by side and find each difference like one of those puzzles he'd done when he'd been a kid. But this time he wouldn't circle anything with crayon, instead dragging his tongue over the sweet imperfections.

It would take a long time to compare them — Annan thick everywhere Wallace was lean. With Wallace's body changing so quickly, Elgin could take extra time to cherish him and show him how beautiful he still was.

He couldn't help himself when Wallace sat next to Annan on the bed. Kneeling, he settled on the ground between them, placing a hand on each of their thighs. Wallace was wearing long pants, the looseness of them hiding some of his thinness, but he was still beautiful — still perfect.

When he looked to Annan, sliding his hand inside a rip in his jeans and settling on the muscle, he squeezed. Annan was strength where Wallace was frailty in his touch, but it had always been Wallace in control and calling the shots. He couldn't imagine Annan doing that.

"You look like you're having a crisis, baby," said Wallace, taking off his sunglasses and setting them on the bed before putting his hand over Elgin's.

I am, but I can't show it.

"Just figuring things out," said Elgin, sliding his fingers roughly through the hole in Annan's jeans and prying it wider until Annan squirmed, clenching his fist in the bedsheets. "Are you guys going to be back here while I drive? Or did you want to come up front?"

He had to resist the draw of these two men or they would never get out of the driveway. That didn't mean he stopped teasing Annan, jamming into the unyielding denim until he brushed against the heat and softness of the top of his inner thigh. Annan bit his lip, looking to Wallace.

The front of the vehicle was bright with sunlight, but back here it was soft and intimate, a small fan circulating cool air through as the summer heat pounded into the vehicle from the outside.

"We should buckle in until we are out of the city," said Wallace, following Elgin's hand with his gaze. "I'll probably need a nap by then, so you two can keep driving." He cracked a yawn, even as he said it.

Wallace didn't pull away, but Elgin could tell that his appetite wasn't there. This was the longest stretch he'd even gone without making love to Wallace, but he didn't care in the least. He could still kiss and hold him, which made up for everything he didn't have.

"Sounds good." He kissed Wallace's knee, brushing against Annan before he pulled his hand away.

* * * *

The traffic in the city was terrible, but Elgin turned the radio on, slowly weaving through the rows as they crawled ahead. Annan was next to him, feet crossed and looking around as if he'd never seen the rush or shops before, while Wallace was seated behind in one of the stowaway chairs and slightly more protected from the sun.

"Where are we stopping tonight?" asked Annan, leaning against his seatbelt as it strained. It was a different perspective from his usual spot low to the ground in the car, and Elgin hadn't quite figured out how to drive all that smoothly. Wallace had already spoken up once about the whiplash, and Elgin had slowed right down.

"I didn't have a set plan," said Elgin. He'd spent the last week studying maps and alternative places they would be able to crash, but he was determined not to set anything in stone. "Depending on how far we get, there are a few campgrounds along the way. Worst case, we spend the night in a supermarket parking lot." It would mean no shower, but they had the bathroom and everything else they would need.

"Let me know if you need me to take over." Annan tensed as Elgin had to stomp the brakes when traffic suddenly slowed. "I've driven the horse trailers around a fair bit, so I imagine this won't be much different."

"Elgin."

Elgin flicked his gaze to Wallace in the small mirror that normally would have acted as the rearview. It gave him a good view of Wallace and the reflection on his dark glasses. Other than looking a bit queasy, he appeared fine.

"If you brake like that again, I'm going to puke all over this RV," said Wallace, the edge of a tease in his voice.

"Maybe you just need a distraction," said Elgin, easing off the brake and taking the exit onto the highway where there looked to be a little less traffic. "Have you seen Annan's thighs today? *Damn.*"

Wallace quirked his lips as Annan flushed, spreading his fingers over the rips in his jeans that exposed his tanned skin.

"Of course I did," said Wallace, a grin on his lips. "At first I wasn't sure if I wanted to ride the new RV or his face."

Fuck.

Elgin throbbed, forcing his eyes back to the road as Annan flushed even brighter. He must've been desperate to be hard so quickly, but Annan's pants looked a little tighter too when he took a quick glance.

Elgin reached across the space, squeezing Annan's thigh. "Get 'em, tiger."

* * * *

Annan

This is the second time my lips have touched his.

Wallace was a sweet kisser—even sweeter than Elgin. Annan lay on his side on the queen bed, the curtains swaying a bit from the changes in speed and a few dishes rattling in the cupboards. They'd hit the highway an hour ago, and Elgin had officially kicked them to the back of the RV.

His hands were on Wallace's hips, keeping him close as they kissed and kissed as if it were the first and last time. There was no rush to it and no goal, only the sliding of lips and the sweet exploration with no time limit. There was a sugariness to Wallace, like he'd had an extra spoonful of it in his coffee, with none of the bitter aftertaste.

Wallace let out a soft moan as Annan tilted his head, taking control of the kiss for a moment before edging back and giving Wallace every opportunity to back down. They were both out of breath, but Wallace was panting heavily, grasping at Annan's shirt every time their touches grew stronger.

Backing off, Annan leaned his head against the pillow, breathing Wallace in. Wallace followed him, shuffling closer so their lips lined up. His chest was heaving, his eyes fluttered shut.

The shift was almost seamless. One moment, Wallace was seeking him, and the next he relaxed, his forehead smoothing out as his grip went lax. The dark lines under his eyes finally seemed to soften as he let out a soft breath, slipping beneath the veil of rest.

Annan leaned in, placing a soft kiss against Wallace's forehead. He was cool to the touch, despite the red blush on his cheeks and the sweat on his skin. His curls were slightly damp but still defied gravity and were the most energetic thing about him.

It was so tempting to close his eyes and settle next to Wallace, letting the dreams take him. But he was a kicker if he napped during the day and would probably wake Wallace up in a few seconds. He didn't expect to sleep well within the metal walls with the sounds so different from his apartment, and giving in now would compound that.

Rolling out of the bed, he did the top button of his jeans back up, stumbling toward the front of the RV. A few minutes into their make-out session, Wallace had shoved his hand down Annan's body, unbuttoning the top of his pants. He'd winced a moment later, but he'd refused to let Annan pull back, instead rolling them onto their sides and slowing everything down.

It nearly killed Annan that even the simplest thing like a kiss pained Wallace. *He doesn't deserve this.*

"Hey," said Annan, sliding into the passenger seat and pulling the belt across him. Elgin looked relaxed in the driver's seat, red sunglasses perched on his nose and an easy focus on the road. "He's out."

"Good," said Elgin, eyes flickering over the road. There was only a small amount of traffic and a few landmarks that Annan recognized, flitting by at their steady speed. "I was worried he would have trouble sleeping with all the movement and noise." Even as he said it, the tire caught a pothole, a few of the dishes vibrating in the cupboard, despite the suspension.

Annan slipped his shoes off before placing his feet carefully on the dash. "Are you holding up okay?"

Elgin nodded stiffly before tightening his grip on the steering wheel for a moment. "Not much I can do but keep on going and try to live each day to its fullest." There was a grim line to his lips, and his easy movements stiffened.

"I shouldn't have brought it up," said Annan, ducking his head and putting his feet back on the ground. His socks were bound to pick up a bit of dirt, despite the RV being so new. "I guess I should just be grateful that you invited me along. I was surprised you guys didn't want to keep this time to yourselves."

The furrow on Elgin's forehead deepened, and he cast a quick glance at Annan before locking his gaze back on the road. "You know we love you, right?"

Annan swallowed, his voice stuck in his throat. No, he didn't. What they were feeling was just a part of the grief. Elgin was latching on to him because Annan was the only sure thing in his life, and Wallace was so determined to find a replacement. There were a hundred guys better than Annan to take that position, but Wallace had settled on him, for some reason.

"From that long, awkward pause, I'm going to assume you're talking down to yourself in your head," said Elgin, flicking his sunglasses as they slid down his nose. At first, Annan had thought they were cheap plastic glasses, but looking closer, they couldn't be.

Elgin sucked in a deep breath, not taking his eyes off the road. "I don't love you because of Wallace. I love you for you. I don't play favorites, and neither does he."

"You should be thinking about Wallace, not about me." Annan's gut immediately twisted. He sounded so fucking cruel. If only every thought each day was Wallace, stamping on his brain for as long as possible. He couldn't imagine how Elgin was feeling. He'd had *years*, while Annan had only gotten a blink of an eye.

"I'd like to think I have a heart big enough for both of you," said Elgin slowly. "Even before I knew Wallace was sick, my feelings were already running deep, and that hasn't changed. I can't promise to always be strong for you, but I'll stick around as long as you'll have me."

Annan rubbed his eyes with his fists as they burned. He'd done enough crying for several lifetimes, and he was so sick of it. They were supposed to be having fun, and he'd promised he'd leave the last of his grief at the barn.

"I'm sorry for leaning on you so much," said Elgin. "I'll try harder."

No.

"Please don't," said Annan, looking to Elgin. Even though he was relaxed, he still seemed exhausted. "I want to be there for you as much as I can. But when it's all over, if you want out, I'd understand. Don't feel like you need to be with me for Wallace's sake."

Elgin didn't reply, but he didn't have to.

Chapter Twenty-Five

Elgin

"I'm not really getting it," said Wallace, tilting his head as he eyed up the massive coffee pot that stood out from the landscape like a giant caffeinated thumb. "Is it art? Was someone *that* obsessed with coffee?"

The massive pot was slightly tilted, pouring an invisible stream into a smaller cup below. It was decorated with huge paintings that looked hand-drawn, the white surface forever marked.

"It's a landmark for the half-way point," said Annan, reaching his arms over his head in a massive stretch. "My mom told me about it when I was little. It's bigger than imagined." He squinted at the coffee pot, which was apparently the largest one in the world.

Elgin rubbed at his chest awkwardly, not able to summon his usual smile or chuckle. He'd searched landmarks before the trip, and so far they had left him very wanting.

From the biggest nickel, the giant red paperclip and now the coffee pot, he'd expected a bit *more*. Not that there was anything wrong with them, but there was something missing about the whole thing.

He wanted to see Wallace giggle with his eyes wide in absolute wonder. There were things in the world that he'd never seen before, and Elgin wanted to be the one to show him. Instead, Wallace squinted at the coffee pot as if he'd never seen something so ridiculous.

"Are you compensating?" asked Wallace, turning a wide-eyed stare at Elgin. "Baby, I assure you there is no need."

That makes me feel a little better.

"I like it," said Annan, putting his back toward the pot before snapping a selfie. "I have to send this off to Milo. That kid has been blowing up my phone with how great his boyfriend is, so it's about time I make him jealous."

Maybe it's not so bad?

"If you filled this thing with every coffee I've ever drank, I feel like it would be close to full," said Wallace, grinning as he took a step closer. He'd had a few rough days on the road, but he'd woken up smiling as soon as they'd entered the flat plains of their current province. "I'm surprised HR didn't request one of these from me when I let them know I wasn't returning. They'd looked stressed as hell, and they'll need the caffeine."

He'd also stood a touch taller since he'd come home to tell Elgin that he was done with work. He hadn't given a notice, just marched into the office of his fellow CEO and HR and told them he was done. Elgin would have paid to see the looks on their faces.

"If it was tea, I would have you beat," said Annan, snapping another picture of Wallace in front of the landmark before tucking his phone into his pocket. He gently slung his arm around Wallace's shoulders, placing a kiss on top of his head.

It was something that Elgin had done so many times, but seeing Annan do it made his heart soar.

"That moose is still my favorite part so far," said Annan, grinning. "Elgin, the look on your face when you spotted it running alongside the RV was priceless."

"I didn't know they were that big…or that fast," said Elgin, flushing as he crossed his arms. "I was expecting an animal about the size of a big goat or something. But that thing's head was bigger than any goat I've ever seen."

"I wish I would've seen it," said Wallace. He'd been sleeping in the back, which he'd done for the majority of the trip so far. The lightless bunk had been his solitude most days, sometimes only coming out in the dusk to blink blearily at the unfamiliar sights around them. He finally seemed somewhat rested today, his sunglasses on and a smile on his lips.

"I'll act it out for you," said Annan, taking a step back so he had more space. He put a look of horror on his face, flailing his arms and lowering his voice. "Oh my God, Annan. What do I do? It's going to run into us. We're gonna crash!" Annan's voice went progressively higher until it cracked and he broke out into a laugh.

"Hey," said Elgin, giving in to his own chuckle. "I may have said all those things, but I was really worried. It would have dented the RV."

"It would've *totaled* the RV," said Wallace, making his way over to a nearby table and taking a seat. There was a small food truck close by and they'd obviously taken advantage of the amount of people as they stopped at the landmark. "Annan, can you grab me an ice cream cone? I could really go for one right now."

"Sure." Annan wiped his hands on his shorts before strolling to the food truck, the sides decorated with all kinds of frozen treats.

Wallace patted the chair next to him, sending Elgin a smile. As he took a seat, Wallace snaked an arm around his waist, leaning into him. "You did really good, baby. We're enjoying ourselves, so don't be worried."

Elgin let out a sigh before shifting a little closer. "How did you know?" He reached for Wallace's thigh, wrapping his hand around it. He was warmer today and not so cool to the touch, his sweater keeping him bundled, even with the warm weather.

"I want you to know that I'm okay," said Wallace, his tone suddenly serious. "You can stop worrying right now, because it's not going to do you any good."

Scoffing, Elgin shook his head. It wasn't possible.

"I'm going to die, Elgin," said Wallace. He didn't seem sad, only steady. "But I'll die a happy man."

Elgin let out a harsh breath, squeezing Wallace a little tighter. *Does he have to say it like that?*

"I'm glad we brought Annan," Wallace continued, looking toward him. He was sliding a few bills across the counter and bouncing a little on his toes. He had a joy to him over the last few days that Elgin had never experienced before. "You love him."

It wasn't a question or even a statement. With the way Annan's hair caught the summer sun and the smile that made his eyes sparkle, how could anyone not fall in love with him? Annan was that constant reassurance that Elgin had never had, slapped together with kindness and understanding.

"I love *you*," said Elgin, wanting to make sure that was clear. "You were my first—"

"And I always will be," said Wallace, running a hand down Elgin's back. "But it's peaceful knowing that you won't be alone, even if it doesn't last. For the record, I think it will." He paused, rubbing his forehead. "I don't think we would have taken this trip if not for him. He brings us both a lot of joy."

True. Even if Elgin was sad, he was still happy, too.

"I don't know if I deserve him," said Elgin. Annan shot them a grin as he was passed three ice cream treats. Two of them seemed normal, but the third was massive and teetered as Annan balanced it, the top scoop shifting to the left.

"You deserve the happiness that I could never give you," said Wallace. "I know I'm not a perfect man— never was. I didn't realize how imperfect I was until I met Annan. He's the best thing that ever happened to us." He patted Elgin's hip. "It won't be so bad. You'll see."

The conversation lulled as Annan approached. He handed Wallace the modest ice cream, keeping one for himself and passing Elgin the massive one. His grin was infectious, along with the sparkle in his eyes.

"This one's not in the Guinness book of world records, but it should be," said Annan, motioning to the huge treat. "Let's hope it's not compensating."

Warmth spread through his chest, heating all but the tips of his fingers where the huge amount of sugar and cream was starting to drip. Flavor burst into his mouth as he took a chomping bite, his head throbbing with an impending brain freeze.

"It's not."

Chapter Twenty-Six

Wallace

I never thought I would see the mountains. A headache had been pounding at his temples all day, but it faded as the flat fields gave way to mountains that had started as a mirage in the distance but morphed into real rock that was progressively getting higher and sharper. The sun cut through the sky but didn't touch the snow on the peaks that sparkled with desolate white.

He reached toward the window, despite the unforgiving light that cut into the main bedroom. If he closed his eyes, he could almost imagine brushing the peaks with his fingertips and how cold and rough they would be. He could plant his hand in the snow, and it would freeze him solid, sucking the last of the life from his limbs.

I'd much rather be here.

Annan and Elgin were talking animatedly up front, as they had been most of the trip. They probably thought he was asleep, but he much preferred to relax with his head against the pillow, listening to the sound of their muted voices.

Elgin was *happy*. He closed his eyes in relief.

Not long now.

Chapter Twenty-Seven

Annan

They stopped once the mountains seemed like they couldn't get any bigger, pulling over in a rest area and setting their lunch out on the picnic table. Stocking up at the last town had been a great idea, especially with Elgin seeming to eat everything in sight, including the chips that he'd sworn he wouldn't touch.

Wallace nibbled at the tip of a piece of watermelon, staring at the mountains with his distant look shuttered by thick sunglasses. He'd been quiet all day, keeping to the darker parts of the camper and spending much of his time resting. Annan had been surprised when he said he was going to join them for lunch, with how drawn and pale his face was.

Elgin seemed to sense his husband's discomfort, talking excitedly, but much quieter than usual. He also had his arm slung around Wallace's waist, rubbing him gently whenever the conversation lulled. Annan was across from them, taking in every moment and committing it to his memory.

He'd taken thousands of pictures on the trip so far and more videos than his phone could store. Elgin had stopped by a box store one town over and had bought him an extra memory card when he'd caught Annan mumbling about his storage being gone.

It was beautiful, with the mountains around them and the two men he was in love with across the table. And he really was. There could be no other word for this than love.

Even the few bees that had found their spot didn't deter the warmth in his chest. He swatted at one that buzzed away, only to return a moment later to rest on the rim of his soft drink. It dipped inside, plunking into the liquid.

I guess I'm not thirsty anymore.

"This is perfect," said Wallace, a soft smile on his lips as he relaxed against Elgin's chest. Elgin leaned in, supporting Wallace and tucking his head against his chest. "They don't look real. It's like I could reach out and touch them."

Annan hummed under his breath, staring at the peaks over Elgin's shoulder. There was a haze that started just off the base of the mountains, like a massive green screen someone had erected. But he couldn't imagine anyone designing something so perfect and positively epic.

"I bet I could hike to the peak and back before nightfall," said Annan, grabbing an orange and peeling the rind. He held one slice out for Wallace, sliding it between his lips once he nodded. "Elgin probably needs the exercise, too."

Elgin spluttered, pointing across the table. "I don't think so. I nearly died on that last hike, and this one contains bears and an actual mountain. There is no way in hell."

"We should go," said Wallace, pulling himself upright. "I could make the shortest trail. I think it was only a few kilometers."

Annan reached for his pop, dropping it again when the bee buzzed inside. It may have been a short trek, but it was over unforgiving terrain and completely uphill. Medical attention was probably a half hour or so away if Wallace became ill.

"Baby." Elgin let out a sigh, reaching for Wallace and rubbing a soothing hand over his shoulder.

"Don't say it," said Wallace, pushing himself out of his seat. "If I say I can hike up a mountain, then I'm fucking going to."

"Hey," said Annan, reaching for Wallace and grasping his hand. "Let me grab a bag with some snacks and drinks. We'll have a picnic at the top."

A grin stretched over Wallace's lips as he looked back to the mountain. If he squinted, Annan could see the small trail between some of the gaps in the trees, the entrance marked by multiple warning posts.

"I can see the trail entrance just there," said Wallace, setting his watermelon back on his plate. "I'll meet you two over there."

Annan gathered up the trash, tossing it into a nearby bin as Wallace trekked over to the posted sign at the entrance. It probably warned them of everything from snakes, bugs, poisonous plants and hunting season, and Wallace appeared to be taking it all in his hands on his hips as he read it.

"You can't be serious," whispered Elgin, trailing after Annan as he ducked into the RV to grab his bag. He upended it on the bed, dumping the rest of his clothes out before grabbing a few things from the fridge. He couldn't imagine they would be gone for long, but he'd rather play on the cautious side.

"You know the easiest way to start a fight?" asked Annan, reaching into the very bottom of the fridge to grab an orange pop for Wallace. They seemed to be his favorite, and he'd been sucking them back the entire trip. "Tell someone they can't do something. You can offer support, guide them along the way and give a shoulder when they get tired, or you can make it clear that you don't believe in them."

Elgin grimaced, crossing his arms over his chest. "This is different. He could get hurt out there. It's a *mountain*, Annan."

"And we'll carry him to the top if that's what it takes." Annan slung the bag over his shoulder. People were volatile. It was something that Milo had taught him almost as soon as they'd met. But people were also the very reason life was worth it most days.

"Elgin," said Annan softly, wrapping his arms around Elgin's shoulder in a brief hug. "I know we're going to carry him most of the way, but I can't take this from him. There's no mountain after this one."

"*Fuck.*" Elgin leaned into him, taking a deep breath. "I-I can't. I fucking can't." He trembled, tears soaking into Annan's neck. "I need him. He's not allowed to leave me like this. He's so young and beautiful and perfect. Why can't he stay?"

I'm breaking. Annan took in a trembling breath, running a soothing hand along Elgin's back. "Let's go.

He's waiting for us now just a few steps away. He's not going anywhere while we're here with him."

Elgin shook his head, burying his face deeper into Annan. "I don't want him to see me like this."

"He'll understand."

* * * *

Wallace was leaning against the entrance sign when they approached, his eyes closed and his head tilted back against the map. Annan smiled at him, sending him a quick wave as he wrapped an arm around Elgin's waist, slowly stroking his side. Elgin hitched his breath.

"You okay?" asked Wallace, slowly looking between them.

"You aren't allowed to ask," said Elgin, his voice trembling as he shook his head. "It's just dirt in my eye, anyway."

Wallace softened, closing the space between them and sliding his arm right next to Annan's as he lay his head against Elgin's collar. "I'm having such a wonderful time." He flickered his eyes open, smiling at Annan. "I love you."

Is that for me or Elgin? Annan swallowed harshly. Elgin might love him, but Wallace? Wallace didn't want him. He wanted Annan *for* Elgin.

"We should start before it gets too warm," said Annan. "I've got drinks, and I downloaded the trail maps earlier. There is a rest stop about an hour into the hike, but some good views before that if the temperature goes up. Who knows? Maybe the altitude will get to me and you'll have to drag me back."

Wallace grimaced, pulling away. "Elgin, I hope you're ready for your workout, because I'm not carrying anything except for these guns." He lifted his arms, curling his biceps. With the baggy shirt and the delicate stretch of his arm, Annan couldn't help but chuckle.

"Oh, baby," said Elgin, slinging his arm over Wallace's shoulders as he started down the trail, Annan a step behind. "You better put those things away, or I'll whip out my Glock."

Annan pulled the straps of his bag tighter, hiking it up as it sagged down his back. "I think you meant cock, not Glock."

Elgin nodded, grinning over his shoulder. "Sorry... I misspoke."

The path narrowed from a wide field to a narrow trail as soon as they breached the treeline, the ground stomped flat by more than a thousand shoes. Mint and evergreen seeped into him immediately, a pure freshness coating his lungs.

Wallace let out a sigh before perching his sunglasses on top of his head. "That's better." The trees thickened, casting a shadow closer to dusk than midday. "It's a beautiful day, but it sure is *bright.*"

Annan squinted in the dim light, trailing after them silently. There was a slight but steady incline as they grew deeper into the forest, his calves pulling from the repeated angle. Wallace slowed, panting as he leaned into Elgin's side. When Elgin cast a worried glance back at Annan, Annan nodded.

"There's a break in the trees up here, Wallace, but I don't think you'll have the best view from there," said Annan, closing the space between them and placing a hand on Wallace's back. He could feel his heart pounding, Wallace's skin sweaty, even through the baggy shirt. His face was pale and shiny, an unhealthy redness to his lips.

"What…do you mean?" Wallace swallowed between pants, bending to rub his thigh that must've been aching. The look on Elgin's face was like a slap to Annan, but he gritted his teeth, trying to keep his face passive.

"You're a bit vertically challenged," said Annan, holding his hand at the level of Wallace's head. The top of his head only came to Annan's shoulders in that perfect package-sized way. "We have to get you higher so you can really see the sites."

Wallace put his hands on his hips with a frown. "And what do you suggest? I didn't exactly pack heels."

"Piggy-back," said Annan. "Elgin was talking about how he wants you to ride him at some point on this trip, and we haven't done that yet."

In fact, the entire trip had been quiet except for the one sleepy make-out session. When they crawled into bed each night, they slept close and soundly, occasionally waking up to find Wallace in the dark bunk. Elgin hadn't even hinted at the desire to fuck him or be fucked, and Annan hadn't noticed until this exact moment.

"Oh, yes please," said Elgin, dropping to one knee and holding his arms back. "Hop up, baby."

Wallace let out a soft sigh, leaning heavily onto Elgin as he wrapped his arms around his neck. As Elgin slowly stood, cradling under Wallace's legs. Wallace went limp, his eyes slitted as he rested his head on Elgin's.

"Better?" asked Annan, adjusting his bag and coming to walk next to Elgin. They picked up the pace, his calves continuing to burn.

It was so different from their last hike, with Elgin panting like a banshee and practically rolling in poison ivy. Now he was walking almost too quick for Annan to keep up, with his head down and a heavy silence between them.

"You're strong." Wallace's murmur seemed to catch Elgin off guard. He paused at the cusp of a break in the trees, turning his head to kiss Wallace's arm. "I was worried, but I think you'll be just fine."

"Don't worry about me, baby," said Elgin.

Annan reached for Wallace's sunglasses, sliding them over his eyes before they stepped into the sunlight. Wallace's eyes were closed, his fingers slack where they clutched at his own forearms.

"Oh wow," said Elgin as they stepped out of the shadows and onto a precipice. It hadn't seemed like they had been walking for that long on much of an incline, but the earth had dropped away beside them. Where the trees had disappeared, the horizon plunged hundreds of feet of sheer rock.

But the best part was the waterfall against the rock, trickling down to a stream that quickly joined a roaring river below. Somewhere high above, the perpetual snow must've been melting in the summer sun, cascading along the groove in the rocks until a rainbow sparkled against the shimmering light.

Annan's heart pounded, louder than the water against earth as Wallace lifted his head. His mouth opened, his glasses sagging low as his eyes went wide, absolute wonder in his gaze.

"Right here," said Wallace, patting Elgin's shoulder. "This is where we stop." He tilted his head back, looking high up the vertical wall. There was a small path that disappeared around the edge of the wall, a promise of more sights to come, but he clearly had no desire to follow it.

"I am fully prepared," said Annan, lowering his bag from his shoulder before grabbing the blanket from within. He stepped off the path, finding a stretch of rock that was relatively flat before laying the blanket out and smoothing the wrinkles.

As Elgin lowered Wallace, Annan set out the drinks, oranges and pretzels he'd brought along. It wasn't much, but Wallace reached for a drink right away, digging in as he sat on the blanket cross-legged.

"I can't believe how beautiful this is," said Wallace, righting his glasses again as he stared at the falls. The rock wasn't just gray, but pink with stretches of dark obsidian that was dyed even darker, some wet portions tinted with a touch of green.

There was nothing but the sound of the water and the beating of his heart echoed by the soft breaths of the two men as they sat close. Wallace reached for Elgin, dragging his head into his lap before long. Elgin squinted against the bright sun before smiling up at his husband.

It was so fucking peaceful. There could have been others on the trail, but the parking area had been nearly deserted, probably because it was a Tuesday and not a weekend. It felt like they could be alone together, their three souls laid bare on the rock. Nothing would change here. Time couldn't touch him.

Letting out a breath, Annan lay next to Elgin, resting his head against Elgin's shoulder. He reached up, placing a hand on Wallace's knee. He could sleep like this — close his eyes against the sun and drift away with Elgin's heart loud in his ear.

"The last time you two saw a view like this, you sent me a very naughty video," said Wallace, breaking the silence as he carded his fingers through Annan's hair. "I got a phone call from Annan, begging for release." He grasped Annan's hand, kissing his wrist.

It was one of the most intimate things that Annan had ever experienced. Those lips against the delicate skin tingled, sensation rushing down his arm and settling in his chest.

If this isn't love, I don't know what is.

"If I would have been there on that cliff with you, I would have asked you to kiss sweet and slow until you could hardly see and your chest was begging for air," said Wallace. He paused, tugging Annan's hair in a loose grip. "I'm telling you now."

Elgin moved before Annan could, grasping at Annan's hips and dragging him higher until Annan's head was in Wallace's lap as well, their lips brushing.

"Should we show him what he missed?" asked Elgin softly, his voice tentative. There was more than lust behind his gaze, his eyes intense and his jaw tight.

"Yeah," said Annan, groaning as Elgin closed the distance and pressed their lips together. There was no other answer. His chest was filled to brimming, the presence of immortality so certain that there was nothing that could ruin this moment.

Tilting his head, Annan tried to deepen the kiss, tightening his grip on Wallace's knee.

"Shhh." Wallace touched his cheek, a stroke of coolness in a pool of heat. "Slow, Annan — soft. You have to make him beg for it. And when he does, slow down until he's falling apart with how much he wants you."

He wasn't sure it was possible to slow down with Wallace breathing that close to him, his words igniting the fire in a burst of heat. But he softened his touch, until Elgin was the one who was groaning, his grip tight.

Time flitted between his fingertips, blood rushing through his ears as they kissed, their tongues slipping together and saliva pooling in Annan's mouth. He swallowed it down, but some dribbled over his lip, soaking into Wallace's pant leg. He didn't seem to mind, petting his fingers through Annan's hair in a soft and steady rhythm.

Each time Elgin tried to pull away to breathe, Annan followed him before wrapping an arm around his neck and dragging him back in — soft, but persistent until his head swam.

Elgin was panting, his cock hard against Annan's leg where he'd casually thrown his leg between Elgin's. Wallace was the only one who seemed calm, his touch as soft as his breath.

"Show me how you want to kiss him, Annan," said Wallace, skimming a finger over Annan's cheek. "Don't hold back."

The thing was, this was *exactly* how Annan wanted to kiss Elgin. He may not have known that at first, because he'd never had the time for simple exploration, always submitting to the lust that had gotten him into so many bad circumstances.

So he gentled his kiss, licking over Elgin's lower lip before gently grasping it between his teeth. Elgin panted in the break, probably trying to clear his fuzzy head, but Annan cut off his air before he could, sealing their lips together with a new sense of urgency.

He couldn't stop — *wouldn't* — because there was no way he was going to let this end.

"You're beautiful together," said Wallace, his voice low. "I could watch you like this for hours — days."

"I'm not going to last days," said Elgin as he tore his lips away. Getting to his knees, he cradled the back of Wallace's head, carefully bringing their mouths together.

Wallace grinned into Elgin's lips, pushing him away with a hand on his chest. "I want to watch."

Elgin was on Annan in a moment, their teeth clicking together at the force of the lunge. The sound of Wallace's chuckle in the background only seared the warmth in Annan's chest, the denim of Wallace's jeans scraping against his neck.

"I said I want to watch. That doesn't mean he's an all you can eat buffet."

These two men. Annan couldn't recall a moment where his urge to laugh was almost as strong as his urge to fuck.

"You're wearing too many clothes for me to eat you," said Elgin, grabbing at the hem of Annan's shirt and tugging it up to expose his nipples. Elgin's mouth was on him, nipping his teeth over the sensitive buds as the humid air brushed his skin.

"Hell," said Annan, shifting his head to the middle of Wallace's lap. Hardness poked at the back of his head, but he did his best to ignore it. He wasn't going to lay a finger on Wallace unless he begged him to. *This works both ways.*

But with Elgin dipping his mouth lower, his resolve was crumbling fast. Annan cast his gaze toward the way they'd come, then over to where the path disappeared around the sheer rock. There was no sign of anyone else, but that could change in a moment.

"I'm gonna fuck you," said Elgin, grabbing at Annan's jeans and dragging them past his hips. They rubbed against his cock painfully before it sprang free, slapping against his belly. *Surprise.*

He felt more than saw Elgin's smirk.

"Commando?" asked Wallace, bringing one hand to stroke the bulge that was now right next to Annan's head. Annan couldn't stop himself from turning his face to nuzzle against his fingers, breathing deep.

"I'm on vacation," said Annan, yelping as Elgin bit into his thigh. His voice carried, echoing against the water before it disappeared into the roar.

"I have to take you places more often," said Elgin, his voice a growl as he eyed up Annan's cock, licking his lips. "I'd rip your pants off, shoving my cock inside before Wallace even gets a look at your hole." He patted Annan's hip. "Turn over, baby."

Jesus. We're doing this. Annan struggled to his hands and knees with his pants still tight around his thighs. When he reached to pull them off, Elgin slapped his hand away, helping him tuck his legs under him instead. Wallace grabbed his hair at the same time, bringing Annan's head back to his lap, but this time with his lips pressed to that throbbing bulge beneath a thin layer of material.

"Did you bring a condom?" asked Elgin, supporting Annan's hip so he didn't topple. His knees ached from the rock beneath the thin blanket, a pebble digging into bone.

Annan shook his head. He hadn't exactly expected this when he'd dumped his clothes out onto the bed in the RV. Among his socks and underwear, he had an entire unused box of condoms, just waiting to be filled by a dick. Next to it were probably the single-use packets of lube, scattered throughout.

"It's fine," said Annan, clutching at the blanket and digging in. "I trust you."

Wallace tugged at him until Annan looked up. Those soft blue eyes were staring at him through the tint of the sunglasses, Wallace's hair that defied gravity, glowing around him as the sun stroked him from overhead.

"Are you sure?"

Annan nodded. "I trust you both."

"We still have a lube situation," said Elgin, using one hand to search through the bag as he stroked Annan's hip with the other. "I'll just use my mouth — Oh, wait! There was one at the bottom."

Elgin pulled the silver packet from within, scrambling to get it open. It must've caught on something in the bag when he'd dumped the rest out. *Thank you.* It had been a long time for Annan — longer still since he'd been with someone as *hefty* as Elgin. It wasn't going to be easy.

"Say the word, and I'll stop," said Elgin, squirting lube onto his fingers before stroking Annan's entrance.

Taking a deep breath, Annan shoved his face back into Wallace's groin, flinching when the cold lube touched him. Elgin's fingers were huge enough by themselves, and Wallace's gaze was burning through him.

"Isn't he beautiful?" asked Wallace, stroking Annan's back before leaning to set one hand on his ass. "Is his hole just as pretty?"

Annan burned, clenching tight, even as he nuzzled against Wallace, taking deep breaths of his soft scent. The only thing that would improve this moment was if Wallace was in his mouth—hard, salty and heavy on his tongue.

"Prettier," said Elgin, slowly easing one finger inside. "*Fuck.* You're so tight."

That didn't seem to stop him from hilting his finger, then easing out, only to add a second digit and slide all the way in.

Annan let out a moan, scrambling for the button on Wallace's pants and ripping it wide. The zipper followed and Wallace didn't stop him as Annan reached for his cock, pulling it out into the air. *So much for making him beg.*

Some of Wallace's cock was hidden in his pants, the position making it impossible for Annan to expose all of him, but what was on display was beautiful. He'd seen Wallace before, but never so close, and he'd never gotten to *taste*. He was perfect and proportionate, the head wet and red.

"C—can I?" asked Annan, his voice catching as Elgin curled his fingers. He was going to hurt tomorrow, but right now, he was drunk with it.

"I thought you'd never ask," said Wallace, curling his fingers into Annan's hair and guiding him in. The first touch was sweetness and sin as Wallace thickened against his tongue, a gasp touching his lips.

"I'm not going to last," said Elgin as he withdrew his fingers, an empty ache following him. Annan wiggled his ass, trying not to tip over as he begged without words.

"Put it in," said Wallace, his voice broken and soft.

As Elgin lined up his cock, breaching Annan for the first time, Wallace suddenly shifted, thrusting his cock all the way inside Annan's mouth. It took everything in Annan not to come in that instant, the ache, pleasure and desperation frying every reasonable sense.

Then he heard it—the smack of lips as Elgin bottomed out with an ache. They were kissing above him, each giving him every inch of themselves as they kissed loud and wet.

Annan couldn't stop himself. He arched his back, curling his toes as the throb in his groin suddenly went tight. Jerking, he sucked as much of Wallace as he could into his mouth, jamming his nose against the soft hairs of his groin. Elgin's breath stuttered as he cursed, Annan clamping down on him from the force of his sudden orgasm.

A few drops hit his abdomen but the rest must've been lost to the blanket as Elgin grabbed his hips, urging him through it relentlessly with the pounding of his hips. He must've been just as close as Annan, because it wasn't long until he stuttered, humping so hard that it forced Wallace's cock even deeper.

Saltiness coated his tongue as Wallace pulled Annan off him by his hair, dragging him up and bringing their lips together. It was hard with Elgin jerking against them, Wallace's lip getting caught between their teeth and the taste of blood blooming over his tongue.

Annan panted, his lungs empty, even as Wallace let him get his fill between kisses, wetness instantly rolling toward his thighs as Elgin pulled out.

"Holy fuck. *Fuck*," said Elgin, collapsing next to them on the blanket with his cock still exposed and shiny with cum. Wallace echoed his words.

It was the second time he'd heard Wallace curse — a long line of explicitness as saltiness coated Annan's tongue.

In the next moment, Wallace was lying back, his eyes slipping shut with a smile on his lips. With his breathing low and soft, Wallace almost seemed like he was asleep, if not for the way he petted Annan's hair, his fingers stripping through the strands.

"I think I'm ready to go home," said Wallace, his smile stretching wider.

Annan turned his head, placing his ear against Wallace's chest as he reached for Elgin, stroking his naked belly where his shirt had rucked up. These men were more beautiful than any mountain or waterfall. Wherever they were was fine with him, as long as he was there.

Chapter Twenty-Eight

Annan

The humidity was so thick that it was almost a shock to his system, even the bugs going silent except for the bravest of blackflies. Milo was stretched out next to him, the pond a few feet away and the shade of the trees the only thing that was keeping him from melting.

Taking a swig of his soft drink, Annan grimaced as the warm liquid crept over his tongue. The ice pack from his packed lunch had been almost completely defrosted by the time they'd taken a break, and his drink had been anything but satisfying.

"What's next?" asked Milo, barely twitching as a fly crawled over his nose. He scrunched his face but didn't move to swat it. His blue hair was completely faded now, just a touch a color left to the blond.

A shower and a dinner with the two best men in the world. It had been so hard being back, the early morning light dragging him from Elgin and Wallace's bed instead of his own. It had only been three days since they'd come home from their trip, but those three days had been lifetimes.

"Annan?"

Annan grunted, finishing off his drink before setting it back in his bag. There were still two granola bars to be eaten, but he had no appetite for it. Sometimes he had to force himself to eat in heat like this, water being the only thing he craved.

"I can't exercise any of the horses like this," said Milo, flopping over to face him. "But we should probably work on that fence."

Annan glanced at the fence, which was about a hundred yards away. It was also in full sun, the heat hazy against the ground. The electric tape had come loose when a yearling had decided to test its luck against it. The fence had come out mangled, while the yearling had trotted away.

"No." He shook his head. "I was thinking we should bring some of the older horses off the field and get them hosed down. The young ones should be fine for a bit yet in the shelters, but I'm worried about Thelma."

Even now, her head was low in the field, but she wasn't grazing, flies probably circling her ears. She was the type of horse who didn't believe in fly masks. He'd tried, and he'd gone through a dozen styles before he'd given up when she ripped off every single one, stomping it in the dirt until it was unrecognizable.

"Okay." Milo groaned, lying back. "You first."

Annan pulled himself to his feet, startling when he felt a buzz against his ass. Blinking, he pulled his phone out of his pocket, staring at the screen. *I must've forgotten to take it out.* He never had his phone on him when he was doing chores, too worried about accidentally smashing it or slipping it into a hay bag.

He furrowed his forehead at the screen, reading Elgin's name twice before he accepted the call.

"Hey? Did dinner plans change?" He'd been looking forward to their shower since he'd stepped onto the farm that morning and the lack of air conditioning had made itself known. That, and those soft sheets that always seemed to caress every part of him. *Holy shit, I'm getting spoiled.*

Elgin was breathing heavily on the other end, each exhale buffeting against the speaker.

Annan pulled the phone back, triple-checking the name before he brought it back to his ear. "Hey. You okay?"

"N-no," said Elgin. A sob cut through his words, everything else garbled between sobs.

Annan's chest went tight, his spine snapping rigid as he grasped at the tree. "What happened? Are you okay? Wallace?"

"He's…he's. I can't fucking say it." Elgin's voice cracked, shoving a cold spike directly through Annan's chest. Bile burned on his tongue, his hands trembling as he tried to keep his grip on the phone.

"Call for an ambulance, and I'll be right there." Annan was already running for his car, ignoring Milo's call after him. He had the keys in the ignition, and the car in drive before the call flipped over to Bluetooth. Elgin's voice echoed all around him, raspy and worn with each breath.

"I did. They already— I'm at the hospital."

Fuck. Annan gripped the steering wheel hard as he accelerated, steering through the potholes as dust rose around him. His car bounced, the change in the cupholder jingling as sweat poured down his face. He blinked it out of his eyes.

"He's gone."

Annan lifted his foot off the accelerator, coasting ahead until he hit the slight rise at the end of the lane. The car slowed, until it was inching ahead, getting closer to the road with every heartbeat.

"The ambulance got to the house quickly, but he was already gone." Elgin sobbed, his voice almost unrecognizable. "I was just talking to him in the garden, and he fell. He's gone, Annan. He's *gone.*"

His heart sank as Annan leaned his head into the steering wheel, finally reaching for the brake before he made it onto the road.

"Did you want me there?" asked Annan, his voice soft, even to his own ears. Tears were ready to pour from him in a long cascade that never ended, but all he could do was shake his head, longing to be with Elgin with his entire being. Right now Elgin was alone in that hospital with absolutely no one. It was everything that Wallace had fought to prevent.

But Annan had to know. *Am I still wanted? Was this all just a dream that was bound to end when Wallace dies?*

"Please. I need you."

Annan let out a shuddering breath. "I'll be right there, baby. Hold on for me just a few more minutes. I'm coming."

Chapter Twenty-Nine

Three months later
Elgin

Elgin stretched his arm across the bed, the sheets and pillow still warm but utterly empty. It was so strange how time worked for different things. He still dreamed of Wallace every night as if he was going to be in that bed when he awoke, his wild hair sticking to his head as he slept.

But the moment he woke, it was Annan he reached for.

There were a few times on the cusp of sleep when he got confused as to why there weren't two people in his bed, but he always sobered quickly as he fluttered his eyes open to sunlight and Annan.

Annan, who smelled like leaves and the bright colors on the trees as fall took hold. Annan, who had been with him every night and came running whenever

Elgin called. Annan, who Elgin wondered if he could ever live without.

He'd once thought that of Wallace, until he'd realized that he was stronger than anyone had given him credit for.

He flicked his eyes open at the sound of cloth, spotting Annan emerging from the bathroom. His jeans were undone and low on his hips, and he hadn't put his shirt on yet. Letting his eyes slip closed again, he feigned sleep before Annan could spot him.

Warm lips pressed against his in a brief touch before Annan kissed his forehead, stroking a finger over his cheek.

"I love you, Elgin. Sleep well, baby."

Elgin reached for Annan before he could escape, grasping the back of his neck and pulling him close. Annan fell to the bed with an *oompf*, landing against Elgin's chest in a heap of limbs.

"You scared me," said Annan grinning down at Elgin as he opened his eyes. "Sorry if I woke you."

Elgin stroked Annan's cheek in the same place that his still tingled from Annan's touch. "I'm glad you did."

The thing was, he *never* dreamed of Annan. When he was asleep, it was all Wallace in the times before they'd known Annan and before Wallace had gotten sick. But there were times that he missed Annan in his dreams.

He wanted to dream of their time at the pond together or when they'd scaled a mountain and had taken Annan between them. It was that time that had made him fall in love with Annan.

But it was the little things every day when he was awake that made him fall in love over and over. And it was the moments he had with Wallace in his dreams that made the days a little more bearable.

"I'll see you tonight," said Annan, sneaking in another kiss before he grabbed a T-shirt from the ground and pulled it on. Despite sleeping there every night, he hadn't touched the closet, only bringing just enough clothes for the next night. He still went home every night before he came home to Elgin in time for dinner, sometimes still smelling of horses and hay.

"Will you move in with me?" asked Elgin, glancing toward the closet before quickly looking away. He'd moved all his own clothes to the spare bedroom, and there was plenty of room for Annan's there, too. "This is your home as much as it is mine."

Annan glanced to the nightstand that still had Wallace's watch perched on it. The battery was one that charged on continual movement, and it had stopped working a long time ago, perpetually stuck on two o'clock.

"You're not ready, baby." Annan smiled, tucking his hair behind his ears. "I'll be here when you are." He grasped Elgin's hand, kissing his knuckles. "I'll see you tonight."

Chapter Thirty

Three years later
Annan

"I didn't think we'd make it this far," said Annan, staring over the landscape as the sun slowly got closer to the horizon. "But we'd better turn around before it gets dark."

They had maybe an hour — two tops — before it started to really get dark, and it had taken them almost three to get to the lookout that seemed to be halfway up the mountain.

Green trees and thick undergrowth impeded every bit of their path, until it opened up to a view that made it all worth it. It must've been the thin air that made the scenery so beautiful, or maybe it was the man at his back. Trees and rock had never looked so good.

"We have to look after tradition first," said Elgin, leaning heavily against his walking stick as he stared at the valley below. It was difficult to imagine that this once would have been flat land, the mountains mere piles as they rose out of the dirt.

"Just let me catch my breath first," said Elgin, putting his hands on his knees. Sweat clung to every part of him, soaking his shirt dark, and the straps of his pack dug grooves into his skin, every wrapper stored safely within.

"You're getting better," said Annan, rubbing Elgin's back as he pulled the bag from his shoulders with his free hand. Grabbing a water bottle from within, he passed it over, taking a few swigs from his own. "But we really should get moving. It's going to be full dark by the time we get back, and I only brought one flashlight."

"We made it fine last time," said Elgin, wrapping an arm around Annan's waist. His skin was blazing hot, sending tingles over his flesh everywhere he made contact. It hadn't changed — not since that first time when Annan hadn't understood why Elgin had come for him from across a packed restaurant.

"No," said Annan, crossing his arms. "Last time you fucked me for four hours, and we ended up sleeping up here."

"Wasn't it romantic?" said Elgin, letting out a hum. "Nothing but the stars overhead and the sound of you sleeping beside me."

"Uh-huh. And the fifty mosquitos buzzing around my head until it got too cold for them," said Annan. Normally, he didn't mind bugs, but the mosquitos in this province had to be on some kind of drug. "The best part was when it started to rain, and we had to trudge all the way back in sloppy shoes and wet jeans."

Their packs had weighed twice as much by the time they'd made it back to the RV. Elgin had peeled

Annan's clothes from him, taking him again on their queen bed with only the sound of their breathing and the rain on the roof.

"Hey, I tried to convince you to go naked," said Elgin, hugging Annan tight. "Come on. Let's take the picture, then I can blow you and we'll head back."

"Jesus," said Annan, looking over his shoulder. About an hour ago, there had been another group of hikers behind them. They may have turned back, or maybe they were behind them and ready to crest the pathway at any time.

"Give me that kiss," said Elgin, holding up his phone and taking the picture as soon as their lips met. He squinted as he glanced at it, zooming in on the picture. "Hell, we look better every year. I'll get it framed as soon as we get home."

It would join the ones from every anniversary of the first. That first picture that had been taken on the trail for Wallace hung next to the others, the blue sky and wind still sharp in his memory. They looked a little older in each one, Elgin filling out with a few grays as Annan gained some lines at the corner of his eyes.

But Elgin was right. They looked better with each year that passed, and the view got higher.

Annan grabbed the phone, taking another picture as Elgin got to his knees. If there was one time his man looked best, it was on his knees with that sexy smirk on his face.

"Like what you see?" asked Elgin, grabbing for the button on Annan's jeans.

"Best view in the world."

Elgin looked over to the side before shuffling so Annan was facing the valley, the sun shining directly onto them. "Now *that's* the best view."

Annan tilted his head back, looking to the sky. *We love you. We miss you.*

Want to see more from this author? Here's a taster for you to enjoy!

It's a Kink Thing: Kinked Up
M.C. Roth

Excerpt

Nav

Nav's apartment key tumbled from his hand as his phone vibrated, rattling his change and his plastic swipe card from work. He fumbled in his pocket, pulling his phone out and groaning at the name on the display.

"This is *not* a good time," he said as he accepted the call, sighing at the laughter that burst against his eardrum. He glanced down, searching for his key that had somehow made it halfway under his apartment door, only the jagged edge visible beneath the crack.

He really needed to get a keychain so the thing didn't disappear on him again. He'd already gone through three keys in the last month, and the hardware store was starting to get suspicious as to why he needed so many spares. There just didn't seem to be much point to getting a sparkly keychain if he wasn't going to keep it for all that long.

"How did it go, Nav?" asked Sasha through the speaker.

No matter how many times Nav lost his things or moved, Sasha always seemed to track him down. He was Nav's self-appointed best friend and number one annoyance.

Nav let out a sigh, leaning his back against the door as he looked down the hall. There were a dozen doors that were identical to his, with grungy numbers barely clinging onto their hastily painted surfaces. At one point, the doors must've been a dreadful forest green, but someone had decided to paint over them with a thin layer of white primer. The results were pale lime rectangles with dark corners where the primer had been rubbed raw. The red apartment numbers completed the nightmarish Christmas look with tacky gusto.

"It went great. Better than great, actually. Everette never wants to see me again, and he got his brother to throw me out of the house." Nav rubbed at his shoulder where he was sure there was a bruise. They'd taken the throwing part a touch too literally, and Nav had found out first-hand how hard concrete sidewalks were.

"Ouch. Not unexpected, though," said Sasha, his laughter booming through the tiny speaker. "Maybe you shouldn't have hit on their dad?"

Nav ran a hand through his hair before he leaned back and let his head rest against the thin door. It sounded hollow to the touch, and it nearly bowed under his weight. "Maybe their dad shouldn't have been so hot. I mean, who the hell walks around in just their boxers then gets offended when they get hit on? I didn't know guys his age could even *have* abs like that. His body was just rocking."

"Gross… I don't need the details," said Sasha, the phone rustling. "How many is that now, though?"

"This year or this month?" asked Nav, sliding down the door until his ass met the thin and filthy carpet. A light flickered overhead, and somewhere a baby screamed. His neighbor down the hall was making their weekly batch of boiled cabbage, if the smell was anything to go by. And who the hell had crushed packets of ketchup at the end of the hall?

"You're such an asshole," said Sasha. "I've never met someone who has as many ex-boyfriends as you have. You must run into one at every bar."

Nav laughed, letting the grief of the situation roll off his shoulders and down the ratty hallway to find a sewer out on the street somewhere. There was hardly any grief there at all, if he were honest with himself. He'd only dated Everette for three weeks, which was two weeks longer than his usual attention span. The guy had been cute, but nothing compared to his dad.

"Most bars are out. Restaurants, too. I ran into Josh the other day, and I swear to God he spit on my salad," said Nav. He'd still eaten the salad, of course. A little spit never turned him off a good meal.

"So, you won't come out for drinks with us tonight?" asked Sasha. "Katie already did her hair up real nice, and I can't wait to fuck it up."

"Your straightness disgusts me," said Nav, letting his eyes drift shut. It had been a long week of too many hours at work and even more wasted on another guy he knew would never work out. His shower was calling to him, and he could definitely hear the cries of his lonely pillow.

"I dunno. I'm really tired, Sash." He leaned his head to the side to cradle his phone against his ear. A noise at the end of the hall made him startle, but he kept his eyes closed. It was probably just one of his asshole neighbors getting home after their day job. They would be able to step by him just fine.

"All the more reason to come out with us. You're in a rut, Nav. You need to relax and stop trying to fuck your way through every gay bedroom in the city. Come out with us tonight for drinks, keep your dick to yourself and I guarantee you'll feel better."

"Drinks do sound good," said Nav, pulling his feet closer when the squeak of shuffling footsteps approached him on the carpet. "Okay, I'll be there tonight. Don't let me fuck up again, okay?"

"Deal." Sasha chuckled. Nav could almost see his best friend's smirk through the phone. "I'll keep you surrounded by women so your dick shrivels up and dies. Then I'll get you so wasted that you forget about Tray."

"Tray was last month, before Scott and Paul, remember? Everette was the guy whose dad I just fucked," said Nav, lowering his voice as the footsteps came closer. He already got enough flack in his life for being gay and he didn't need any more shit from anyone.

"You are fucked up, man. I'll see you tonight. Nine sharp at Pinty's. Bring your long underwear and a chastity belt." Sasha ended the call with a click and Nav sighed, letting his phone slide to the ground with a hollow thump. He could sleep against the door, even with the floor jamming into the bruises on his ass.

Who *actually* threw someone? Concrete was not a fun place for his skinny ass to land. At least they had tossed him his pants.

"You okay?"

Nav's opened his eyes and cursed to himself, scrambling to get up to his feet.

Of course, the person to see him crumpled outside of his door had to be his smoking-hot and totally unreachable neighbor. He was gorgeous, with short blond hair that models would die for, and the softest blue eyes Nav had ever seen. Top that with thick shoulders, strong arms and thighs that could kill and he was everything Nav dreamed of.

The guy was also completely and totally unavailable. His boyfriend was the most average person in the world but had something that Nav couldn't even fathom — commitment. Every time Nav saw his him, the boyfriend was usually close by.

"Sorry... I just lost my key," said Nav as he pushed back against his door, his knees wobbling as his neighbor got closer. His mouth went dry, his throat constricting like nobody's business. His palms went damp as he suddenly began to sweat, his face flushing. Hunger evaporated in his gut like he'd just gotten a whiff of fresh ass, and his priorities had spun one-hundred-and-eighty degrees.

He was also the only one who did *that* to Nav. The beautiful blond specimen transformed him from a bonified slut who was proud of it into a blushing virgin.

Nav had fucked and been fucked by more guys than he could remember, but something about that tall, built frame and those crystal-blue eyes sent him back to his high school days when he'd seen his first cock and decided he was gay for life.

"Oh crap, that sucks," he said, running a hand through his blond locks that were probably softer than actual silk. "Did you call the superintendent?" He shifted a brown paper grocery bag in his hands, reaching into his pocket for something.

Of course he was environmentally aware, too, which made Nav want to drool. There was nothing worse than a hot guy who used plastic bags and drove a car that guzzled more fuel than a loaded transport truck. *Can you be any more perfect?*

Nav shook his head. "N-not yet. I think I probably just dropped it somewhere." Nav wanted to crumple into a ball. His voice was so soft and weak that he probably *sounded* like a virgin, too.

Virgins were the literal enemy. Clingy, flustered and nervous, Nav always steered well clear. He'd been there, done that and returned the T-shirt.

Knowing how thin the walls were in the building, Nav guessed the guy had probably heard his sex adventures from across the hall, which was probably why he was looking at Nav with confusion and concern etched onto his perfectly sculpted face. Statues were probably made of this guy—hopefully the ones with the big dicks and not the little ones.

Nav slid his foot sideways to where he remembered dropping the key, hopefully concealing it. He was such a fucking idiot, but he couldn't even think straight with his neighbor staring at him, his gaze piercing straight through his defenses.

"Did you need a hand? Just let me put my groceries in the fridge and I'll help you look for it." A soft smile settled on his lips as he pulled his own key out before opening his door with one hand.

"No, it's okay," said Nav, his face burning. He slapped his hands to his cheeks as the guy looked away, hoping to draw the heat out with his frigid fingertips. The sight of his wide, strong back had Nav flushing all over again. He looked away and into the apartment instead, his jaw dropping as something caught his eye.

There, on the wall, and hidden in the most unlikely of places, was a painting that he'd never thought he would see again.

"Oh my God, you have one of Brian Maeckery's paintings?" He stumbled across the hall, his key and his bag forgotten as the art drew him through the open door.

Seeing it again was the same as seeing it for the first time. The piece was one that had caught Nav's eye when it had been in the studio. His breath stuck in his throat as his cock swelled against his will, his groin pulling tight.

He couldn't help it. The brushstrokes were perfection, each one laid with such sensual purpose that Nav could almost feel them against his skin. The lovers on the canvas were wrapped around each other in an intimate embrace that made Nav's blood boil. They looked at each other in the peak of their pleasure, love and commitment frozen on their features. It was as unreal as a dream.

But what was his favorite painting of all time doing in a run-down apartment building? Sure, his neighbor had spruced up his place from what Nav could tell, but the painting didn't belong.

"Yeah." He set his grocery bag on the counter, before turning to Nav. "He's actually a friend of mine. He owed me a favor, so he gave this to me as payment. It's a beautiful piece." He shifted, flickering his gaze over Nav once before he turned and started unloading his groceries.

Butterflies erupted in Nav's belly. Brian Maeckery was nearly famous—like a shiny, untouchable doll on television. Nav would have worshiped the ground that he walked on, if only he had been able to find his house.

"I'm so jealous. I'm such a huge fan of his." He let out a sigh, reaching for the muddled color where the lovers' legs met. He hovered a few inches away, his hand trembling. The last price tag he'd seen on it was over one-hundred-thousand dollars. "It must've been one hell of a favor."

It still smelled fresh, the flavors of the paint rolling over his tongue as he inhaled sharply. The wooden frame was pristine, without a hint of dust or fingerprints, but how long would that last? It was something that should have been hanging in a temperature-controlled gallery for the rest of its life behind a pane of thick glass, not in a shitty apartment building soaking up the faint smell of cigarettes and cat piss.

His neighbor paused, a tray of chicken breasts clutched in his fingers. He furrowed his forehead before he let out a small laugh, his eyes lighting up. "Not really, no. My fiancé and I modeled for the painting, so Brian thought it was best if we were the ones to get it."

"Wait...what?" Nav took a step back, his gaze flashing between him and the painting. The faces on the canvas were in shadow, with only their lips visible and a hint of their partially closed eyes. But it *did* look like them, and the hair color was spot-on. And their bodies...*oh God*. Was that really hiding beneath the guy's T-shirt and jeans?

"Shit, I've jerked off to this painting," said Nav, flushing as he smacked his hand to his forehead. "I-I mean, shit. You're Theo?"

His boss had relayed the entire story as they'd hung the painting in the gallery together—how Brian had claimed that Theo was his muse and how he had called to him with each brush stroke. Nav had agreed from the bottom of his balls. That had been the first time the painting made him hard — but not the last.

Nav dropped his gaze, flushing so fiercely that he wasn't sure his cheeks would ever cool again. He couldn't look at him. In fact, it was probably best if he turned around and crawled back to his apartment before begging for forgiveness through the door.

Nav started as his neighbor chuckled. His gaze was dragged back to the gorgeous blond, his heart thudding as he stared at the man with his head tilted back and his lips curled and open as the beautiful sound emerged.

"Theo's my fiancé," he said, wiping the gathering tears from his eyes as he continued to chuckle. "I'm Maverick, but everyone calls me Trick. Thanks for the compliment." He let out another laugh, his body shaking as his chest heaved.

"I'm so sorry. I'm just really tired, and I always say things I'm not supposed to when I'm tired." He bit his tongue as Trick laughed even harder. Trick was stunning when he was silent, but when he laughed, he transformed into an actual Adonis.

Nav looked at the painting again, something new surging from the base of his gut.

As much as he had longed to be the one in the painting in the past, it had always remained an unattainable figment of Brian's imagination. It had been fitting that the only thing that he would ever love was an imaginary scene with a fictional man.

But they were *real*...and the man he'd been fantasizing about was Trick. His heart rate picked up, his chest rising and falling like he'd just run a marathon.

Trick was obviously in love with Theo. He'd smiled, the corners of his eyes crinkling when he'd said Theo's name. And the painting…? Nav hadn't known what true love looked like until he had seen the canvas.

An ugly green monster twisted in his gut, leaving a foul taste in his mouth. It seemed that everyone could fall in love except him, even the not-so-fictional characters in a painting. He was going to be cursed to chase brief hookups for the rest of his life, ditching them before they lost their new boyfriend smell and shine.

"Sorry. I didn't mean to upset you by laughing at you. I was just surprised," said Trick, his humor falling away. "You sure you don't want me to help you find your key? Or I can get you a drink if you want to call the super and wait here."

"No, it's okay. I don't want to intrude," said Nav. He looked back to the painting, but the magic that had enthralled him for months was gone. His stomach lurched as he took a step back.

I'm just overtired. Alcohol required STAT.

"Well, it was nice meeting you…" Trick paused as if he were waiting for something.

"Nav." He shrugged, filling the uncomfortable silence.

"Nav. Just knock if you need something or if you change your mind." He smiled, parting his full lips to reveal white teeth that were perfectly straight. His smile was dazzling, pulling a wave of fresh heat from Nav's core.

"Thanks. Bye." Nav rushed into the hall, shutting the door before Trick could say anything further. His heart was still pounding, and for some strange reason, he felt the first prickling of tears at the corner of his eyes.

He took a deep breath and pinched the base of his nose. He must've been more exhausted than he'd thought if he was already starting to get teary-eyed. He usually didn't hit that level until he'd worked sixty hours in one week. He'd only done fifty-five hours in the last five days, so he should have still been in the glaringly frustrated and angry phase.

He reached for his key, easing it out from where it had squirmed through the crack under the thin door. He grabbed his bag, hauling it over his shoulder and turning the key in the lock before pushing inside.

Unlike Trick, he hadn't spiffed up his floors or counters in his apartment. There really was no point if his stay was going to be brief.

The paint was the original faded ivory with a few cracks around the corners and a smudge of purple along one baseboard. The floors were roll-on linoleum with a few holes in the kitchen where someone had repeatedly dropped a sharp knife. It could have been anyone's apartment.

Except for the art that he'd hung on the walls. The art was all his. Most of the paintings were little pieces he'd picked up in estate and garage sales in the city, with a few originals from up-and-coming artists. His work in the studio gallery put him in reach of a few artists who hadn't hit it big yet and had prices that were within his reach.

He stepped up to one of his favorites. The artist was known simply as *Rachel*, and they had a way with traditional techniques that wasn't too common anymore. A frog on a lily pad would have made most artists scoff, but Rachel had elevated the simple idea and done something beyond anything Nav could have imagined himself. The frog was made of stars, and the lily pad was the cosmos, according to the gods. It always managed to take his breath away.

All the works he had managed to collect were beautiful and unique, but nothing like the scandalous and sensual canvas of Brian's work. It was so far beyond his price range that he didn't *deserve* to be close enough to touch it.

His throat clogged as he thought of the painting in its dismal setting across the hall.

"Christ, I need a drink." He pulled his clothes from his body, letting them trail on the ground on his way to the shower. As the water cascaded over him, he tried to push the painting and Trick from his thoughts.

About the Author

M.C. Roth lives in Canada and loves every season, even the dreaded Canadian winter. She graduated with honours from the Associate Diploma Program in Veterinary Technology at the University of Guelph before choosing a different career path.

Between caring for her young son, spending time with her husband, and feeding treats to her menagerie of animals, she still spends every spare second devoted to her passion for writing.

She loves growing peppers that are hot enough to make grown men cry, but she doesn't like spicy food herself. Her favourite thing, other than writing of course, is to find a quiet place in the wilderness and listen to the birds while dreaming about the gorgeous men in her head.

M.C. Roth loves to hear from readers. You can find her contact information, website details and author profile page at https://www.firstforromance.com/

PUBLISHING

Sign up for our newsletter and find out about all our romance book releases, eBook sales and promotions, sneak peeks and FREE romance books!

www.ingramcontent.com/pod-product-compliance
Lightning Source LLC
Chambersburg PA
CBHW020822260626
47169CB00003B/779